Secretariat Reborn

T0159296

Secretariat Reborn

A Novel

Susan Klaus

OCEANVIEW PUBLISHING
SARASOTA, FLORIDA

Copyright © 2013 by Susan Klaus

All rights reserved. No part of this book may be reproduced in any form or by any electronic or mechanical means, including information storage and retrieval systems, without permission in writing from the publisher, except by a reviewer who may quote brief passages in a review.

This book is a work of fiction. Names, characters, businesses, organizations, places, and incidents either are the products of the author's imagination or are used fictitiously. Any resemblance to actual events, businesses, locales, or persons, living or dead, is entirely coincidental.

Illustration © 2013 by Emily Baar

ISBN: 978-1-60809-130-0

Published in the United States of America by Oceanview Publishing, Sarasota, Florida
www.oceanviewpub.com

10 9 8 7 6 5 4 3 2

PRINTED IN THE UNITED STATES OF AMERICA

To my father, Leonard Meyer,
who passed on to me his love of animals and
the optimism to never give up.

To Hold on Chris, my Thoroughbred stallion
who gave his foals his gentleness and tremendous heart.

ACKNOWLEDGMENTS

A big thanks to Henry Colazzo, my Miami horse trainer, whose knowledge and help were invaluable. Christopher and Kari Klaus, my children, and Sharon Burns, my sister, for their support. Bobbie Christmas, my Atlanta editor; Susan Gleason, my agent; Jana Hoefling, my niece and copy editor. Cliff Klaus for legal research. To my friends Janet Albright and Maryann Burchell for their encouragement. To my critique boys: Ray, Pat, and, especially, Bill Carrigan who taught me how to write. To my family for always being there for me.

Secretariat Reborn

Secretariat ran a mile and a half in 2:24 4/5, matching the world record time for that distance on any surface. He won the 1973 Triple Crown with ease and still holds the track record for the Kentucky Derby and Belmont Stakes, winning the Belmont by a phenomenal thirty-one lengths. He was included in ESPN's Fifty Greatest Athletes of the Century, *the only nonhuman to make the list. It is doubtful that we shall see his like again.*

PROLOGUE

Kentucky, 1985

The young man stuffed the paper bag in the pocket of his jeans, looked up and down the aisle of the deserted barn, and slipped his beanpole frame out of the stall. His jittery hands managed to bolt the latch. He hustled outside into the cool autumn air and fading light. The sun was sinking behind vast blue hills as he crept along the checkerboard of white fencing, flanking a dirt lane that lead to the employee parking lot.

Darkness and a heavy mist had settled over the horse farm when Wendell reached the lot. He took a deep breath and strolled to his banged-up Datsun parked under a light. Once in his car, he placed the small, crumpled bag on the passenger seat and fumbled with his keys.

The glare from a flashlight hit his face. “Oh, shit,” he muttered and raised his hand to shield his eyes.

“What are you doing here?” called the approaching security guard.

Wendell rolled down the window. “I’m one of the grooms. A mare—she went down, looked like she might miscarry, maybe colic. I, ah, I had to keep an eye on her.”

“Well, you’d better get going. It’s past hours.”

Nodding, Wendell started the engine and pulled away. He drove down the long lane under a canopy of moss-draped oaks and left the farm. Patches of fog obscured the quiet country road and slowed his speed to town. He turned into the parking lot of a closed restaurant and through the eerie mist, he saw a green Chevy pickup. He pulled up alongside it and climbed out.

"You're late," growled the man in the driver's seat.

"I'm . . . I'm sorry, sir. It took longer than I thought."

"You got it?" asked the man with a low, unsettling voice as he eased out of his truck and flicked a glowing cigarette butt onto the asphalt.

"Yes, sir." Wendell handed him the bag. "I did exactly as you said." He shifted from foot to foot and stared up at the tall man, thinking this guy could double for Clint Eastwood in his early spaghetti westerns.

The man rested against the fender and inspected the bag's contents. "If you've fucked me, boy, I'll be your worst nightmare."

"No, sir, I wouldn't do that, I swear."

The man tossed him a rubber band-wrapped wad of grimy twenty dollar bills and climbed back into his truck. The Chevy taillights vanished into the haze.

CHAPTER ONE

Florida, Present Day

The trainer stood on the lush Bahia grass, several yards from a semi horse van. A cigarette dangled from his lips, and his blue eyes squinted in the hot August sun. Hank Roberts, though middle-aged, still had his rugged good looks and trim frame. He spoke with a soft southern twang, yet had an edgy manner that was short on words and short on patience. But when it came to horses, Hank was as cool and calm as the azure sky. He took a last puff of his Marlboro and crushed it under his boot as he watched Juan, his young groom, lead a two-year-old Thoroughbred to the loading ramp.

The sleek bay filly snorted nervously at the monstrous van and flung her black mane. At the loading ramp, she put on the brakes and planted her spindly legs on the grass. Her wide, shifting eyes betrayed her terror as she twitched her ears, listening to the men; one on her right flank, another at her rear, and Juan halfway up the ramp with her lead rope.

"Easy, girl," said Juan, shaking a bucket of sweet feed to coax her inside the trailer.

"That's it, Juan. Don't tug," said Hank. "She's ready to jump out of her skin." He slowly walked to the filly's left side and stroked her neck. "Good girl," he whispered. "There's nothin' gonna hurt you." He gazed into her startled eyes and waited until they became serene. More relaxed, she took a bite of food.

Hank ran his hand over her shoulder and down the front leg. "Pick it up, baby," he said, applying slight pressure to her ankle. The filly lifted her foot as if for hoof trimming, and Hank gently set it back down on the slanted ramp. She withdrew her hoof at once from the unsettling rubber padding and placed it back on firm ground.

"Let's try again, girl," Hank said and repositioned her foot on the ramp. She nibbled the feed and left the hoof in place. "All right, Larry, set her other foot on the ramp."

Larry, a stout man with a piggish face and personality to match, had worked for Hank only a few days. He picked up the filly's front leg and let the hoof plop down hard on the ramp. The filly spooked, rearing and pulling backward.

Juan dropped the bucket and struggled to hold the horse's lead. "Easy, girl, easy," he called as the other men leaped clear of her crushing body and flying hooves. Twenty feet from the trailer, the frightened filly settled with all four feet on the ground. Juan petted and calmed her.

Larry shrugged in Hank's direction. "Ain't my fault that Thoroughbreds are nuts."

Hank shook his head and grumbled, "Goddamn idiot." He called to Juan, "Bring her back around. We'll try again."

Juan walked the filly in a wide circle and led her back to the ramp. The men retook their positions.

The van driver, standing at the horse's rear, added, "Mr. Roberts, I've got some tranquilizers in the cab."

Hank studied the filly. "Naw, she's already sweaty and excited. Instead of helping, it might turn her into a fearless drunk, a bigger problem. Let's give her more time."

A half hour passed with no success. "Time for a new approach," said Hank. He got a blanket and slowly wrapped it around the filly's head, covering her eyes. Taking the lead from Juan, he pulled back on the halter and gently pushed against her chest. "Back, sweetie, back."

No longer able to view the scary trailer, she allowed herself to be guided backward up the ramp, but stopped halfway. "Okay, guys, push," Hank said, goading the filly back with the lead as the others pressed against her chest. The horse kept stepping back until she was finally inside. Hank walked her into a stall, attached the crossties, and removed the blanket.

"Good girl," he said, patting her neck. "Next time won't be so bad." He locked the stall gate and stepped down from the trailer ramp. "One more, but this colt shouldn't take long. He's on a layoff from the track. Been loaded plenty."

"Good, I'm ready for a beer," said Larry.

Hank raised an eyebrow and growled, "Drink on my farm, boy, and you're out of here." He turned to Juan. "Fetch that dark colt in the third stall."

Juan jogged to the long barn and soon returned with a flashy sable colt trotting alongside. "Want me to take him right in?" he called.

"Give it a try," said Hank.

At first the colt seemed ready to leap into the horse van with Juan at his side, but at the ramp, he, too, refused. "Come on, boy," said Juan, pulling on the lead. "There's a pretty girl in here."

Hank ran his sweaty hands over his threadbare jeans and wiped his damp forehead with his sleeve. "Going to be one of those days. All right, Larry, let's lock hands behind his butt and shove him in. He isn't afraid, just being stubborn."

Hank placed one hand on the colt's rump and with his other hand, he reached for Larry, but before they could clasp hands to muscle the colt in, he kicked out and struck Hank's hand.

"Son of a bitch!" Hank examined his injury. "It's always the one you never expect." He glared at the colt and thundered, "Son, you better get your ass in there." The colt, sensing trouble, bounded up the ramp, and Juan backed him into a stall.

The men gathered around Hank and looked at his bloody fingers.

"Jesus, Mr. Roberts," Larry said. "That horse nailed you. Those look broke."

The trailer driver nodded. "You need to go to the emergency room."

Hank cringed, trying to move his fingers. "Think you're right. Can't budge them." He glanced at the driver. "Get going, Joe. Don't want those horses overheating."

"Okay, Mr. Roberts, got one more pickup, but I'll offer them water before I head south." He slid the ramp up and closed the doors.

Juan said, "I'll get you a clean towel from the tack room."

As the semitrailer took off down the long drive, Larry asked, "Want me to take you to the hospital?"

"I'll drive myself," Hank said. "Just help Juan feed and finish up. He's in charge while I'm gone."

The husky white man scowled at the smaller dark-skinned Juan entering the barn. "But, Mr. Roberts," Larry said, "he's Mexican. I don't take orders from them."

"You'll take orders from Juan or collect your pay and be gone."

As Juan approached them, Larry put out his foot and tripped him. Juan hit the ground, but in seconds was on his feet with fists raised.

"Leave it, Juan," Hank said. He straightened, facing Larry. Although slighter than his helper and with an injured hand, the trainer had a no-nonsense attitude that could intimidate most men with a glance. "You're about to spit teeth. Now get off my place."

Larry backed away. "Fucking wetbacks," he snarled and strode to his pickup.

Hank drove to the hospital in his tired truck using the wrist of his injured hand to steady the wheel as he puffed a cigarette and glanced at the bloody towel serving as a bandage. *How am I going to train horse with only one hand? Hell, a couple of splints, some stitches maybe, and it should be healed in a few weeks. Managed with worse horse injuries.*

At the hospital, Hank learned that his broken index and second fingers would require more than splints and stitches. After X-rays, the emergency room doctor said, "The bones are shattered, Mr. Roberts. You'll need surgery."

Hank next met with a surgeon who examined his injury. "I'm scheduling you for an operation tomorrow," the surgeon said. "You'll be too groggy to drive home, so have someone accompany you."

The following morning Hank and Juan sat in the hospital's waiting room. A nurse explained to Hank that it was standard procedure to take a chest X-ray before surgery.

"You're just padding my bill," he complained and followed her.

Shortly after, he reclined on a gurney in the operating room. The surgeon entered and Hank lifted his head. "Let's get this over, Doc," he said with a nervous grin. "I got horses that need tending."

The surgeon placed his hand on Hank's shoulder. "Mr. Roberts, I have bad news. It's your chest X-ray."

CHAPTER TWO

Christian Roberts's lanky body rested comfortably in the seat as he tapped the steering wheel of his SUV in sync with the classic rock blaring from the radio. The song "Last Chance" came on. He shuddered, shaking his sun-bleached hair, taking a deep breath. Even after the tune changed, the lyrics played on in his head, making him focus on the purpose of his trip.

He pushed his Ray-Bans up against the bridge of his nose and massaged his chin. "Fuck," he muttered.

Until the day before, Christian's life had been good and uncomplicated. He had youth, looks, and brains and was cruising in a new red Ford paid for with his flourishing boat business. And he was dating one of hottest chicks to grace Sarasota nightlife.

Then the phone call came from his mother, telling him the bad news. His father was dying from lung cancer and wanted Christian to drive up. Now, after four years, he felt old insecurities kicking in, bringing memories of being unwanted, unloved, and a disappointment to a man Christian had idolized.

He exited I-75 and drove past rolling green pastures dotted with oak hammocks and horses. He gazed at the mansions and well-kept barns with paddocks and exercise tracks that screamed "horse money." If not for the humid air and an occasional cabbage palm, he could have been in Kentucky, but this was Ocala, the only place in Florida where horses outnumbered cattle.

At Citra, a tiny town north of Ocala, he turned off the main road onto a narrow side street. After a mile of potholes, he saw the familiar yellow sign: MAKE A WISH FARM. He slowed and turned into the entrance.

Six-foot-high dog fennel grew around the faded sign and in the ditches along the drive leading to the house and barn. The pastures, too, were overgrown with weeds. He moved on and noticed that most of the four-board fencing on both sides was either broken, warped, or completely down.

This place has gone to hell, he thought, glancing at the dilapidated fifty-acre farm, so out of place with its immaculate neighbors. He noticed the pastures were empty. *He wouldn't have sold his horses, not all of them. They meant too much to that miserable old man.*

He pulled in front of the two-bedroom wooden house that paled in comparison with the thirty-stall, concrete-block barn farther down the drive.

"Nothing but the best for the nags," he mumbled, and slid out of his vehicle. Pushing the sunglasses up, he turned his sapphire-blue eyes on the rundown track that surrounded a small lake, used for exercising young Thoroughbreds. A gentle wind tugged at his Tommy Bahama shirt and blew his shaggy locks off his collar. As he stared at the sandy track, he recalled the day when his world collapsed and he gave up winning his father's love.

Christian had been only ten when he sneaked into the stall of a promising gray colt and put on the tack. He had led the colt from the stall and hopped on. His hope was to make his father proud, showing him that he could handle a Thoroughbred as well as any hired help. He guided the colt down the path leading to the track where his father stood at the railing, watching two exercise riders put their horses through the paces.

As Christian approached the open track gate, he saw the two horses and riders making their last turn, and they were breezing, a full-out gallop that was clocked in preparation for an upcoming race. As they came in his direction, he felt his colt's body tense and hump up as it prepared to dash after them. "Whoa, boy, whoa," he said, gripping a handful of the horse's silver mane.

"Christian!" his father screamed from fifty yards away.

Christian immediately recognized his error. Although he had started riding at age three on the gentle teaser pony and later on his father's quiet quarter horse used to lead and calm the high-strung Thoroughbreds, none of his riding experience had prepared him for a thousand pounds of hard muscle moving like a launched rocket. The colt, believing it was bursting out of a starting gate, took the bit in its teeth, and left Christian with no control.

His father yelled again. The colt lunged forward, and Christian tumbled off its back, crashing to the ground. Dazed, he lifted his head from the dirt and saw the departing hooves of the gray colt that charged down the track after the other horses.

"Pull him up, pull him up before he hits the rail!" his father had yelled to the riders.

Christian sat, holding a throbbing arm, and watched one of the riders grab the runaway's reins and gallop him slowly to a stop. The rider hopped off and held his mount and the gray.

"Is he all right?" his father had hollered to the man and jogged onto the track without a glance at his son or his welfare.

Only after the colt was examined and led back to the barn did his father hotfoot it to Christian. "Goddamn you, boy," he cursed. "What the devil were you thinking?"

Christian, in tears, scrambled to his feet. "My arm hurts, Dad."

"I don't give a shit! Do you know how much that colt is worth? Your ass is about to hurt."

Lucky for Christian, his mother had heard the commotion and raced onto the scene. "Look at his arm, Hank!" she screamed. "It's broken! You care more about a lousy horse than your own son. I've had it!"

That day marked the end of his parents' marriage. Before the cast was off Christian's arm, he and his mother had left the farm and moved 150 miles south to Sarasota and her relatives. Six months later, his parents were divorced.

During the summer, Christian would stay with his father, but over the years, the visits became shorter and less frequent, realizing he couldn't compete with the horses for his father's time or affection.

His mother married a wealthy lawyer, and Christian spent the later part of his childhood on the snow-white beaches of Siesta Key with Sarasota Bay his backyard and playground. He became an avid sailor, fisherman, diver, and surfer. In his late teens, he stopped going to the northern horse pastures. His childhood devotion had faded, replaced with resentment, and every discussion with his father ended in an argument. As an adult, he closed his mind to a father who never cared.

Now, a familiar man's voice came from the house and snapped Christian out of his reflection. "Christian?"

Christian put the Ray-Bans in his shirt pocket and turned. "Hi, Dad," he said and walked toward the porch.

"Nice ride. Is it a rental?"

"No, it's mine," said Christian, swiping the blond hair back from his forehead, "Bought it a few months ago."

"Don't you know buying new is a waste of money?"

Christian bit his lip, feeling the squabble coming. Quickly, he changed the subject. "Mom called and said you weren't doing too well." Opening the screen door, he lowered his head to conceal his shock. Gone was the vibrant fifty-year-old with the lean, muscled frame, fiery eyes, and thick brown hair. Even his low, subtle voice, the one that commanded respect among men yet could seduce any horse and most women, was listless. His father resembled a corpse. At six-foot-two, Christian now towered over the pale, emaciated man with sunken eyes. The cancer had ravaged him.

"Yeah. Go figure. I went to the hospital with broke fingers from a horse kick and walk out learning I'm dying of lung cancer." Hank forced a dry smile. "Well, I'm glad you drove up. We need to settle on what I'm leaving behind." He coughed for nearly a minute and clutched the back of a porch chair for balance. "Come in, come in," he rasped and shuffled back inside the house.

"There's nothing the doctors can do?" Christian asked and followed him.

"Been through radiation; it didn't help. And I'm not about to spend my last days bedridden and sick with chemo." He glanced toward the kitchen. "Can I get you somethin' to drink?"

Christian saw how difficult it had been for his father to greet him at the door, and instantly his animosity toward him lessened. The heartless dictator was now a pathetic old man. "Sit, Dad. I'll get it." His bitterness began to be replaced with pity, and he vowed there would be no sarcasm or quarreling on this, perhaps his last, trip to the farm.

Hank nodded and collapsed in his overstuffed chair. "I get pretty winded these days."

The small kitchen had cluttered counters, dirty dishes piled in the sink, and an overflowing trash bin. In the refrigerator, Christian found open cans of soup, containers of spoiled food, and meager supplies. "Dad, are you getting any help here?" he asked, removing a couple of Cokes.

"Oh," Hank called, "sorry about the dirty dishes. If I'd known you were coming today, I'd have asked Juan to help me clean up."

Christian returned to the living room and popped the soda can for Hank. "Juan, whoever the hell he is, should be fired. The whole place is a mess." He eased into a chair opposite his father's. Still stunned by his father's gaunt appearance, he shifted his gaze to the window.

"Can't fire someone you don't pay." Hank grinned. "Juan stops here every morning, takes care of the horses, and gets me what I need before heading off to work on another farm. He stops again in the afternoon. He won't take money, says he owes me for teaching him the horse business. That little Mexican is a darn good friend."

"I see." Christian popped his own soda can. "So, you do have a few horses left?"

"Still have Chris, my old stallion, and another one in the barn, plus two brood mares in the back pasture."

"Can I get you something to eat?"

"You can fetch my Marlboros in the bedroom."

Christian frowned.

"Look, the doctors give me less than six months. I ain't giving up the few pleasures I got left."

Christian retrieved the pack and lighter for his father, noticing the oxygen tank by the bed. Hank lit up and coughed slightly with the first drag. He shoved the pack up into his t-shirt sleeve, securing it against his arm.

Christian eased into a chair, took a sip of Coke, and glanced into the kitchen. "After I clean up in there, I'll head to the store for some real food."

Hank scoffed. "I didn't ask you here to play housekeeper or nursemaid." He took another drag, rubbed his forehead, and looked up, struggling to speak. "Look, Christian, I've never been any good with people and wasn't much of a father, but I'm hoping to make it up to you before it's too late."

"Don't worry about it," Christian said, but thought, *you're already way too late.* He felt the urge to run, get back to his carefree life on the water, away from the smell of death.

"No, no," Hank said. "Now, listen to me. Out in the barn is a two-year-old colt out of a stake-winning mare and old Chris. I want you to have him."

For a moment, Christian was speechless. "Jesus, you wanted me here so you could give me a horse?" He chuckled, the sarcasm emerging despite his vow to himself. "No thanks, Dad. Give the plug to Juan or, better yet, sell it, so you can get some help around here."

Hank leaned forward and glared, his red eyes like neon. "He's no damn plug, Christian, and not for sale." He sat back and seethed with each puff on the Marlboro.

Christian stared at the floor as the two men sat in an uncomfortable silence. Tobacco smoke filled the room, the haze representative of the wall that had always stood between them and prevented a father-son bond.

Hank smashed the butt out in an ashtray. “Christian,” he said, calmer now. “This is a really good colt, probably the best I’ve ever bred. I can’t explain, but he’s more than a racehorse.” His gaze became distant. “This colt is the start of an incredible journey. He’s going to fulfill a lifelong dream of mine.”

CHAPTER THREE

Christian discounted his father's ramblings about the colt and his stupid dream. He'd heard it before. Just to own a racehorse, a person had to be a dreamer.

When Hank went to his bed and the oxygen tank, Christian kicked off his sandals, more comfortable barefoot, and began cleaning the kitchen. After an hour the room was habitable. Living aboard a sailboat, he had learned to keep things tidy in cramped quarters. In his father's bedroom, he queried Hank. "I'm going to Winn Dixie for some steaks and supplies. Is there anything you want?"

Hank pulled off the cannula, a flexible tube with two projections that attached his nose to the oxygen tank. He lifted his head from the pillow. "I want you to look at that chestnut colt."

"I'm not interested. I really—"

"He's fast, Christian. He'll make you a ton of money. That colt will square things between us. You'll see."

"All right, I'll look at him." Christian left the house and strolled to the barn, laughing to himself. *The old fart's delusional. No hay burner will make up for the grief he's put me through.*

In the first stall, his father's old bay stallion rumbled a friendly hello with his deep-throated nickering. "Hey, Chris," he said and rubbed the stud's head under the long forelock. They shared the same name and were close in age, twenty-five. "I wouldn't be surprised if I was named after you," he said, patting Chris's powerful neck.

In the last stall, a greyhound-looking red colt tossed its head and whinnied. Christian reached in and scratched behind its ear. The colt tilted his head and flattened his ear, enjoying the massage. "So you're supposed to fulfill Hank Roberts's dream. You look ordinary to me."

"He is not ordinary, mister."

Christian turned to see a short Hispanic man in his late twenties, walking toward him with a plug of alfalfa hay. "You must be Juan."

"I am Juan."

Christian backed up so Juan could drop the hay in the stall. "I'm Hank's son, Christian."

Juan's brown eyes brightened and his lips curved upward into a broad smile. "Oh, welcome, welcome. Mr. Roberts must be very pleased. He was worried you might not come."

Christian grimaced. "We're not close, but he *is* my father, and he's dying."

"That is what I told Mr. Roberts—that you would not let him down." Juan turned to the horse. "This is a fine colt. You are lucky to have him. I exercise him every morning, and he is ready to win a big race."

"Don't get me wrong. I appreciate what Dad is trying to do, but I don't want this colt. I got burned out on horses a long time ago. They're big, dumb, and dangerous, plus very expensive."

"That is true," Juan chuckled. "But Thoroughbreds are also noble creatures and have great hearts. No other creature will break its legs to win for you. I saw you scratching his ear and how he responded. You have a way with horses, like your father."

Christian's drive to the store involved thumbnail chewing. "What am I doing here?" he asked himself. "The old man never gave a shit about me, but now I'm supposed to do him a favor and race his fucking horse. In a few days I'm outta here. He can take that colt and stick it up his ass."

Back at the farm and unloading the grocery bags, he glanced at the orange-and-pink horizon laced with purple clouds, sinking beyond the silhouette of moss-covered oaks. At sunset, the ever-changing Florida sky was more than beautiful, it was engrossing. It made him feel good, lucky, alive.

Not so at the house, now only a shadow of his childhood memory and a forlorn place barely holding death at bay. He exhaled deeply. No sunset would help here. Sighing at his mixed emotions, he fried steaks while the potatoes cooked in the microwave. He set the small kitchen table and called to his father. "Dad, dinner's ready."

Hank ambled into the kitchen. "Smells good, but don't hold it against me if I don't eat much. Kinda lost my appetite."

Christian pulled back a chair for his father. "I could've brought a plate into your bedroom."

Hank sat down. "No," he said. "While I'm able, I want to get up. Keeps the bedsores away." He looked around and grinned. "My goodness, boy, you've been busy. This place looks spotless."

Christian smiled his thanks, but he had to say his piece. "Dad, I'd like to stick around, but I'm leaving Saturday morning. I have a business to run."

Hank took a bite of potato. "And what business is that?"

"I told you about it four years ago." He inhaled deeply through his teeth. His father still didn't know or care about his life. "I have a few docks at a marina off Sarasota Bay. We rent out WaveRunners, Hobie Cats, and Sunfish. I also restore boats in my spare time."

"I remember now," said Hank. "That's the business your stepfather helped you with."

"Frank loaned me the money, but I've since paid him back."

Hank put down his fork and stared at Christian. "Your mom did a good job raising you. You're a hard worker; seem responsible." He sighed. "I'm trying to say you turned out okay."

Surprised, Christian could barely swallow his food. He had waited all his life to hear those words. He managed a weak smile. Was this what dying did for people?

"About you leaving in a few days—that should work out fine. It'll give you and Juan time to check out my old two-horse trailer for the trip to Miami. I've already put the colt's Jockey Club papers in your name and, while you were at the store, I called a big trainer at Calder. He's got an open stall for the colt. I told him—"

Christian broke in, "Wait a minute, Dad. You're jumping to conclusions. I haven't agreed to take the colt, much less trailer him three hundred miles to Miami."

"Three-fifty," Hank corrected him.

"Whatever!" Christian stood and paced the kitchen. Like a punctured balloon, his feel-good moment had deflated. "I know all about your gambling . . . how you'd spend your last dollar on a horse. I don't want anything to do with your so-called dreams. Don't you understand? They made my life miserable."

"Now you sound just like your damn mother," Hank retorted. "Get it straight. I'm no gambler. I never bet at the track."

"Bullshit, every time you put a ton of money and energy into a yearling, it was a gamble," Christian argued, "hoping he'd turn out fast, hoping he didn't break down, hoping you'd sell him at a profit, hoping—" Before he crossed the line and said too much, he stormed outside, slamming the screen door. In the yard he pushed back his hair and held his head. Nothing had changed. Even dying, his father's foremost concern was his horses, not his son. And like four years ago on his last visit to the farm, he and his old man were fighting and he had been here only one day. He heard the creaky door and turned.

His father stood in the doorway. "Christian, you won't have to put a dime into the colt. I promise."

"Are you telling me the Miami trainer, the vets, the farrier won't charge anything? Give me a break, Dad. I'm not stupid."

Hank nodded. "Oh, they'll charge and charge plenty, but by the time you get their bills, you'll have the money. This horse is going to win. Please, son, I can't explain now, but this dream—It's bigger than me or you, but I'm running out of time. I need you, Christian."

Christian looked at his defeated father leaning against the doorjamb. "Last Chance" again started playing in his head. This could be his last chance to know his father and perhaps have some kind of relationship that's worth remembering. He gazed up at the first star of the night, deep in thought. *Even if we don't connect, I might regret that I didn't take his frigging colt. At least when Dad dies, I can say I did my part and walk away with a clear conscience. So I'll do it for me, not him. Besides, how much trouble can one lousy racehorse be?* He glanced back at his father. "All right, Dad, you win. I'll take the horse."

After dinner Hank reclined in his living room, smoked, and watched TV. He had barely eaten. Christian dumped the steak and potatoes into the garbage bin, washed the dishes, and stepped outside to make a call. No reception on his cell phone, *fuck it*.

He returned to the house. "Dad, I need to make a call, but can I use the phone in your bedroom?"

Hank smiled. "Girlfriend?"

"Something like that." Christian walked into the bedroom, shut the door, and, sitting on the bed, he placed the call.

"Hello," Kate said.

"Hey, it's me."

"Why are you calling from this number?"

"No cell signal in this backward place. I'm using the farm phone. So—what are you doing?"

"Painting my nails," she said. "Wait until you see the black dress I bought for Saturday night, low cut. You'll love it."

"Look, about that, I'm sorry, but I'm not going to make it back until Sunday. I have to do something for my father."

"But we had plans. Chad's party at his beach condo is this weekend."

"I know. You go ahead."

"I'm not going by myself," she griped. "Everything is more important than me."

"Kate, you *are* important, but—"

"I'm tired of your excuses, Chris."

"Excuses?" he grumbled. "You mean like spending time with my dying father? I have responsibilities. I don't have the luxury of attending every party that's thrown in Sarasota."

For a moment there was silence. "I just get the feeling, baby," she said, her voice softening, "that you don't care about me anymore."

He hesitated and rubbed his forehead. "I do care, Kate. When I get back, I promise I'll make it up to you."

"Fine, Chris," she snapped and hung up.

Christian leaned back on the bed and stared at the ceiling fan, wondering if this high-maintenance woman was worth all the aggravation. Four months earlier, he had met the long-legged knockout with high cheekbones, luscious large lips, and bewitching green eyes when she Porsche-d up to the marina and asked him about sailing lessons. Her wit kept him so off balance that by evening, she had him in her Longboat Key condo, where he lost himself in layers of her coffee-colored hair during incredible all-night sex.

He and Kate soon became a couple. Heads turned when they entered a nightclub. She introduced him to a wealthy circle of friends and prodded him to replace his little pickup for the expensive SUV. After several trips to the islands and Mexico, he had thought she might be the one, but, lately, the romance seemed as rocky as his sailboat in a squall.

Christian saw himself as easygoing and capable of adjusting to most situations. He could hang with crusty sailors, beer-toting fishermen, and country rednecks, fitting in as one of the good ol' boys. But then, chameleonlike, he could adapt; clean up, put on a suit, and ramp up his charm and intellect to blend in with a rich, sophisticated crowd. With a craggy horse trainer father and an affluent lawyer stepfather, he had learned to mingle with comfort in both worlds.

At first he had adopted Kate's lifestyle with enthusiasm. Little by little, though, the constant parties, Kate's demands, and her stuck-up friends caused him more and more grief.

When he later learned Kate wasn't interested in sailing, the outdoors, or nature, the things he loved, he became even more disillusioned. Her request for sailing lessons had been a ploy to lure him in. Her creamy-white skin should have been a clue that she was an inside girl. Really, the only thing holding them together now was sex.

Christian sat up on his father's bed and placed a second call. "How's everything going?" he asked Jake, his eighteen-year-old employee.

"Good," said Jake. "I rented the Hobie Cat this afternoon to some Yankees, but the fools got caught in New Pass on an outgoing tide—couldn't tack against the current. They ended up in the gulf, freaking out. I had to take the Whaler and rescue them. Other than that, everything went okay, but it was a little slow."

"Well, it's May. Things will pick up next month when the schools let out and the tourists come down. Jot down this number in case you need to reach me. My cell's not picking up. I should be back on Monday."

"Okay, boss, I can handle things. How's your dad?"

Christian sighed. "Not good."

He hung up and glanced at the phone, realizing that Kate hadn't had the courtesy to ask about his sick father. When I get back, he thought, things have to change. He walked into the living room and slumped on the worn couch. An old black-and-white movie played on the TV. His father was dozing, and a Marlboro burned in the nearby ashtray.

Early the next morning, Christian woke in his old bedroom to the smell of brewing coffee and the drone of men's voices. In the dark, he stumbled out of bed and looked out the window. A dim glow showed on the horizon, and the pastures were shrouded with shadows and mist. "What time is it?" he mumbled, rubbing his eyes. He glanced at the digital clock on the nightstand. "Five thirty!"

He slipped on his pants. In the kitchen, Juan and his father sat at the table.

Juan smiled. "Good morning, Mr. Roberts."

Christian gave him a nod. "Call me Christian or Chris."

"There's coffee, Christian," said Hank.

Christian scratched his back, yawned, and shuffled to the coffeepot.

"Juan breezed the colt this morning," Hank said. "He did a thirty-five and change."

Christian poured a cup and took a sip. "Is that good?"

"On my slow dirt track, that's a damn good time," Hank said. "A decent horse averages thirty-eight, thirty-nine seconds over three furlongs. He's ready."

Juan stood. "I have to go, Mr. Roberts, or I will be late."

"Okay, Juan," Hank said.

After Juan left, Christian eased into his vacant seat. "When it's light, I'll look at the trailer. Where is it?"

"Behind the barn. I haven't used it in years. In the past, I'd have a big van company take my horses to the track, but that costs money. Besides, it'll be good for you to take the colt down, talk with the trainer, get a feel for things."

Christian felt his frustration rise in his throat. "Dad, I don't plan on switching occupations and getting into this horse game, if that's what you're hoping. I already said that."

Hank gave another of his ghoulish grins. "Yeah, this business is a curse, a contagious disease. You catch the fever, and nothing else matters. Don't wish that on you, but I reckon if you get a little taste, you'll understand where I've been coming from all these years." He broke into another coughing fit, but went on. "You're about to enter the sport of kings, boy, the most exciting two minutes of all sports. I want my son to feel that rush. After, you can go back to your boats."

CHAPTER FOUR

After coffee and a piece of toast, Christian walked to the barn. He examined the dry rot cracks in the tires on the two-horse trailer and frowned. "Sure, Dad," he said to himself. "The colt won't cost me a dime. What a fucking joke." He would have to replace the tires if he hoped to make it to Miami. And that would be one dirty job. He returned to the house and changed to a pair of tattered cutoffs, a faded t-shirt, and his paint-spotted sneakers. *Figured I'd need them*, he thought.

After putting on a baseball cap, he glanced in the mirror. "Well, I fit in now—look like a true cracker." He took the jack from his SUV and plodded to the horse trailer. After two hours of cursing, sweating, and scraping his knuckles with the tire iron, he had the trailer on concrete blocks and had removed the tires. Annoyed and tired, he walked back to the house, soaked with perspiration, filthy, and smudged with grease.

His father met him at the door. "You should have waited for Juan."

"The tires were dry rotted and had to be pulled. No sense in waiting for him." Christian wiped his damp face on his sleeve and slipped past his father. "Where's the best place to buy tires? I want to get this shit over with."

"There's a store a few miles south on 441."

In his bedroom, Christian retrieved his wallet and returned to the living room. "I'll need an old blanket so those tires don't mess up the inside of my SUV. I should be back in an hour or so."

"There are blankets in the tack room." Hank said. He looked so pleased that Christian felt less aggravated. He gave his father a nod on his way out the door. As he loaded the old tires, he reflected on his father's smile; his way of expressing appreciation. Although he had long been convinced that he didn't need his father, he was starting to realize that, in truth, he longed to knock down the barriers that had separated them and have this bond.

His eyes watered. "I wish we had more time."

Juan arrived later in the afternoon as Christian tightened the last lug on the new tires.

"You have been busy, Mr. Christian," Juan said with a grin.

"Yeah, I greased everything and checked the lights. It's good to roll." Christian removed his cap and wiped his sweaty brow with the tail of his shirt.

"Have you checked the inside, the floorboards?" Juan opened the back door of the trailer and stepped inside. He stomped the wooden floor panels. "I think we should replace this one," he said, looking down. "I have heard of horses that fell through the floor and arrived at a barn missing half their leg. Very bad."

"Jesus," Christian said, flinching.

Juan hopped out of the trailer, saying, "There are some two by sixes in the back shed."

As evening approached, Juan and Christian had finished replacing several floorboards in the old trailer. Christian tried to pay Juan for his help, but he refused, saying he was doing it for Mr. Roberts. Christian walked to the house hungry and longing for a shower. To his surprise, he smelled food cooking.

"Bet you're whipped," Hank said, standing by the stove. "I cooked up some burgers."

"I could've cooked."

"I ain't totally useless."

That must have taken a lot for the old man, Christian thought. But Hank didn't appear tired. He seemed invigorated. After cleaning up, Christian joined his father at the table.

"When you get to Miami," Hank said, "tell the trainer that Glade Hunter breezed a thirty-five and change and should be entered in a maiden special weight, not a claimer."

"Dad, you'll have to explain some of these racing terms to me."

Hank put down his fork and leaned back into the chair. "Okay, your colt is a maiden. That's any horse that hasn't won a race. A maiden special weight race is for top horses that are expected to win quickly. Once your colt breaks his maiden, wins a race, he should be entered in an allowance race that has special conditions and weights plus bigger purses. Next is the stake race. Only the cream of the crop can run in those and the races are graded one, two, and three. The Kentucky Derby is a grade-one stake race."

Christian noticed his father's voice was stronger, clearer, and he breathed easier. The importance of teaching his son about racing seemed to improve his health. "What about the claiming race?"

"In a claimer," said Hank, "every horse has a price tag and can be bought or claimed for that price. A buyer puts in a request for the horse prior to the race. After the race, he's the new owner regardless if the horse wins or loses, is injured, or drops dead on the track. The old owner gets any purse, and the new owner gets the horse. But like I said, Glade Hunter has great times and doesn't belong in a claimer."

"I like the colt's name, Glade Hunter. When will he run?"

"It's up to the trainer, but if Hunter adjusts well to the track, probably roughly a month. He'll also need to come out of the gate and get his gate card and the lip tattoo."

"A month, huh?" Christian said and massaged his chin. He wondered if his father would be around to see this race.

Hank reached over and patted Christian's shoulder. "Son, I'm excited for you. When you see *your* horse racing toward the finish line, see pure determination and courage on four hooves—" He shook his head. "There's nothing like it. It gives you goose bumps and can bring tears to a grown man."

The rest of the evening's conversation was lively. Christian felt for the first time that he and his father had the same goal, getting Hunter to the races. He was enjoying his father's company and sensed the feeling was mutual. When he crawled into bed, he went over possible reasons why their relationship had changed. Maybe dying, his father was more tolerant, more eager to have a final father-son bond. Perhaps he, Christian, had also changed, no longer a negative, smart-mouthed teen, but a twenty-five-year-old man, time tempered with the knowledge that everyone—himself and his father included—was flawed. Then there was the colt that gave them common ground. He didn't care if Hunter could win a race, just grateful that the creature had brought them together at last.

At five in the morning, he woke to watch Juan ride Hunter. He dressed in the dark and pussyfooted outside. Juan's old pickup was already parked under the barn lights. Christian hustled down the drive to the distant barking of dogs, an owl hooting its final goodbye to the night, and the whinny of the old stallion. When he reached the barn, Juan emerged riding the chestnut colt.

"Good morning, Mr. Christian," he said. "Come to watch him work?"

"Yeah, I wanna see all this speed you and Dad are talking about."

"Oh, not today," said Juan. "He ran hard yesterday. Today we slowly gallop."

Christian stared at the lean-muscled colt with the white star that tossed his head in anticipation of the ride. Under saddle, Glade Hunter seemed totally different from the horse Christian had petted in the stall. His red coat shimmered in the floodlights as he pranced, his hoofs barely grazing the ground. He had the dazzling look of a champion.

"He's awesome," Christian said, a word he never thought he'd apply to a horse.

"Come," said Juan. "Watch your boy move."

Juan took the colt to the track and loped him under the lights. Christian stood by the rail, a cool predawn breeze bearing the scent of orange blossoms blowing against his face. The powerful animal seemed to glide over the dirt and only the rhythm of pounding hooves conveyed that the creature was still earthbound.

The colt was no normal horse; it was *his* horse, and he felt the excitement of possibilities. It didn't matter if Hunter came from a rundown farm, a dying trainer, and an old stallion with an mediocre pedigree. Hadn't he heard his father say that every Thoroughbred enters a race as an equal, ready to prove he has the most speed, stamina, and heart? Plenty of long shots had won the Derby.

Christian pondered that his father had stood at this very spot by the rail, probably having the same thoughts. Was he following in his father's footsteps? "No, I'm not," he said firmly. "I'm just dealing with this one horse, and only to make Dad happy. I won't get caught up in horses and racing." As the gorgeous colt galloped past, Christian's determination weakened, and he felt the thrill pulling him in.

After Juan brought the colt back to the barn, he removed the tack and hosed the colt down. "Mr. Christian, would you like to walk him until he is cool?"

Christian shrugged. "I haven't handled a horse since I was ten."

"It is something you do not forget." With a grin, Juan handed Christian the lead, a stud chain laced through the halter over the colt's nose. "Take him around the barn under the shed row ten times while I clean and feed."

"Come on, boy." Christian tugged slightly on the lead and briskly walked the horse beneath a roof that extended from the barn, recalling a lecture his father had given him when a boy. "Patience is a must when handling horses that are bigger and stronger than you," his father had said. "If you're not patient, you'll end up as a hospital patient."

When they had finished ten rounds, he stopped the colt at his stall, and the horse nuzzled his arm. "Good boy." He chuckled and led Hunter into his clean stall and unsnapped the lead. Hunter nibbled some hay while Christian stroked his neck.

His father strolled toward them, a lighter gait in his step.

"Dad, what are you doing down here?"

"The pain isn't too bad today, and this will probably be the last time I see this colt." He stood in the stall doorway and gazed at Christian and Hunter.

The colt stopped eating and playfully nudged Christian. He rubbed Hunter's head. "He likes being messed with."

"I was watching you lead him," Hank said. "You got the gift. Very few can look into a horse's mind and sense how they're thinking. And horses instinctively trust such a person. As a little kid, you were always in here and crawling around the horses. You never got kicked, bit, or stomped. Even the rankest mare dropped her head and let you pet her. I knew you had the makings of a great trainer."

Hank lowered his gaze. "I've been such a fool, so damn occupied with horses that I turned my back on my own son. It takes dying to learn what's really important in life." He ran his hand over his thinning hair. "I'm sorry, Christian, sorry I wasn't there for you."

Christian chewed his lip. "It's okay, Dad. I'm happy with my life. But I'm glad you gave me the colt."

The rest of the morning Christian and his father sorted papers: horse records, the farm mortgage, car titles, insurance policies—depressing work, getting one's life in order before death. Hank grumbled and cursed; Christian longed to be elsewhere.

The afternoon was even worse. Christian drove his father into Ocala and waited while he and an attorney updated the will. Next, they traveled to Johnson's Mortuary, where the director and his father discussed contracts and prices. In the end, his father chose a cheap pine box, small headstone, and a burial plot in an out-of-the way cemetery.

When they finished, his father slowly rose. Now, unlike this morning in the barn, Hank was slow and halting. "Sorry about all this, Christian, should have taken care of it earlier." He patted Christian's back. "I think we've earned a drink. Let's hit my little watering hole, so I can buy us some beers."

Christian drove the SUV into the shell-paved lot and stopped before a shabby brick building. Surrounding it were weeds, trash, empty beer cans, and bottles. Three dented and rusted pickups languished out front. "This place is pretty fancy," he joked. In the dark window a neon sign flashed, "Shirley's." It could just as well have read "Strangers Not Welcome."

Hank cringed when he slid slowly out of the passenger seat. "Yeah, it's a redneck bar, but close to home and cheap."

"Are you sure you're up to this?"

"Whether I'm here or home, I'll still be hurting. Let's go in."

When the door of the bar closed behind them, blocking out sunlight, the room grew as dark as a tomb. The place reeked of cigarettes and stale beer. Christian pushed up his sunglasses and moved toward the tattered vinyl booths, thinking they offered the most comfort for his father. A pool table rested in the center of the room, with the bar on the other side. Four men sat at the end of the bar, absorbed in a baseball game on an overhead TV.

The bartender, a robust woman with short curls called out, "Hank, is that you? Haven't seen ya in a dog's age."

"Hey, Shirley," Hank said. "I want you to meet my boy, visiting from Sarasota." By the time they were seated, she stood beside their table. "Shirley, this is Christian."

"Hank, you never told me you had a son, and, my Lord, he's handsome. Could pass for a movie star." She raised her eyebrows. "Christian, I'll have to make you feel right at home."

Hank grinned. "He's too young for you, Shirley girl. Why don't you get us some Buds on tap."

Christian spoke up. "I'd rather have a Cuba libre."

"A what?" Shirley questioned.

"Rum and Coke with a lime," Christian explained, "preferably Bacardi."

"Call brands are fifty cents extra."

"That's fine," said Christian.

The bartender reached over and patted Hank's shoulder. "Your son's not only cute, but he's got some class. Must get it from his mother." She broke into a yuk-yuk chuckle.

"Very funny," Hank said.

She soon returned with the drinks. "Hank, I heard about your troubles," she said, her tone somber. "If there's any way I can help, just call. And the first round is on me. You've always been a good friend." She sauntered back to the bar.

Hank took a sip from the cold mug. "Ya know I brought your mother here on our first date."

"Mom? Here?" Christian laughed. "That's hard to believe. Only the Ritz-Carlton is good enough for her now."

"I suppose that lawyer changed Angie, but she used to be a hell of a cowgirl, real spitfire. I met her at a rodeo, running barrels on a flea-bitten gray. Ugly swayback horse, but boy, was she gorgeous. Long blonde hair flying in the wind—" He sighed and lit up a Marlboro. "I sure messed up."

"Mom still looks good," said Christian. "And sometimes, I think, she misses you, too. But Frank's a nice guy and treats her like a queen."

"I'm glad. Angie deserves to be happy."

Christian looked past his father at a big man who had been seated at the bar and was now walking toward them. "You know him?"

Hank glanced over his shoulder. "Oh, Christ, the guy used to work for me." He turned back around, and the man stopped at their table. "What do you want, Larry?"

"I hear you're eaten up with cancer." Larry smirked. "That's too bad. I was wondering if that fucking wetback is still working for you."

"Just move on," Hank said.

"Look, old man, I don't work for you anymore, and you're in no condition to give me orders."

Christian slid out of the booth and glared into the man's moronic eyes. "You were told to move on. But if you got a beef with my father, you can take it up with me." Although he and Larry were close to the same age and height, the guy was built like a bulldozer. Christian topped the scale at 175 pounds, but the bum outweighed him by nearly a hundred.

"Christian, sit down," Hank said. "He's not worth the effort."

"Yeah." Larry laughed. "Sit your ass down, pretty boy, before you get hurt." He gave Christian's shoulder a slight shove.

Instantly, Christian's temper rose like a flash flood. He lunged at Larry, caught him with a right hook to the jaw and sent him crashing backward against the pool table. Larry rubbed his jaw and slowly straightened. "You skinny fucker, I'm gonna kick your ass." He stomped forward.

Christian's fists were up and ready. Larry swung. Christian ducked and punched his opponent's beer gut. Larry doubled over and coughed. The three men at the bar moved in. Christian grabbed a cue off the pool table. He wielded the makeshift weapon and shouted, "You want a piece of me? Come on!"

"Leave him alone!" Shirley screamed from the bar.

One of the men rushed Christian, who swung the stick, breaking it against the man's temple and sending him to his knees.

"Get 'im, boys," Larry yelled. His other two buddies leaped at Christian, who managed to cuff one's nose before they wrestled his arms down.

Larry clopped in front of Christian. "Hold him! Hold him still," he said to the men. "I'm gonna teach this fucker a lesson." Larry pulled back to swing, but he was struck from behind with a bar stool. He collapsed on the floor, unconscious.

Standing over Larry, Hank dropped the broken stool and muttered, "Son of a bitch."

With the men's attention diverted, Christian elbowed the ribs of one of his captors. His arm free, he turned and flew into the second man, hammering at his face. Christian and the two men exchanged blows when Christian heard the sharp ratcheting sound of metal against metal, the unmistakable and nerve-shattering noise of someone pumping a shotgun.

Everyone froze.

Shirley stepped toward them, holding the deadly weapon. “Get out of my place,” she growled, aiming the gun at Larry’s friends. “Or else you’ll be digging birdshot out of your hide.” The man who had been whacked with the cue stick stumbled to his feet, and the threesome dragged Larry, now semiconscious and moaning, out the door.

Christian breathed hard, so charged up that it took a few moments to lower his fists and calm down a little. He tasted blood from a split lip and glanced at his bruised knuckles.

“You all right?” his father asked.

Christian felt his aching cheek and jaw. “Yeah, thanks for the help. Not bad for a sick guy.” He walked to the window and watched the men leave, making sure they didn’t take out their hostility on his vehicle.

Shirley was picking up the broken pieces of wood and glass. “I’m so sorry, honey,” she said to Christian. “That bunch is nothin’ but trouble. Always lookin’ for a fight.”

Hank eased back into his seat. “Shirley, I’ll pay for damages.”

“Don’t be silly. The stool and pool stick aren’t worth beans.” She put her hands on her wide hips and gazed approvingly at Christian. “Hank, your boy is one hell of a scrapper. He’s definitely a chip off the old block.”

Hank’s eyes twinkled as he beamed at Christian.

CHAPTER FIVE

Saturday morning, Christian woke early, stiff and sore from the bar brawl and groggy from one too many drinks in Shirley's bar after the fight. He touched his bruised cheek and ran his tongue over his busted lip. "Shit," he said and awkwardly rose. He wandered through the house and, out a window, saw Juan's truck parked near the barn. He found his father still in bed, using the oxygen tank.

"Dad?" he asked softly.

Hank opened his eyes and his lips curled. "Little too much excitement yesterday, but it was worth it. Can't remember having so much fun."

"Yeah, it was fun, despite being a little sore," Christian replied. "Look, Juan is waiting to help me hook up the trailer and load the colt. I'd better get going."

"Give me a call when you're back in Sarasota and let me know how things went in Miami. You can leave the trailer at the track."

"I'll be back up in a few weeks."

Hank shook his head. "Don't bother with me. Go to Miami instead and make sure your colt is being treated right, that he's not losing weight, and he's coming out of the gate okay. The trainer will see you're involved, not an owner who just sits in the clubhouse, drinking and paying the bills. Be sure to slip the groom and exercise boys a few bucks. They'll take better care of your animal. You got his papers, health certificate, and Coggins test? The track won't let you in the backside without them." The energy required for Hank's lecture took several breaths of oxygen.

"I know, Dad, we've gone over all this."

His father nodded. "You'll do all right, son. Just use good common sense."

"I will. I really . . . I really had a good time with you, Dad." Christian tried to swallow the lump stuck beneath his Adam's apple. "I'm glad I came up."

"Me, too."

"We'll stay in touch." Christian hustled outside into the dark and felt moisture form in his eyes. After a moment, he sniffled and cleared his throat. He drove to the barn, and Juan helped him hitch up the horse trailer to his SUV. They loaded the colt with little trouble. He thanked Juan for all his help.

"Your father and I will watch Hunter race on the big TV at OBS," Juan said. "I plan to bet my whole paycheck. He will make us all some money."

Christian recalled the excitement he felt as a kid at the Ocala Breeders' Sales when buyers, sellers, and hundreds of horses gathered for the yearling, two-year-old, or mix auctions. He climbed into his SUV. "Let's hope he wins. Dad says he should run in about a month."

Christian was soon traveling south in the slow lane on I-75. Although he had hauled plenty of boats, he was anxious with a horse. He could feel the thumps from a stomping hoof and the slight tug on the wheel when the colt shifted his weight or moved from side to side in the old trailer. At the Orlando exit, he turned onto the Florida turnpike that would lead to I-95. He wasn't looking forward to the congested traffic ahead or old people that barely moved.

Halfway through the trip, he pulled off at a rest stop to check on the colt and grab a drink, feeling dehydrated from the slight hangover. On the way back from the vending machines, he saw several people standing by his trailer, including a preteen girl.

"He's real pretty, mister," she said. "What kind of a horse is he?"

"Thoroughbred, a racehorse."

"Ohhhhh." She turned to a woman. "Mom, he's like Barbaro."

Christian started his engine. "Hope he doesn't end up like poor

Barbaro," he mumbled to himself, reflecting on the Kentucky Derby winner that had won with ease. Barbaro remained undefeated until he broke his hind leg in the Preakness, the second race in the quest for the Triple Crown of horse racing.

Christian had felt sick when the horse ambulance carried Barbaro to a clinic. Wanting an expert's opinion on the horse's injury, he had made the rare call to his father.

"He's done," Hank had said. "They should've put the colt down on the track."

His father's matter-of-fact tone left Christian aggravated. "Dad, you don't know for sure. They're saying they might fix the leg with surgery."

"The break ain't his biggest problem," Hank said. "It's his other three legs that will have to support his weight for months. The flesh inside the feet will give out and detach from the hoof wall. There's no fix, and he'll founder with laminitis. That's what killed Secretariat."

"You could be wrong." Christian hung up, more disturbed after the call than before it.

Christian, along with a captivated nation, followed Barbaro's medical roller coaster of hopes and setbacks in the media as the champion fought to survive. After nine months, the *New York Times*, *Washington Post*, and thousands of other publications ran the front page headline that Barbaro had lost his battle and was put down, his other three feet giving out from laminitis. His father had been right.

In the late afternoon, Christian pulled into the backside of Calder Race Course, west of North Miami Beach near the Sun Life Stadium. He strolled into the office, believing it wouldn't take long to check in. After handing over the colt's health certificate and Coggins test, he faced what seemed like never-ending paperwork. He was photographed and given an ID for himself and his SUV so he could enter the stable area.

A guard checked him at the gate, and he slowly drove the fifteen-mile-an-hour speed limit down the narrow, winding roads dotted with shade trees and rows of barns with countless stalls. Between each barn and shed row was a grassy courtyard where a few horses were being led around and washed after a race. The mostly Hispanic grooms chatted in Spanish as the horses whinnied to one another. Chickens, cats, and an occasional goat or dog roamed freely among the Thoroughbreds and workers. The smell of hay and pine shavings filled the humid Miami air.

Christian followed the road until he ended up in the parking lot near the smaller back training track that included an employee cafeteria, tack shop, and gift shop. The place had the makings of a small city that catered to horses.

With the correct barn number in hand, he pulled into several parking spaces. He left his SUV and trailer to question an old man leaning against a large banyan tree.

"Is this Ed Price's barn?" Christian asked.

"*Sí, señor*, Ed Price," the man answered.

"Is he here? I'm dropping off a horse."

"*No comprendo*." He called in Spanish to a man in the shed row.

The younger Hispanic man jogged to him. "Can I help you, sir?"

"I'm dropping off a colt for Ed Price's stable."

"You must be Mr. Roberts. I've been waiting for you. My name is Jorge. I will be seeing to your colt."

"Where's Price? I want to speak to him."

"Mr. Price has a horse in the seventh race and is at the track, but I doubt he will return to his barn today," Jorge said. "He should be here in the morning." He opened the back of the trailer and declared about Hunter, "He is nice." He untied the colt and backed him out of the trailer.

Christian followed them under the shed row and into an empty stall. He held Hunter's lead and stroked his neck while Jorge squatted and removed the shipping wraps from the colt's legs. When the groom had finished, Hunter took a sip of water and then got down to chomping on hay. He seemed perfectly at ease in his new home.

Christian detached the lead from the colt's halter, but continued to massage his lean flank and deep chest.

Jorge must have guessed his thoughts and said, "Do not worry, Mr. Roberts. I will take good care of him."

Christian handed Jorge a twenty dollar bill. "You do that. And tell Price I'll be back in the morning."

"Thank you, sir, thank you. I will tell him."

Christian started toward his vehicle and turned. "Say, where do I park my horse trailer?"

Jorge explained that Christian would have to go back to the main road, turn left, and go past the guard and entrance. Then he would see the mountain of new pine shavings and garbage bins. Beyond the maintenance building, the horse trailers would be parked against the fence that was the backstretch of the race track.

Christian drove by the yellow pile of wood shavings stacked twenty feet high and then the trash bins that overflowed with stall waste. Unlike other animal feces, horse manure had a pleasant country odor. In the distance, he saw the horse trailers parked in a row along a mesh fence. Some trailers were big and new, their aluminum siding glistening in the sun, but others were small, rusted, and paint-peeled like his. As he passed the maintenance building, he noticed a large tarp. The wind had lifted the tarp corner back and exposed a mound of brown fur. With the same curiosity that draws a crowd to a car wreck, he stopped, got out, and walked to the tarp. Ten feet away, he gasped at the sight of a dead filly with a mangled front ankle. Earlier in the day, she had probably dashed around the track to the roar of a cheering crowd, but she now lay on the asphalt like discarded trash.

Covering his mouth, Christian flashed back to Juan's words. "They will break their legs to win for you," he had said about Thoroughbreds.

Christian inhaled deeply, the reality of the words hitting him hard. He wondered if he had the stomach for this business. With horses running in a tight pack at top speed, injuries and death were bound to happen. How would he feel if this happened to Hunter?

Oddly, he had no problem beating the daylights out of a jerk like Larry, but he became emotionally unglued when an animal suffered. Possibly he had inherited this trait from his father, who cared more about horses than people.

He unhooked the trailer and drove to the hotel overlooking Calder Race Course. In the hotel lobby, the desk clerk asked him if he wanted a room with a track view.

"Sure, why not?" Christian said. "Oh, I almost forgot. I have a horse at Calder." His father had told him that owners received a discount at the hotel.

"Can I see your track ID?"

Christian dug into his back pocket, found his new card, and plunked it down with his Visa card. In his room on the eighth floor, he pushed the heavy curtains and sliding glass door aside and stepped onto the balcony. A row of tall Australian pines and a small street separated the racecourse from the hotel. With the view, he saw the grandstands and eight horses trotting to the starting gate for the last race of the day. To the left, he caught a glimpse of the trailers parked along the fence. Although out of sight, the ghastly image of the lifeless filly still tormented him. Rather than watch the race, he shut the curtains.

In the dark room, he turned up the air conditioner, called room service, and took a shower. When his Reuben sandwich and fries arrived, he ordered a new-release movie for the TV, hoping for a distraction to get his mind off death—the filly's and soon his father's.

Even with the noisy air conditioner, Christian woke to a faint rhythm of pounding hooves. He climbed out of bed and pushed the curtains aside. Between the silhouette of tall buildings, dawn was breaking. Below, two Thoroughbreds and their riders hugged the rail and thundered around the turn. On the outside of the track, forty or more horses slowly galloped, trotted, and walked as they performed their morning exercise.

Christian made coffee and stepped out onto the balcony. Even at that early hour, Miami was steamy—well into the eighties. *This is great*, he thought as hundreds of horses paraded past. After coffee and a half hour of watching the show, he dressed and went downstairs, eager to get to the stables.

He drove past the guard and, unlike the quiet of the afternoon before, the morning bustled with activity. Each courtyard contained twenty to thirty horses. The grooms rushed around cleaning stalls, feeding, leading, and washing the animals while trainers and their assistants supervised. The hot-walkers that resembled carousels with live horses were full, the horses walking in a circle to cool down after a workout. Exercise riders twirled their whips, waiting for their next mount as others walked their mounts, warming up in the courtyard. Vehicles filled the parking spaces in front of the barns, and veterinarian and farrier trucks parked along the road. Groups of mounted horses walked down the road, going and coming from the track. At the crosswalks, Christian stopped, allowing several to pass.

Christian felt privileged to witness this behind-the-scenes circus that occurred daily beyond the grandstands. The betting public was prohibited access, never seeing the effort it took to maintain racehorses, probably the most pampered animals on the planet. As Hunter's owner, Christian had just been initiated into a private club, its members thinking, breathing, and dreaming Thoroughbreds.

He parked in front of Ed Price's barn and strolled to his colt's stall. "Hey, Hunter," he said and patted the colt's neck. Hunter paid him little attention, also entranced with all the doings.

A tall, middle-aged white man with brown wavy hair and a mustache strolled down the shed row toward Christian. Dressed in a spiffy white sport shirt and trousers, Ed Price looked more like a golfer than a horse trainer and stood out among his employees, who wore jeans and dirty t-shirts. In Spanish, he spoke to several men taking tack off a horse and called to a rider in the courtyard. His accent was good, but his high-pitched voice was similar to a horse's whinny.

Price walked up to Christian. "You must be Mr. Roberts," he said and offered his hand. "I'm Ed Price, your colt's trainer."

Christian reciprocated and noticed Price's unsoiled hand and manicured nails. Unlike his father, the guy was obviously not a hands-on trainer.

"Your colt is a nice animal," Price said, glancing at Hunter, "but I pulled up his pedigree and the racing stats on his sire. The stallion didn't earn much and is only stake placed—never won a big race, plus he hasn't had many starters. You don't see too many studs by Hold Your Peace."

Christian crossed his arms and lifted his chin, taking a slight dislike to this pompous trainer who was critical of his father's horses. "Meadow Lake is by Hold Your Peace, and he's produced some great stake horses," he said. "Chris didn't breed many mares, but he has an eighty-seven percent win rate from starters. I believe that's above average." Christian had absorbed every word when his father discussed Hunter and his old horse, Chris.

"Yes, that's a better percentage than most studs. Watch out, Mr. Roberts." Price motioned Christian to step near the stall so several horses with their grooms could walk past.

Christian resumed the conversation. "Hunter also breezed a thirty-five and change on a slow dirt track a few days ago. I believe that's also above average, Mr. Price."

"It's a good time." Price produced a dry smile and began to backpedal. "Look, Mr. Roberts, I'm not putting down the stud or prejudging your colt. If your colt has talent, he'll prove it on the track. I pull the pedigree and stats so your horse is entered in the right race. The stud and his other colts ran on dirt and most of his races were six furlongs. But your colt's mare has some great milers and European grass horses in her pedigree. She also won two grass stakes and produced several winning grass horses. That leads me to believe your colt could possibly fit into any kind of race."

"My father says Hunter should run on dirt."

"That's good. There are more dirt races. Sometimes it takes a month or two to find a maiden grass race with the right distance and purse to fit a horse."

Price abruptly said something in Spanish to Jorge, who nodded, put the lead rope on Hunter, and walked him out of the stall.

"Is he going to the track today?" Christian asked.

"No, he'll be walked for a day or two. By the end of the week, I'll pair him with another horse, and he'll start on the training track. Once he has some workout times and his gate card, I'll find a race that suits him."

"That sounds like a plan," Christian said and unfolded his arms. He watched Jorge lead Hunter around the shed row with other horses and their handlers.

"Do you have his Jockey Club papers and Florida-Bred registration?" Price asked.

"They're in my SUV."

"I'll need to put them on file in the track office," said Price. "While you're here, you might as well drive over to the grandstand and apply for a racing license in the state office and get fingerprinted. They usually open at noon."

"Fingerprinted?" Christian frowned.

"They check your record. Can't be a felon and race a Thoroughbred."

"There's sure a lot involved in racing."

"Everything has to be on the up-and-up. These aren't hobbyhorses."

Christian returned to his cool hotel room, showered, shaved, and packed his bag. From the balcony, he saw the show was over. The track was empty except for a lone tracker grading dirt in preparation for the afternoon races. If not for needing the license, he would have started the two-hundred-mile drive back to Sarasota.

Instead of checking out, he rode the elevator up to the top floor restaurant and enjoyed a leisurely breakfast of bacon and sunny-side-up eggs. While eating, he glanced through the *Miami Herald* Sunday classifieds. Since he restored and sold sailboats in his spare time, he was searching for a cheap fixer-upper.

A twenty-two-foot McGregor with a trailer and ten-H.P. motor caught his attention, and it was only a thousand bucks. On his cell phone, he spoke to the owner and made an afternoon appointment to see the sloop.

Might as well make this trip profitable, he thought and made another call.

Kate answered, "Chris, why are you calling me so early?"

Christian glanced at his watch. "It's almost eleven."

"I didn't get home until three."

"Guess you had fun at the party. Well, I'll be back tonight if you want to hook up."

"Call later," she said and hung up.

He sighed, slightly annoyed. *She never says good-bye, as if good manners might kill her.*

Through the window, he saw cars filling the grandstand parking lot. He paid the restaurant bill and headed for the racecourse. At the gate, a woman scanned his track card for free admission. He wandered past the covered saddling paddock, the grassy riders-up arena, the jockey room, and entered the quiet grandstand. With the race time still an hour away, spectators were few. He took the elevator to the various levels and checked out the poker rooms, clubhouse restaurant, more snack bars, a gift shop, gaming machines, and the box seats reserved for trainers and their clients.

He found the state licensing office, but it was still closed. He saw three security guards leaning against a raised table, talking and drinking coffee, so he walked over. "Think the licensing office will open soon?" he asked and glanced at its door.

The largest of the men set his cup down and said, "You own a horse?"

"Yeah, first one. My trainer is Ed Price."

The oldest guard held his chin. "Price's horses win a lot, but didn't he lose a filly yesterday? Second race, I believe."

"Sure did," said the big guard. "Broke her leg in the homestretch, but kept running. Still managed to win before the jockey could pull her up. Damn shame."

Christian's jaw dropped. "I saw her. A dark bay lying by the horse trailers. Price trained her?"

The older guard nodded. "Sometimes it happens, but don't you worry, son. Your horse will be fine. You come with me to my office. I do the fingerprinting here. By the time we're done, the state office should be open."

Christian paid forty dollars for the fingerprinting and another hundred for a license. The money was adding up. Before leaving the track, he heard the crowd cheering and hotfooted to the rail. He got there in time to see the horses in the first race blow past. As he left the grandstand, a TV monitor said that the trainer of the winning horse was Ed Price.

It took a half hour to find the sailboat owner. The neighborhood was called Hibiscus Terrace, tired-looking with small lots and faded single-story block homes built in the 1960s. The surrounding chain-link fences were lined with old boats, boxes, and junk. He saw the sailboat a short block away, parked in the grass alongside a potholed driveway.

He stopped in front of the faded pink house and began inspecting the McGregor.

A balding, middle-aged man opened the house door and walked out. "You the one that called about the boat?"

"Yeah," Christian said, inspecting the hull. He then walked to the stern. "Can I climb aboard?"

"Go ahead," said the man. "She's a beauty and a bargain. My son owned her but doesn't have time to sail anymore."

Christian climbed up the ladder and slipped past the small outboard onto the deck. He looked at the washed-out teak trim and hatch, its varnish half peeled.

"She's pretty rough." Christian pushed up the hatch leading to a hot cabin that contained two bunks in the front hull, a tiny head, and a table with wooden benches.

"Why was the kitchen gutted?" he called to the man.

"My son raced her, wanted to make her lighter."

"How are the sails and motor?"

"The main and jib are nearly new, and she has two spinnakers. The ten-horse Johnson runs fine."

Before leaving the cabin, Christian tried to turn the crank that lowered the retractable keel, but nothing moved. Back on deck, he looked down at the man. "It's gonna take a lot to fix this boat."

"That's why she's only a thousand." The man grinned.

Christian hopped down and climbed under the hull, reinspecting the keel. "The keel is warped and it's stuck up inside. It'll have to be pulled. That repair alone costs more than the boat is worth." He ran his hand over his mouth, adding up the money and labor involved to salvage the boat. After examining the old iron trailer, he turned to the man. "Providing the sails are good and the motor runs, I'll give you six."

"Six hundred?" The man frowned. "The sails alone are worth seven."

"The sails are the only thing I'm really buying," Christian said. "Take it or leave it." There was an old saying: the best days for a boat owner are the day the boat was bought and the day it sold. For this guy, the saying rang true.

"Fine." The man grunted. "I'm tired of mowing around it."

Christian paid the guy, getting the title and trailer registration. He hooked up the trailer to his SUV and was grateful the brake lights worked. He left Miami as the thunderclouds rolled in.

• • •

Driving west on Alligator Alley toward a brilliant pink-and-orange sunset, he witnessed the spectacular lightning storms that moved across the vast plain of swaying cattails raked by the wind and laced with narrow waterways. Except for the highway and its traffic, the Everglades was empty, endless, and breathtaking. "This is the way Florida was meant to be," he mumbled.

The Glades turned into cypress and pine forests, signaling an end to the hundred-mile journey across the state. At Naples he would face the monotonous drive north on I-75. After another hundred miles, he would be home, soothed by his comfortable sloop on the peaceful bay.

At dark he pulled off the interstate at the third Sarasota exit and drove though the quiet town toward the beaches. May and a Sunday night, traffic was sparse. He arrived at the Sarasota Sailing Squadron on City Island and stopped at the chain-link gate. After punching in the code, he drove past rows of dry-docked boats. He found an empty slot and backed his newly acquired boat into the narrow space.

He unhooked the trailer and placed a call to Kate. Tired from the long day, he was glad she didn't answer. He grabbed a flashlight from the SUV and wandered though the small, breezy park of Australian pines to the bay.

His dinghy sat on grass, just beyond a narrow beach where large broken clamshells and dried seaweed had come to rest. He flipped the small boat over, shoved it into the water, and soon was paddling toward *The Princess*, a forty-eight-foot Morgan that was moored a hundred yards offshore. *I can't wait to hit that bunk.*

The bay was several miles across, sandwiched between the barrier keys and town. A slight chop reflected the sparkling lights of the surrounding high-rises as the moonlight guided him past other anchored sailboats. In the distance to his left, he heard the blowing noise of the local bottle-nosed dolphins.

He reached his broad sailboat, built more for comfort than speed, and tied the dinghy to the ladder off the stern. In the dark hold, he stripped off his clothes and crawled onto the bunk, grateful to finally be home. What a journey it had been over the last several days. Listening to the whistling wind, the halyards clanging against the aluminum mast, and the waves lapping against the hull, he quickly forgot his worries: the horses, racing, and his sick father as *The Princess* gently rocked him to sleep.

CHAPTER SIX

Over the next few weeks, Christian's life returned to normal. During the day, he rented out his small boats and WaveRunners, sometimes giving private sailing lessons. Jake, his freckled-faced employee, bused dishes at night in a seafood restaurant and worked for Christian on weekends and afternoons. Since the easy job involved the water and boats that attracted plenty of female customers, the poor, red-headed kid probably would have worked for free, desperate to find a girlfriend.

On weekday evenings, Christian restored the McGregor that had been moved to the boatyard area. With the promise of free beer, he enlisted the help of friends and, together, they managed to remove the eight-hundred-pound lead keel. After Christian sanded, added new fiberglass, and gave the keel a fresh coat of paint, the men set it back inside the boat with new cables.

Christian next started on the gutted cabin, rebuilding the kitchen cabinets, replacing the counters, cold storage, and adding a small sink. After the cabin work was done, he planned to overhaul the motor and varnish the outer wood trim. To restore a boat, one had to be a carpenter, painter, and mechanic—a jack-of-all-trades.

When finished and sold, the McGregor might net him four or five grand, not much money considering all his time and effort, but for Christian it was a labor of love. If he hadn't purchased the McGregor, the old girl surely would have been stripped of her sails and motor and ended up at the dump. He now breathed new life into her, giving her a second chance to adorn the seas.

Although inanimate objects, boats, he felt, had a persona, and to save one was a worthy cause. Like other sailors, he could cherish, curse, or plead with a vessel as if it contained a soul. He reflected that no horse could compete with his love for boats and the water.

Christian's weekend nights were reserved for Kate, for partying with her friends and sex. He could never find the opportunity to discuss his mounting frustration with their relationship.

He told Kate that his father had given him a colt, and to his surprise, she was delighted. Dating a Thoroughbred owner gave her bragging rights, because she believed only the prominent and wealthy possessed racehorses.

When he mentioned he would be returning to Miami soon to check on the horse, she asked to come along. He agreed, thinking that on the long drive he could discuss his unhappiness and perhaps improve their relationship. Also, it might be fun going to the track, watching some races, and having someone share his enthusiasm. Within days, he regretted his decision. Kate flatly said she had no interest in horses, only in their owners. She was looking forward to shopping, dining in fine restaurants, and taking in the South Beach nightlife.

At the Sarasota Sailing Squadron, he reminded her that this was a business trip. Its purpose was to see the colt, watch him work, and talk to his trainer. Only if there was time would they follow her agenda.

She blew him off, complaining they hadn't taken a vacation together in over a month, that he owed her. "And it should take you only a few minutes to look at a horse," she huffed.

He foresaw the coming conflict and grief. She expected him to chauffeur her around, wine and dine her, and party until dawn. He decided in that instant he would not be bullied.

"Look, Kate," he said. "The horse is the priority on this trip. If you have a problem with that, maybe you shouldn't come."

Her green eyes took on an open-mouthed gaze, and she withdrew a step. "You're an asshole, Chris!" She flung her long, brown hair, gave him the finger, and stormed off to her car.

Christian watched the powder-puff blue Porsche race down the road. "This is getting old," he mumbled. He realized he was first attracted to Kate because she was beautiful and polished with a teasing, witty charm. And then there was her voracious sex drive, so erotic that he had initially felt like a virgin on their first night. She was exciting and, unlike past girlfriends, she was a challenge. But now he was seeing the real Kate, the demanding, selfish Kate. For him, the hot romance was cooling faster than an overnight cold front.

The next day Kate phoned. "Hi, baby." She always called him "baby" when she wanted something. "I'm sorry I got mad. I realize this little horse your daddy gave you is important. I always sleep late, so you'll have all morning with it. We can work things out. You know I get lonely and still miss my family. You're all I have, Chris. Please let me come."

Kate had inherited her money at seventeen when her parents were killed in a car accident. He massaged the back of his neck, feeling the sympathy for a young woman on her own winning him over. And maybe with an honest talk, he could fix things, turn their troubled relationship around. "All right, Kate."

"That's great. Lately you've been so testy. This trip will be good for us. You know I love you, baby," she said and hung up.

Christian called his father and said he was heading back to Miami for the weekend to check on Hunter. He would call again when he got back with an update. He also mentioned the dead filly that Price had trained.

"Accidents happen," Hank said, "even to the fittest horses and the best trainers, but I'm sorry you had to see that. You've always been thin-skinned when it comes to animals. I remember when your old collie died and you cried for a week. Never saw a little kid take it so hard."

Christian reflected on his childhood pet. Growing up on the farm and miles from other kids, he had relied on Lady for companionship. "Yeah, I loved that collie, still miss her. But getting back to Price, besides the dead filly, there's something about him I don't like. I can't put my finger on it. It's just a gut feeling."

"Well, he's listed as one of the top trainers in Miami and his horses win. Go down and inspect your colt. If you find a problem, we'll switch trainers, but that delays his first race and eats up more money and time."

Time my father doesn't have, Christian thought. "It's probably nothing. Price just comes across like an arrogant S.O.B., but I'm sure Hunter's in good hands."

"Give me a jingle when you get back."

They ended the call, but Christian had noticed his father's wheezy voice and the breathlessness. He decided that after the trip to Miami, he would drop Kate off in Sarasota and continue to Ocala. His concern over the loss of business and work would have to take a backseat to the reality that his father was dying and, oddly enough, he wanted to be with him.

Late in the morning on Friday, Kate propped her bare feet up on the dash of the SUV and sipped a soda as Christian drove east on Alligator Alley. They reached the halfway point in the Glades, and he pulled off at the rest stop.

"Why are we stopping?" she asked and straightened in the seat.

"I thought we'd take a break and look around." He pulled into a parking space. "The Everglades are awesome, Kate."

"Of course you *would* love it," she said. "It's flat, hot, and full of mosquitoes. There's nothing to see."

"Yeah, no civilization. That's what makes it great. Come on and check it out."

"No, thanks, I'll wait here. Keep the air on."

He left the engine running and walked to a canal. A large alligator meandered down the center. On the far bank, a few roseate spoonbills waded near a blue heron. He stared out at the immense landscape with an endless horizon. The Glades resembled a green ocean and had been fondly called the river of grass. After several minutes, he returned to the SUV.

"You missed a big gator," he said and backed his vehicle out of the parking space.

"You know I don't care about that stuff. The only alligator I want to see is on a new purse." She giggled. "The sooner they fill this swamp in and put up condos, the better."

He slammed on the brakes, pushed up his sunglasses, and glared at her. "You really think that way? That the Glades shouldn't be preserved?"

"Please, don't start your homeboy ranting. If left alone, you crackers would still be living in huts on the beach."

"Exactly, there'd still be a goddamn beach instead of a coastline of concrete." He pushed down his irritation and drove out of the rest stop, merging with the highway traffic.

Kate raised her eyebrows. "When we reach Miami, what do you want to eat for lunch?"

"I don't care."

"Hmmm, I feel like shrimp cocktail."

He had planned to have that honest talk about their relationship on the ride home, but decided to bring it up now. "I've been thinking, Kate. Besides sex, what do we have in common?"

"Chris, you're blond." She smirked. "Don't try to think." When he failed to smile or respond, she went on, "Baby, we're the beautiful people, and people like us belong together. And you're my equal in bed. You're my boy toy, baby."

"I'm serious, Kate. There are things that bother me."

She put her soda down and turned toward him. "You're not thinking of breaking up?"

"I didn't say that."

"Good." She relaxed back into her seat and twirled a lock of her shoulder-length hair through her fingers. "Chris, I do love you. And besides my dad, you're the only man with the balls to stand up to me. I respect that, and you're an excellent lover. We're perfect together."

"I'm not so sure we are perfect for each other. You hate everything I love—my boat, the water, the Glades. I'd like to share more than bed with someone. The boy toy thing is wearing thin. You say you respect me, but you don't show it. It'd be nice if you were a little more flexible and less critical. I'm not real happy with the way things are."

He glanced over at her to see how she had taken the truth, but she turned her head toward the window. Ten minutes passed without a word, unusual for Kate, who normally had a quick, cutting comeback. He began to think she was considering all he had said and might be more reasonable. But he was a guy, not in tune with the mysterious mind of a woman.

She turned and glared at him. "You've met someone else, haven't you?" she snarled. "Probably some sailing slut who showed up at your crummy business. Who is she, Chris?"

He choked a little, shocked by her conclusion. "There's no one else. I was hoping if I told you how I felt it would improve our relationship. But just forget it." He shook his head. "Forget I said anything."

But she couldn't. Like a cat with a stepped-on tail, she puffed up, her eyes became slits, and her voice elevated to a screeching hiss as she berated and accused him of cheating. When he clammed up and took the abuse, thinking she'd calm down, she upped the ante. Her ranting turned to threats. "If you leave me, Chris, you'll be fucking sorry, one sorry fucking prick!"

Startled by her hateful tone and scare tactics, he lashed out, "What the hell do you mean by that?"

"I meant . . ." she seethed and then hesitated for a moment. Her voice softened. "I meant you'd be sorry because you'd never find anyone to replace me." She covered her face and started crying. "Chris, I love you. I can't live without you. Promise you won't leave me."

"You're not listening. I'm not going anywhere. There is no other girl." He pulled her close so she could rest her head against his side. "Please don't cry." She put her arm around his waist, clinging to him, and continued to whimper. A sucker for a woman's tears, he felt guilty he had hurt her.

She stopped grasping his waist, and her hand moved to the crotch of his pants. He knew a blow job was coming. Like all their unresolved arguments, Kate's resolution was sex.

"Not now, Kate," he said breathlessly. "We'll be at the hotel soon."

She ignored him.

At noon they arrived at the hotel off the track, but Christian knew the sex was far from over, that a long marathon on the bed awaited him. For now he'd do his best to satisfy her, not wanting to revisit the cursing and crying jag that occurred on the ride.

In the dark, cool hotel room, their clothes came off. After four months, he knew that the what and how with her never involved tender kisses or caresses. A few hours later, he collapsed on his stomach, totally spent.

She pushed his damp locks from his closed eyes and kissed him. "You did good, baby," she whispered.

"Glad you're happy," he murmured. After several minutes, he managed to gather his limbs under him and rise.

"What are you doing?"

"Taking a shower," he said and walked toward the bathroom. "I have to go to the track and tell the trainer I'm here so I don't miss Hunter's workout in the morning."

"You're leaving me for a horse?" she called.

He glanced around the corner at her slender nude body stretched across the bed. "Kate, we talked about this. Why don't you come with me? You can see my colt, and then we can go to the clubhouse and watch some races over lunch."

"Not interested, horses and barns are filthy. I'd rather order room service and rest up for South Beach tonight."

In the shower, he closed his eyes, hoping the coursing water would revive him. He felt physically and mentally whipped.

Kate was wrapped in the sheets when he walked back into the room, damp and naked. He dug out a pair of clean jeans from his bag as she watched.

"God, you are one gorgeous creature, Chris. I can never get enough of you." She smiled and pushed the sheets aside. "Sure you have to go?"

He pulled up his jeans and grabbed a fresh shirt. "I won't be long. Could you order me a sandwich from room service?"

"Fine." She re-covered herself with sheets and reached for the TV remote.

Christian walked down the hallway to the elevator and reflected on the hellish trip through the Glades. He was accustomed to Kate's rudeness and sarcasm, but had never been subjected to her vicious name-calling and threats. It surprised him. Furthermore, it gave him a good taste of what would happen if he actually left her. He flung his wet bangs out of his eyes. *Always figured men were spineless jerks when they used a note or text message to break up. Now I'm not so sure.*

At the track, Christian parked in front of Ed Price's barn and walked to his colt's stall. Hunter stuck his head out immediately for a caress.

"Hey, boy, remember me?" he said and stepped into the stall. "How've they been treating you?" Stroking the colt's neck, he noticed the new shorter coat. The full-body clip kept the horse cooler in the Florida heat. He ran his hand across the animal's withers and first two ribs.

"You've lost a little weight." Next he examined a few cuts on the front of Hunter's back legs. "What happened here?" He left the stall, looking for Jorge. He found the groom in a stall several doors down from Hunter's, tending a charcoal filly with silver-dappled rings on her rump. Her mane and tail were also silvery white. Jorge picked up a pail and poured ice into the loose wraps on the filly's front legs.

"Hi, Jorge," Christian said. "What're you doing?"

"Hello, Mr. Roberts. I take care of this row of horses, and this filly is in the eighth race. I must keep her legs cool. I call her my sweetheart." When the filly nuzzled his face, he smiled. "You see? She loves me. She will do anything if asked and has won many big races. She will win today."

"She's a beauty." Christian reached in and petted the filly. "So how's my colt doing? Is he eating all right?"

"He finishes all his grain and is doing well. He is very calm. Already he goes to the racetrack. He breezed the other day, and I heard the exercise rider tell Mr. Price that your colt is a Cadillac."

"A Cadillac?" Christian knitted his brows. "Does that mean he's slow?"

"No, it is very good, Mr. Roberts. It means he is no cheap horse."

"That's great. Look, I'm staying at the track hotel and want to see him exercise in the morning. What time does he go?"

"Between five thirty and six," said Jorge. "I will tell Mr. Price you are here and wish to see your horse gallop in the morning. We will wait until you arrive."

Christian nodded. "I'll see you tomorrow." He thought about asking Jorge about Hunter's cuts and weight loss, but figured he'd wait for his expensive trainer to explain. He walked back to Hunter. The colt curled and smacked his lips, normally the gesture of a foal when begging for food or acceptance from a strange horse.

"What do you want, more petting?"

Hunter tossed his head up and down as if he understood.

"I'll be damned." Christian chuckled. He spent another half hour fooling with Hunter until the colt had enough and began eating his hay.

Christian left the track and returned to the dark hotel room. He found Kate sitting cross-legged on the bed, staring at the TV. She wore a black silk robe, and her wet hair was wrapped in a towel. On the sheets before her were plates of a half-eaten shrimp cocktail and salad.

She glanced up at him. "I ordered you a BLT."

"Thanks," he said and stepped out of his shoes. He walked to the window and opened the curtains. "You don't want to see the horses? They're racing right below us."

"I saw them, but I don't watch horses unless I have a bet on one. Could you close the curtains? I can't see the TV with the glare."

"Sure." He took his sandwich off a tray and joined her on the bed. Leaning against a pillow and the headboard, he sat with his legs stretched out, ate, and watched a corny sitcom on the TV.

Kate curled up next to him. "Chris, I'm sorry I screamed at you earlier and calling you names. I freaked out, thinking I was losing you. I've had boyfriends, but never been in love like this."

Christian stroked her head, and after Kate drifted to sleep, he changed the channel to Discovery. An hour later, she woke and spent an enormous amount of time in the bathroom, getting ready for the evening.

Before sundown, they left for lower Miami Beach. Colorful Art Deco buildings lined the streets, and the couple took in the local food, dining in a Cuban restaurant. Afterward they hit the posh nightclubs that bustled with young people and blaring music. They drank mojitos and danced into the night. Kate was in her element, flirting and fast becoming friends with an ethnic blend of strangers.

At midnight, Christian suggested they leave, since he had to rise early, but Kate brushed him off. By one o'clock, though, he insisted. "Kate, we have to go. As it is, I'm only going to catch a few hours of sleep."

"You go back to the hotel and get your beauty rest," she sniped, her words slurred. "I'll get a cab."

If they had been in Sarasota and among friends, he would have walked out and not argued, but here, he wouldn't dream of leaving his intoxicated girlfriend with this crowd. He took her arm. "Come on, Kate. We're leaving."

She pulled, attempting to get free. "Let go of me, Chris."

A tall Jamaican man with beaded dreadlocks migrated to Kate's side. "Hey, mon," he said to Christian, "de lady wants to stay with us. Let go of her." Several of the man's friends moved in, encircling them.

"That's right," Kate chimed in.

Christian held on to her and grumbled, "Shut up, Kate." He straightened to his full stature and glared at the Jamaican. Having a long, rough day and then several cocktails to give him blind courage, Christian was pumped up and ready to punch someone. "She came with me, and she's leaving with me. And, mon," he mocked, "you don't want to fuck with me."

The black man tilted his head, analyzing Christian and his incensed demeanor. A cocky grin slowly emerged and he said, "No problem, mon, no problem. She's yours."

Christian escorted Kate through the packed dance floor and outside, with her bitching all the way. Her griping continued on the ride back to the hotel and stopped in their hotel room only when he screwed her so he could get some sleep.

The room phone rang, and Christian, half awake, fumbled to answer it, knowing it was the hotel clerk with his five o'clock wake-up call. His head in a fog and hurting, he staggered from the bed and entered the bathroom. With no time to shower and shave, he splashed water on his face and threw on his clothes.

He glanced at Kate before leaving. She was still passed out cold. He no longer saw the gorgeous woman he had fallen for months earlier, and the trip that he had hoped would bring them closer, was instead driving him away.

In the dark, he drove to Price's barn. The place was alive with horses coming and going with their grooms and riders. He found the trainer in the shed row, talking on his cell phone, stopping only to shout out orders in Spanish to the men.

Christian waited patiently nearby and watched five horses and riders walk in a wide circle around a tree within the courtyard, warming up before going to the track.

Price closed the cell phone. "Mr. Roberts, Jorge told me you were here. Your colt breezed a few days ago, but had I known you were coming, I would've waited. In the future give me a heads-up when you decide to drive down."

"I'll do that," said Christian. "Jorge said the colt is doing great, that the exercise rider called him a Cadillac."

"These grooms, they slay me." Price cackled. "They tend to exaggerate, especially with a new client. You want information on your horse, you ask me. He worked a thirty-eight and change on a fast track, about average."

Christian rubbed the stubble on his jaw. "That's odd. My father breezed Hunter before I brought him down and said his time was better than that. Dad wants him in maiden special weight."

Price used a strand of hay like a toothpick and poked it in his mouth. "Every mom-and-pop operation in Ocala tells me they've bred a stake horse. Unfortunately, the track clocker is exact and doesn't lie," he said. "Your father must have had a fast watch. But don't worry, Mr. Roberts, your colt should do well in his maiden race."

Price called down the shed row to Jorge and another man, and turned back to Christian. "They'll get your colt saddled, and the rider will take him to the track. We'll ride to the grandstands in my golf cart and watch him gallop." Abruptly, he walked across the courtyard and began talking to an exercise boy.

Christian stared at Hunter and felt pangs of disappointment, learning of the colt's unimpressive workout time. The track clocker had to be accurate. He reached into the stall and massaged the white star on Hunter's forehead. "You probably just had a bad day."

Jorge held the colt's lead as another man put on the tack. When they finished, Jorge led the colt out and the other groom gave an exercise rider a leg up into the tiny saddle. In the courtyard, Hunter walked in the wide circle, following five other mounted horses.

Price returned. "Are you ready, Mr. Roberts?"

"Call me Christian." He followed Price to his golf cart that sat under the banyan tree near the parking lot. In the predawn darkness, they followed Hunter and his rider along with the other horses down the street toward the track.

"I noticed Hunter's lost some weight and has several cuts on his back legs," said Christian.

Price glanced at him. "For a new owner, you're very observant."

Christian realized that Price had not only checked out the colt's pedigree and his stud's racing history, but had also checked on him, learning he was an amateur in the business. "Hunter might be my first racehorse, but my father is a trainer, and I know something about Thoroughbreds." In the world of racing, it wasn't wise to come across too dumb.

Price made a crooked smile. "Then you should know those are speed cuts, caused when the front hooves nick the back legs when a horse runs. The farrier fixed the problem and adjusted the new aluminum plates. It shouldn't happen again. As for his weight, most horses are nervous when they first arrive and lose a little. But he's eating and sweating well. That's more important."

Price spoke with such authority that Christian was temporarily assured. Perhaps he had misjudged Price earlier, and the man was a good trainer. Between the first grandstand seats and the track railing, Price came to a stop on a wide stretch of asphalt. Other golf carts with trainers were scattered about, facing the finish line.

"Here comes your colt." Price pointed. "He's working in company with another chestnut."

Christian eased out of the cart, and the two red horses galloped past under the floodlights. Beyond the racetrack, a pink-and-gold horizon was engulfing the night sky. The fiery horses and brilliant sunrise left Christian awestruck.

A dark bay reared up on the first turn, dumping the exercise boy, and taking off down the backstretch.

"Loose horse," called a voice from the PA. Riders pulled up their horses, and the pony riders chased after the runaway, trying to capture it before the horse hurt itself or others. An outrider on a paint gelding quickly cornered the bay, grabbed its reins, and galloped it to a stop. Immediately, the other Thoroughbreds in training continued their daily exercise as if incident had never occurred.

Christian glanced down the track at the rider, who slowly rose from the dirt with no help. "I hope that guy is all right."

"Exercise boys are a dime a dozen," Price retorted. "It's the horse that matters. That damn kid should've hung on, risked injury to that horse."

Christian reflected on the painful event in his childhood when the gray colt had dumped him and he broke his arm. Like Price, his father had only been concerned about the horse. What was it with this breed of men with their all-consuming passion for horses? They seemed to have little sensitivity left for a fellow human being, for a son.

Christian lowered his head, nagged for the hundredth time that he had lacked a father's love in his formative years. He believed he would eventually outgrow this insecurity, but realized the anxiety would most likely haunt him forever.

Price's cell phone sang out. "They're already here? Okay, okay, tell them I'm on my way." He flipped the lid shut. "I hate to cut this short, but I need to get back to the barn."

With the morning radiance, the cart and barn lights were no longer needed when they sped through the back lot. A white stretch limo was parked on the road in front of the barn. Price whipped the cart into its spot under the tree and hopped out.

"I'm sorry," Price said, "but I've gotta run. I'll call if anything comes up about your horse or when I get him in a race." He made tracks to the limo.

Christian hung around and watched Jorge give Hunter a bath and a cooling-down walk around the shed row. The colt was placed back into his stall, a foot deep in clean wood shavings. Hunter lay down, rolled a few times, and stood. Starting with twisting his head, the colt's shaking motion traveled down his body and ended with a flick of his tail, ridding himself of the clinging shavings. Jorge stuffed alfalfa hay into the hanging mess bag in the colt's stall before he left to tend to other horses.

Christian stroked the colt's head while Hunter gobbled up the rich hay and enjoyed the cool breeze of a stall fan. "I hope you like it here, boy," he whispered. "It's costing me sixty dollars a day."

Leaving the stables, Christian noticed Price across the courtyard. He was deep in conversation with a group of dark-skinned men with black beards, dressed in Arab garb of white kaffiyehs and long robes. So they were the limo's occupants.

Christian understood why the trainer had brushed him off earlier. These rich Middle Eastern sheiks were probably the trainer's bread-and-butter clients, while he was a small-time, one-horse owner, always worried about money and costs.

He gave Jorge and the exercise kid a modest tip and patted Hunter good-bye. As he walked to his SUV, he noticed that Price and the Arabs watched him. He nodded to Price, and the trainer responded with a thumbs-up grin.

Since Kate would be out for hours, Christian drove to the employee cafeteria near the training track. He needed coffee. In the restaurant, the crude tables and plastic chairs were occupied by several Hispanic laborers. The hardworking Mexicans seemed to him to be the backbone of the Thoroughbred industry.

He wandered through the buffet, rejecting the rubbery scrambled eggs and greasy bacon in the heating pans and choosing a bagel and cream cheese to go with his coffee. Last night's late partying had left him feeling queasy and drained. Maybe some food would help. He headed outside to eat and watch the horses on the smaller training track. Holding his food and drink, he backed against the door to get out and bumped into someone coming in. Coffee flew onto his shirt. "Ah, shit," he cursed.

"Oh, I'm so sorry."

Christian glanced down at a young blonde woman, whose head reached only to the middle of his chest. "It's my fault. I should've watched where I was going." The splattered coffee and stained shirt suddenly vanished from his mind.

Her deep-brown eyes stared up at him, and Christian felt breathless, nervous. Even with no makeup and in a dirty white blouse and worn jeans, she was stunning.

She shook her ponytail and focused on the stain. "Let me get a towel before your shirt is ruined." She walked to a cafeteria worker and quickly returned with a damp cloth. As she dabbed away at his shirt, Christian's chest pounded and his mind went blank. Finally, he mumbled, "Do you work here? I don't mean the cafeteria. I mean at the track—ah, with horses. I mean you're dressed like you work with horses." He gulped down some air, aware he sounded like an idiot.

Her smile was easy and full. "I know what you mean," she said, her voice restraining a laugh. "I'm a trainer." She raised an eyebrow. "And judging by this expensive shirt, you must be an owner."

"I have one, one horse, I mean. I have, a-ah several shirts." He now felt like slapping himself.

Why was he losing it? He was normally confident, felt he could talk intelligently with women and dazzle them with his looks and charm. But with this girl he was flustered and totally disarmed.

She finished wiping his shirt. "When you get back to your hotel, rinse this in cold water. I think it'll be all right."

"Thanks. Um—my name is Christian. Maybe we'll run into each other again."

"If we do, I hope you're not carrying coffee," she jested and turned away, gliding through the restaurant, disappearing beyond the doors that led to the tack and gift shops.

Christian lumbered outside. *That went well. Came across like a moron. If she saw me again, she'd run.*

At the hotel, Christian managed to get Kate up before eleven and halfheartedly asked if she'd like to have lunch at the clubhouse and watch some races. She declined, saying she wasn't up for it. They headed home with Kate sleeping most of the trip. She woke when they reached the outskirts of Sarasota.

He drove out to her Longboat Key condo and pulled into the bottom-floor garage, parking alongside her Porsche. He grabbed her bag, and they rode up the elevator in silence. At her condo, she unlocked the door, dropped her keys and purse on a side table, and sashayed in.

He placed her bag just inside the doorway and stood outside. "Kate, I'll talk to you later," he called.

She turned and wrinkled her brows. "Aren't you coming in?"

"I told you, I'm worried about my father. I'm heading straight for Ocala, but I'll be back in a few days." She walked back toward him, and he expected a good-bye kiss.

"Fuck you, Chris," she said and slammed the door in his face.

He gazed upward at the ceiling. "That's it. That's it." He breathed. "I'm done."

CHAPTER SEVEN

At six in the evening, Christian pulled into Ocala, stopping at a Kentucky Fried Chicken to pick up supper before going to the farm. Entering the house, he called to his father.

"Christian, is that you?" his father answered from his bedroom.

Christian walked into the room and held up the bucket of chicken. "Thought I'd bring dinner."

His father slowly swung his legs around and sat up. "I told you not to come up here," he complained. "You should be in Miami, checking on your horse. He's more important."

"That's your opinion, not mine. Besides, I just came from Miami."

His father's eyes lit up. "How is he? Did the trainer breeze him yet?"

"The colt is fine, Price worked him, and said he should do well in his maiden race."

"Damn right," his father said and stood. "That colt is probably the best horse in his stable. What was the time?"

Christian hesitated and fearing the mediocre time might upset his father, he lied. "I'm sorry, I don't remember."

Hank gave his son a disapproving stare. "Christian, you need to remember these things. The breeze time determines the race that he's fit to run."

Over dinner, they discussed other aspects of the colt's training. Christian mentioned the minor speed cuts on the horse's back legs and slight weight loss. His father wasn't too surprised. He got a kick out of hearing that the exercise boy had called Hunter a Cadillac.

Christian sensed that his father was willing himself to stay alive long enough to see the colt run, believing the win would make up for his fatherly failings. After dinner, Christian crashed, wiped out from driving and getting only two hours of sleep in two days. The next morning, he rose early to talk to Juan.

He found Juan cleaning the stallion's stall while the horse was turned out. "I'm worried, Juan. Dad is growing worse. He needs to be in an assisted living or a hospital."

Juan stopped raking. "Your father would not go. He is too proud. And in such a place, the unhappiness would kill him faster than the cancer. He says he wants to die right here."

"Well, something has to be done. He can barely get up." Christian kicked some shavings back into the stall. "He can't stay alone anymore. I'll call his doctor and see if hospice can help out."

"I have told Mr. Roberts that my mother is available. She would not charge much to come during the day and cook, clean, and wait on him, but Mr. Roberts said no."

"Did he?" Christian said. "Tell your mother that she's hired and to be here tomorrow."

Juan grinned. "She can come with me in the morning when I take care of the horses and leave with me when I'm done feeding them in the afternoon."

Early the next morning, Juan's mother, Rosa, knocked on the door, and Christian let her in. "Thanks for coming," he whispered. "Dad doesn't know I hired you. We'll let it be a surprise."

The plump, middle-aged woman nodded. "*Sí, señor*, I will start with the kitchen."

"Christian, who's here?" his father called and shuffled into the kitchen, an ever-present cigarette between his fingers. He stared at Rosa, washing dishes. "What's she doing here?"

"I hired her," said Christian. "She'll be here every day, helping you out."

"Wait just a darn minute. I don't need or want help."

"And I didn't want the colt," said Christian, "but I took him for you, so do this for me. I'll feel better if someone is here."

Instead of answering, his father turned and crept back to his bedroom. Christian heard him start a fit of coughing as if reproaching his son's meddling.

Christian finally drove toward home. For the last several days, he'd felt like a fireman, racing up and down the state, putting out flames, making sure the colt was okay in Miami while trying to please a bitchy girlfriend, and making sure his father got help in Ocala. Now he headed to Sarasota, anxious about his boat business and lack of income caused by his absence.

He reached Sarasota and mumbled, "Screw it. Jake can close up. I'll deal with the business tomorrow." He longed to kick back on *The Princess*, watch the sunset, and sip a cocktail all by himself.

As he pulled into the Sailing Squadron, his cell phone chimed. He recognized Kate's number on the caller ID, but didn't answer it.

He had received five phone messages from her while in Ocala, the first one predictable. Calling him "baby," she had sweetly explained she was sorry for being short. Her apologizes had grown old, and he didn't return her call. In the following messages, she grew angrier.

Outside his SUV, he flipped open his cell and hit the voice mail key to hear her latest ranting.

"What the fuck, Chris!" she screeched. "Answer your goddamn phone!"

He closed the phone. "I'm really ready for that drink now."

The following morning Christian woke in the cabin to the gentle rolls and a cool breeze that swept across the bay. He turned on the small propane stove to heat up water for coffee, and by the time he slipped into some cutoffs and brushed his teeth, the water was boiling. He fixed a cup, slipped on his sunglasses, and ascended the three steps to the open deck. On the port side, he noticed a stir of water and looked down at a young manatee munching sea grass on the bottom. "Hey, fella. You sure don't look like a mermaid." He reflected on reading that ancient sailors had once mistaken these sea cows for mermaids, starting the myth.

While taking a sip of coffee, he glanced toward City Island. Instead of swallowing, he choked at the sight of Kate's Porsche parked alongside his SUV and her marching back and forth on the beach, waiting for him to come ashore. "Oh, shit," he said and wiped the dripping coffee from his chin. *Getting up this early, she must be really pissed.*

He gulped down half the coffee while grabbing a t-shirt from the berth. Tossing the shirt into the dinghy, he climbed down the ladder and rowed toward the Squadron.

"Why haven't you answered your fucking phone?" she yelled across the water. "And don't give me the damn excuse you had no reception. You were avoiding me."

He didn't respond and took his time, rowing. In foot-deep water, he stepped out of the dingy and plodded toward shore, pulling the small boat behind him. On the beach he slipped into his t-shirt and gazed at her. "I haven't returned your calls," he said somberly, "because what I need to say should be said in person."

Her irritation instantly evaporated, and her fleshy lips curved into a seductive smile. "Baby, I know I was a bitch, slamming the door in your face, but I said I was sorry."

"And I'm sorry too, Kate," he said, figuring he should get to the point, "but it's not working out between us."

"So you lied." She huffed. "You were trying to break up with me on that trip to Miami."

"I was trying to tell you how I felt and save our relationship, but that trip—" He bit his lip and shook his head. "It convinced me there wasn't anything to save."

"But we're meant for each other. Besides my daddy, you're the only man I've ever cared about. I lost him. I can't lose you, too. I love you, baby."

"You might need me, Kate, but you don't love me. Look, I'm done arguing with you. The fact is I'm fed up with this one-sided relationship where there's no give on your part. We have nothing in common except sex, and even that's not worth all the bullshit."

"Chris, I promise I can change. I'll treat you right. We'll go sailing more often."

"It's too late. I'm not sure what we've been playing at for the last few months, but I'm not happy and want out." He dropped his head and said quietly, "Kate, I'm sorry. I just don't see a future happening with you anymore."

She shrank away and slowly sat down on the edge of the dinghy. She twirled her hair and her face looked like she had been punched in the stomach. She glanced up at him, her eyes watery and bewildered. "This time you're not just angry," she mumbled. "You really are leaving me."

"No, I'm not angry, just tired. I'm sorry, Kate." Like on the trip to Miami, he expected her to break down into tears and stepped closer to comfort her.

She leaped to a stand and hauled off, slapping his face. "You sorry fucker!" she said, her tone and gaze spiteful. "If you think you can dump me and get away with it, you'd better think again. You'll regret this, I promise."

Startled and speechless, he held his smarting cheek, her mood swings leaving him with whiplash; sweet and needy one minute and hateful the next. She marched to her car and floored the gas, leaving tire grooves on the shell lot.

"Wow," he said and watched the Porsche drive off. "How could I've been so blind?"

Over the next several weeks, Christian focused on work. He finished restoring the McGregor in the evenings, and during the day he stayed busy renting out his boats and giving lessons. Schools had let out and the summer tourists were coming down, so thankfully business was picking up.

Although he missed the sex, he didn't miss Kate. He was surprised but relieved she didn't contact him. He figured she had replaced him with a new playmate and pitied the poor sucker.

He called his father every few days. After the first week with Rosa, Hank had stopped complaining. Apparently, Rosa and Juan now made a habit of staying for dinner, his father welcoming the company.

Once a week, Christian also called Ed Price, keeping tabs on Hunter's progress. Price said that his colt was doing fine and his first race was fast approaching.

At the end of a hectic Sunday, Christian was hosing down the last WaveRunner while Jake sat at a picnic table under a shady tree and tapped the keys on his laptop computer.

"Jake," Christian called, "are you going to help me clean up and put the sails away?"

"Just a minute," Jake said, still focused on the screen.

Christian puckered his brow, shut off the hose, and walked to him. "What are you doing?"

"I'm on Kaneva, and my avatar is dancing with five awesome chicks."

"Kaneva?" Christian stared at the screen, watching a tall blond male figure dance in the animated bar with the five female avatars. "That's pretty cool. You're the blond guy? He doesn't even look like you."

"I'm drumming up business for you. These chicks are driving down from Atlanta so they can meet you and take sailing lessons."

"Why would they . . . how do they know about me?"

Jake turn from the computer screen and looked up sheepishly. "I kinda put your picture on my profile, saying I was you. Man, I've gotten three thousand hits and loads of friend requests."

"What! What picture?" Christian scowled.

"It's a good picture. I took it when we were sailing. You look good, a real babe magnet. You know, no shirt, great tan, blond hair, sunglasses. Girls say I'm, well, really, you look like a young Brad Pitt."

"Jesus, Jake, I have enough damn problems and I sure don't want to be hounded like Pitt. Get my picture off there." Christian's cell phone chimed in his pocket. Taking it out, he added, "And Jake, if you ever steal my identity again, I'll kick your butt."

Christian flipped the phone open and said, "Hi, Mom, I didn't forget about tonight. After I fuel up *The Princess* and get water at the marina, I'll be over." Every other Sunday, he made a habit of having dinner with his mother and stepdad at their Siesta Key home.

"Try not to be late," his mother said, "and don't forget your laundry. Are you bringing Kate?"

He realized he hadn't told his mother about the breakup. "We're not together anymore."

"I'm glad. Kate was a pretty girl, but call it female intuition, I never trusted her. I'll see you at eight."

He closed the phone, a little stunned. When it came to his personal life, his mother rarely commented. "Jesus, am I the only one who didn't see through Kate?"

At eight o'clock, Christian sat down with his mother and Frank to a surf-and-turf dinner. He dunked a piece of lobster into the bowl of melted butter, realizing he was eating too much junk food. "Great dinner, Mom," he said and glanced at her. Although in her mid-forties, Angie could pass for an attractive thirty. Christian had inherited many of his mother's features; the blond hair, blue eyes, full lips. When mother and son were together, strangers often thought Angie was Christian's older sister, making his mother's day.

Frank, on the other hand, had a toadyish appearance. He was potbellied and shorter than Angie, with a balding head of dark hair and a large, flat nose. But what Christian's stepfather lacked in appearance, he made up for in character.

When Christian first arrived in Sarasota with his mother, age ten, he was bitter and confused, losing his father and home. With his whole world turned upside down, he lashed out at the slightest provocation and got into numerous school fights with his classmates. But when his mother married Frank, the man was kind to Christian, gave him stability, and made him feel worthwhile. Frank patiently mentored Christian and loved him like a son. His stepfather was easygoing, generous, and a gentleman. Christian considered him his most trusted friend.

"So fill us in," his mother insisted. "What have you been up to?"

Christian told them about his hectic life—work, the colt, Hank's failing health, and the breakup with Kate. He admitted he felt like a fool, putting up with her for months.

"You're not a fool, Christian," said Frank. "You're a nice guy who doesn't like to give up on people."

Christian swirled the ice in his Cuba libre glass. "Are we talking now about Kate or my father?"

"Maybe a little of both," Frank said. "But for your sake, I'm glad you're resolving issues with your dad. It's a weight you've carried around too long."

Christian nodded. His stepdad knew him and his insecurities.

After dinner, his mother helped him fold his laundry. He placed the basket of clean clothes in his SUV and headed home.

Leaving Siesta Key, he drove through town, passing Marina Jack and the bayfront. He approached the first bridge, the Ringling Causeway, and glanced to the right, since it offered a full view of north Sarasota Bay and the large group of sailboats, including his own, moored offshore near City Island. He felt his heart skip a beat. "Holy shit," he cried. One of the sailboats was in flames. Surrounding it were the flashing red lights of several firefighting boats. More emergency red-and-blue lights from fire trucks and police cars streamed though the Australian pines on the island.

He stepped on the gas, recklessly swerving around the slow-moving traffic and raced over the bridge, trying to make out the boat, praying it wasn't *The Princess*.

Past the two bridges, he flew through the back neighborhoods on St. Armands, avoiding the circle shopping area. On the home stretch down City Island, his SUV reached ninety. At the Squadron, he slammed on the brakes, his vehicle sliding in the shell lot. He leaped out, ran to the beach, and shoved his way through the crowd of onlookers.

On the shore, he panted with anxiety and stared out at his beloved *Princess* or what was left of her, the flames billowing up from the sloop's remaining hull. He bit his lip hard, the pain preventing moisture from growing in his eyes. Everything he owned was stowed on the boat, every extra dime earned had gone into restoring her over the years. "Crazy fucking bitch!" he growled. He plunked down on the sand, covered his mouth, and watched the firemen extinguish the flames.

Jack, another boat dweller, walked up to him and patted his back. "Chris, man, I'm so sorry. We saw the fire and called it in, but by the time they got here, she was already engulfed."

Christian nodded to the scruffy, long-haired sailor. "Jack, did you see anything, anyone, maybe a blue Porsche in the lot?"

"No, man, didn't see anything. A few fishermen and their cars in the park earlier, but when I went below, no one was here. The cops questioned all of us."

A policeman walked to Christian. "You're the boat owner?"

Christian stood and brushed the sand off his seat. "Yeah, it was mine."

The officer filled out a report, telling Christian that the fire department investigator would determine if the fire was accidental or arson and the following day the detective handling his case would contact him.

Hours later, the police, firemen, and Coast Guard had left along with the spectators. Alone, Christian sat at a picnic table in the shadowy park and stared at the dark water. He knew the fire was not an accident and he had no doubt of the arsonist. Only one person was angry enough to torch his sloop.

He reflected on Kate's threats, the Miami trip, and again on their breakup. *She said I'd regret it. Why was I so damn naïve, thinking there'd be no repercussions with that demented bitch?*

With his elbow on the table, his hand cupping his jaw, he thought about how Kate had planned her revenge. She was the only person who knew he would be gone tonight, eating dinner at his mother's. She also was aware City Island was quiet on Sunday evenings and knew where to hide her car and avoid motion lights and security cameras so she could climb into a dinghy and board his boat. With motive and opportunity, Kate was his prime suspect, but he had no proof.

Guess it could've been worse. He rose from the picnic table and wandered to the shore, realizing she could've locked the hatches while he was sleeping aboard, trapping him in, and then set the fire.

CHAPTER EIGHT

Around two in the morning, Christian trudged into the shadowy boatyard and crashed out in the McGregor's berth. The twenty-two-foot sailboat and its cramped quarters was okay for overnight or a weekend cruise, but he couldn't launch her and live aboard. With no diesel motor to run a generator for electric and no water for a shower, he might as well pitch a tent on the beach.

In the morning, he called his mother and told her about the fire. She offered him his old bedroom, and he accepted the temporary living arrangement until he could find an apartment or purchase a larger sailboat. Disgusted and beat, he still opened up for work at the marina. In the afternoon, Detective Samuels, who had his case, showed up. Samuels, in his forties, clean cut, and wearing a tie, handled himself like a seasoned cop, but Christian caught his slight drawl, giving away that he was also a native. He questioned Christian about his whereabouts during the night and if he had insurance on the sailboat.

"When I first bought the Morgan," Christian said, "I took out a minimal insurance policy in case she broke free of the mooring and damaged another boat, but I never got around to upgrading the policy. Since then, I've invested thousands into restoring her. Even put a new diesel in two years ago. The insurance isn't going to cover what she was really worth."

"That's too bad," said Samuels. "Most boat fires are caused by a knocked-over candle, overheated engine, or electrical, started from the battery." Samuels flipped through the report. "But according to the fire inspector, the burn patterns and depth of char suggest the fire started at the bow. This is also consistent with eyewitness statements that said the initial flames were orange with oily black smoke, indicating an accelerant like gasoline was doused on the deck. The inspector ruled out an accidental fire and labeled this case as arson."

"I figured," said Christian.

Samuels cocked one eyebrow. "Son, you got someone in mind who might wanna burn your boat?"

"I broke up with a girl a few weeks ago. She threatened me, said I'd be sorry, plus she's pretty temperamental."

"Give me her name. I'll question her and check out her alibi and background, but I gotta be honest. Unless there's an eyewitness, arson is the hardest crime to prove. All the evidence goes up in smoke, including fingerprints. Since no one was injured or killed, your case doesn't have high priority."

Christian gave Samuels Kate's name, address, and phone number. Samuels wrapped things up, saying he would notify Christian if anything developed.

At City Island, Christian next met with the insurance investigator and answered similar questions while he watched a towboat take away the charred remains of *The Princess*. His cherished sloop would go to a marina, be hoisted out, and carted to the landfill. The adjuster informed him that an arson case must be investigated, and he wouldn't receive the claim check right away.

A few days later, the calls from Kate began, but he let the voice mail pick up. Although he would have loved to cuss her out, he realized it might only make matters worse. He listened to her messages, the hysterical yelling and swearing, outraged he had given her name to the police and suspected her of burning his boat.

After a week, he got fed up and answered her call. "Kate, I don't give a shit if you're fucking upset. You threatened me, and then my boat was torched. If you're not guilty, you shouldn't be worried about cops. Now stop calling me."

He met with Detective Samuels at the police station and asked if anything was new on his arson case.

"I saw Kate Winslow," Samuels said. "That woman does have a temper. She wouldn't let me in, said to talk to her lawyer, and slammed the door in my face."

"Sounds like Kate," said Christian.

"I did a background check. She's never been arrested, but seven years ago, the upstate New York police questioned her about her parents' deaths because of the large inheritance and substantial life insurance policy."

"Yeah, her parents died in a car crash when Kate was seventeen. That's how she got her money."

Samuels frowned. "There was no car accident. Miss Winslow's folks died in a house fire while sleeping."

Christian's jaw dropped. "You're kidding me? Why would she lie to me, unless—" He rubbed his forehead.

"She's hiding something," Samuels said, finishing Christian's sentence. "The New York fire was ruled accidental, a gas leak, and the case was closed. But, son, if she's guilty of starting these fires, she's not just an arsonist, but a murderer. You'd better watch your back."

"Christ," Christian said and chewed his thumbnail.

"Unfortunately, the New York case is out of my jurisdiction. And without proof that she burned your boat, my hands are tied."

Christian settled in at his mother's spacious Siesta Key home on Little Sarasota Bay. Although enjoying the luxuries of a soft bed and warm shower with meals waiting for him, he couldn't wait to find his own private space.

He had left home at eighteen, living on his own for seven years. His mother and Frank seemed delighted to have him under their roof again. After work, he dived into their pool and swam a few laps while Frank fixed him a cocktail. They'd kick back and talk, man to man on the patio until his mother called them in for dinner.

Another week flew by without hearing from Kate. Perhaps she had gotten her revenge and would leave him alone. On Wednesday evening, Price called him and said Glade Hunter was entered in the fourth race at Calder on Friday. Christian decided to drive to Miami Thursday night. He next called his father with the good news.

"What kind of race, dirt or grass?" Hank asked. "And what's the distance and purse?" His voice was weak and raspy, like fall leaves rustling in a strong breeze.

"I'm sorry, Dad. I forgot to ask, but Price knows you want Hunter in a maiden special weight."

"That's good; that's good. Price is a top trainer. I'm sure he put the colt in the right race." His joy was ardent despite the pain.

"Will you get Juan to drive you over to the OBS track so you can watch it on their big screen?"

"Don't think so, but order the disc of the race. I'll see it later on my TV. Son, this is it, the first part of my dream come true."

"After the race, I'll drive straight to Ocala and bring champagne."

Christian hung up the phone and felt weariness settle into his spine. To miss watching this race in real time, his father had to be much worse. Christian mentally kicked himself for not having visited the farm the previous week. Ending his relationship with Kate, losing his boat, and keeping his business afloat were all fixable problems, but death was final, and a father irreplaceable. Christian leaned over the kitchen counter and covered his mouth.

His mother walked in and massaged his shoulder. "He's bad?"

Christian swallowed hard and nodded.

She patted his back. "I'll leave for the farm in the morning. We've had our differences, but Hank doesn't deserve be alone now."

Early Friday morning, Christian was once again at Price's barn. He felt a hundred years old until Hunter stuck his head out of the stall and greeted him. Christian stroked the colt's neck. "Are you ready, boy? Ready to win today?"

"Hey, you ain't supposed to touch the horses," barked a strapping woman marching down the shed row.

"This is my horse."

"Oh, well, you sure don't look like an owner. Most of them are older." The woman snapped a lead on Hunter's halter and jerked his head out of the way. "Get back! Get back," she snarled at the colt as she entered his stall. "Need to wrap his legs."

Christian took an instant dislike to the female groom. "Where's Jorge?"

"You mean that no-account Mexican? He got fired," she said, tying the colt's head up short. "I'm taking care of your horse now."

"Why was he fired?" he asked.

"How the fuck should I know, mister?"

Christian watched her wrap the colt's front leg, his aversion growing toward the new groom. He was about to give her a piece of his mind when a woman yelled on the other side of the courtyard and distracted him. At the opposite barn a small blonde stood on her toes while angrily venting into the face of Ed Price.

"Look, asshole, you and I both know you fucked me!" she said, loud enough for the whole barn to hear. "When you sold me the gelding, you knew he was a piece of shit."

Price's face reddened. "Get the hell out of my barn or I'll call security."

"You haven't seen the last of me, motherfucker!" The woman stomped off toward the parking lot, her ponytail swinging like a pendulum. Christian recognized her. She was the attractive horse trainer who had bumped into him and his coffee ended up on his shirt.

Christian jogged to the parking lot and headed to a timeworn green pickup. The annoyed woman had climbed into the driver's seat and slammed the door. "Hey, remember me?" he asked through the window. "A few weeks ago, the cafeteria, we ran into each other, literally, and I got coffee on my shirt."

She ignored him, glaring ahead at Price, her face flushed, and her knuckles white on the wheel. With each breath, she almost shuddered.

Christian rocked back and forth on his heels, waiting for her response. Obviously, he had left her with a bad impression or no impression at all. He halfway turned to leave.

"Christian, right?" she said, still staring at Price.

"You remembered me." He gave her one of his woman-killing smiles and pushed his sunglasses up to the top of his head, exposing his deep blues, his best heart-melting feature.

But she barely gave him a sideward glance. "Don't tell me that son of a bitch is your trainer."

"Afraid so. Price has had my colt for a little over a month. I'm here because my horse is entered in the fourth race today."

"Get a new trainer, Christian. Price is a snake. If I were a man, I'd knock the crap out of him."

"What's the problem?"

"I'm too pissed to discuss it, and this isn't the best place. I'll be in the employee kitchen in an hour." She turned the ignition key and her old pickup truck fired up.

"Wait," Christian said. "You never told me your name."

"Allie," she said and jammed the pickup into reverse, gunned it, and peeled out.

Christian found Price at his side. "You know her?" he asked.

"Not really," said Christian. "I bumped into her last time I was here. She certainly isn't happy with you."

"Yeah, sorry you had to hear that. She's pretty, but has one foul mouth. A good beating would straighten her out."

Repulsion caused Christian's neck and shoulders to tense up. He gave Price a penetrating stare of disgust. "A good beating? You believe in hitting women, Price?"

Price's brown eyes grew big and he retreated one step. "Christian, I was only joking," he said, wringing his hands.

Christian crossed his arms. "I don't find it funny."

Price nodded. "I'm just upset. Last week that woman talks me out of a nice gelding with decent times. Then she comes back here, cursing, and accusing me of cheating her in front of my barn staff, claiming I sold her a plug, when she probably ran the gelding too hard and bled his lungs. These small-time trainers don't belong here. Stay clear of her. She's bad news."

Christian remained quiet, still chastising the trainer with a hostile gaze while Price fidgeted and wiped the perspiration off his brow. "So—your first big race," he said, finally. "You should be excited."

"I am." Christian said somberly. He took a breath and decided to let the beating comment slide. He hated violence against women. More than once, he had stepped in and pulverized a sorry excuse of a man. He began to realize that the backside of a track might be as rough as a redneck bar.

"The fourth race should go off around two," said Price.

"What's the distance and purse?"

"The racing daily is in my office," said Price. "With so many horses, I can't remember them all."

They walked to his office in the middle of the barn, and Price opened the door to a small air-conditioned room with a cluttered desk, worn-out couch, and a few chairs.

Price sat down at the desk, picked up a paper, and studied it. "He's running a mile on dirt and is the number three horse in the fourth race. The purse is twenty thousand, the winner taking sixty percent plus a few thousand in the Florida-Bred awards." Price leaned back in the chair. "But don't hold your breath. Horses get rattled first time out, but if he doesn't run into any trouble, he should finish in the money."

"Twenty thousand? What kind of race is this?"

Price glanced back at the sheet and mumbled, "Twenty-five thousand maiden claiming."

"Claiming?" Christian scowled, knowing Hunter could be purchased for twenty-five grand after the race. "My father wants him in a special weight."

"He's not fast enough." Price handed Christian the paper. "Here, look at his morning workouts below his name and compare them with the other horses in this race. They're close to the same time.

He's running in the right company, the right race. The majority of horses start as claimers, even some Derby winners. Without claiming races, a fast horse would keep cleaning up the cheap purses. This way, the owner risks losing his horse. Keeps the business honest."

Christian scanned the race sheet. Some horses had even better times than Hunter. He gnawed his thumbnail, a nervous habit he couldn't stop. "I don't understand. How could Hunter have gotten slower? My father isn't going to be happy."

"Like I said, your dad must've had a fast watch. If your father is any kind of a trainer, he knows you never outclass a horse, don't want him to run his heart out, only to finish dead last. A Thoroughbred runs because he wants to lead the herd. It's ego. No training or jockey can instill that desire and make him go faster. But pit him against better horses enough times, and he'll lose his confidence and stop trying."

Price stroked his mustache. "That's what happened to Seabiscuit back in the thirties. As a two-year-old, he was worked against other horses and not allowed to beat them, then he was over-raced and tired. He lost his motivation. A good trainer and a lot of patience fixed that little horse, and he went on to beat War Admiral, a Triple Crown winner."

Two employees came into the office and said something in Spanish to Price.

"Excuse me, Christian," said Price. He glanced at a schedule and relayed orders to them, also in Spanish. They left, and he turned back to Christian.

"Where were we? Oh, yes, your colt," he said. "If he runs today and manages to blow away the field, you'll end up with roughly thirteen thousand, including the breeder's awards, and that's minus the jockey's and my ten percent of the purse. If he wins, we'll move him into an allowance race next time out, and he'll be more ready. Or I can scratch him, but it might be several weeks before I find another race that fits him. It's up to you. Has your father seen his workout times?"

"No, he's sick with cancer. I don't want to upset him."

"Well, if he knew the times, he'd surely agree with me." Price grabbed an envelope off his desk. "By the way, here's my bill. Might as well hand it to you and save myself a stamp." His grin carved into his cheeks below the mustache.

Christian took the bill out of the envelope and scanned down to the total, $2,300, which included the training fee, shoes, body clip, and other extras, and there would be another bill coming from the track vet. He had yet to receive the insurance check on *The Princess*, and when he paid Price, he would be wiped out. Today's purse money was looking better and better.

Price seemed to be making sense, and if Christian scratched Hunter and waited for a maiden special weight race, his father might not be around for it.

"Well," Price asked. "Run or scratch him?"

"What are the chances of him being claimed?"

"A first race with his run-of-the-mill times," Price huffed. "I'd say slim. No one spends twenty-five thousand for an unproven two-year-old with his pedigree."

Christian fidgeted in his seat. What would his father do? What will he say after this race? Christian had to make a decision. "Okay, let's race him."

CHAPTER NINE

After writing out a check to Price for the training bill, Christian left the office with a few hundred dollars left in his account. Price had told him they'd meet in the saddling paddock at the track prior to the race. Christian paid a visit to Hunter's stall and found the colt standing quietly, the bottom half of his front legs in wraps.

"I don't care about your times," he said, patting the horse's neck. "I know you're going to win today. You'll do it for Dad." The colt lowered his head into Christian's arms.

After spending a half hour with the colt, Christian drove to the employee cafeteria to meet the female trainer, despite Price's warning. Allie wasn't the classic statuesque beauty Kate was, nor was she meticulously groomed and dressed, but she was pretty, like Price said, and had a down-to-earth appeal. And after seeing her fearlessly tear into Price, he found her even more fascinating. He couldn't wait to hear her side of the story. And perhaps she could give him advice, ease his worries with his decision to race Hunter in the claimer. With the race still hours away, there was still time to change his mind and scratch his colt.

He rushed into the cafeteria, but she wasn't there. Five more minutes, he thought, and waited with a cup of coffee. At the exact time they were to meet, she walked through the door.

He vaulted out of his seat. "You're on time."

She frowned slightly. "It's inconsiderate to be late."

Christian reflected on his frustration with Kate, who was always late. He pulled out a chair for Allie. "Can I get you a coffee, Coke, something to eat?"

She raised her left eyebrow and eased into the seat. "You're quite a gentleman. I'll take a sweet tea, please."

Christian hurried back with the tea and slid into a chair, anxious to query her about her assertion that Price had cheated her.

"I don't think he cheated me. I know it," she said. "I took out a second mortgage on my farm and let it be known around the track that I was in the market for a really nice colt. Price approaches me, tells me he's got this unraced two-year-old gelding with super times. I look the gelding over, checked his workouts, and made Price an offer, forty grand. I should've known." Her lips tightened and she glared at the tea glass. "The damn deal was too good to be true. The gelding was easily worth twice that, yet Price didn't quibble about the amount. I get the horse back to my place, work him, and he's slow as dirt."

"Maybe something happened to him," Christian said, recalling that Price had said Allie probably overworked the horse.

"That's what I thought at first. I put another couple of thousand into him, paying for a full body scan, scoping his lungs for bleeding, everything. The gelding appears sound, no respiratory problems or lameness after a workout. Maybe he pulled a back muscle, something that doesn't show up. All I know is that I paid forty thousand for a horse that's barely worth four. Price knew he was selling me a dog, but there's nothing I can do about it." She took a sip of tea.

"That sucks," Christian said and leaned back, taking in Allie's large, brown eyes and thick lashes, her tiny nose, and unlike Kate who was vampire white, Allie had an outdoorsy tan that rivaled his. Strands of blonde hair that had escaped her ponytail hung on each side of her cheek, tapering around her slender jaw. She rested her chin on her hands, and her bemused eyes stared back at him with a pointing-the-finger smile.

She had noticed his gawking, and Christian quickly dropped his gaze to the table and felt a flush of embarrassment. He took a drink of coffee, cold with a bitter aftertaste. He licked his lips. "Coffee's nasty here," he said, but was thinking, *I like her, like her a lot.*

"So you have a horse in the fourth?" she asked. "How many times has he run?"

"This is his first race; mine, too. I'm pretty keyed up."

"You should be. It takes a lot of time, money, and luck to get a horse to the starting gate. Half the Thoroughbreds born never see a race."

"The colt is really my father's. He bred and trained him, but Dad has cancer and gave me the colt. I was hoping you could help me out, give me some friendly advice about this race. My father wanted the colt in a maiden special weight, but Price entered him in a claimer. I haven't told my father yet. He doesn't need the additional stress. And Price says there's not much chance of the colt being claimed."

Allie pulled a daily sheet from her back pocket and stared at the fourth race. "Twenty-five thousand claimer with a twenty grand purse. That's decent money."

"His name is Glade Hunter, the third horse."

"Hell, I hate to agree with that asshole, but Price is right. According to your colt's workouts, he's where he belongs. He's going off at twelve-to-one odds, not even a favorite. Your father shouldn't be upset that he's in this race."

"Thanks. That makes me feel better." Although he did need Allie's advice, he also hoped to drum up points, knowing women usually appreciated a man who wasn't above asking for help.

Allie stood. "I'd love to hang out and talk, but I gotta get home. My truck's been giving me grief, and I don't want to break down in the dark. Good luck with the race."

"How far do you have to go?"

"A couple of hundred miles," she said. "I have a forty-acre farm in a little place called Myakka City. It's not really a city—doesn't even have a red light. Doubt you've heard of it."

He couldn't believe his luck. Stuttering from excitement, he said, "But, but I know Myakka. I live in Sarasota, only twenty-five miles west."

She sank back into the chair. "Talk about a small world."

A fabulous idea came into his head. And, not willing to lose her, he asked, "Allie, how much do you charge to train and race someone's horse?"

"Forty-five a day," she said, "plus extra for hauling the horse to the Miami or Tampa tracks."

"To tell you the truth, I'm not happy with Price. He's rubbed me wrong from the get-go and, even before hearing your story, I had the feeling he wasn't on the up-and-up. He charges a lot and has so many horses he can't keep track of them all. I also met Hunter's new groom today and got real turned off. She's a callous Amazon."

"What are you suggesting?"

Christian explained he had an old trailer at the track, and after the race, they'd load Hunter into it, and he would follow her back to Myakka. "I know my colt will get better care with you, and I won't have to drive two hundred miles to see him. What do you say?"

Allie grinned. "Stealing one of Price's clients out from under his nose? That's sweet. Okay, I'll take your colt." She reached in her purse and handed him a business card. "And because I *also* like you—" She teasingly batted her eyelashes. "I'll charge only forty a day."

"Great." Meeting Allie was the best thing that had happened to him in some time.

Christian spent the rest of the morning with Allie, watching the horses on the training track, visiting the tack shop, where Allie bought some horse wormers. At noon, they drove to the grandstands and had drinks and lunch in the clubhouse restaurant. They watched the first two races, their conversation mostly about horses.

As the horses for the third race of the afternoon entered the track, Allie said, "Less than a half hour before your fourth race goes off. Let's get out of here."

Christian took the last swallow of his cocktail and hailed the waitress. He turned back to Allie, and his gaze lifted from the table to meet hers. "I'm glad you're here so I can share this big moment with someone."

Allie puckered her brow. "Christian, you're an incredibly good-looking guy and a nice guy. I can't believe you don't have a girlfriend. Why isn't she here?"

"I had a girlfriend, but we broke up a few weeks back. I could say the same about you. You must have a significant other in your life?"

"No, and I'm not looking for one, either. Last year I went through a lousy divorce with my lying, cheating husband. The only good that came from it was I was able to keep my farm. He hated the country anyway. I do better alone." She lifted an eyebrow. "And living alone doesn't mean I'm lonely."

"You got a point. Some of the loneliest people I know happen to be married." He paid the waitress as the horses in the third race blazed over the finish line. They hustled downstairs to the saddling paddock. From behind the spectator's chain, they watched the horses and their grooms arrive, each stopping before an official, who checked the horses' lip tattoos.

Christian noticed a groom leading a handsome liver-colored chestnut into the five-horse stall. "That's Jorge," he said to Allie, "Hunter's previous groom. Price fired him."

"I met him," Allie said. "He helped me load the gelding that I bought off Price. I'd like to talk to him and find out if the horse was injured." She pulled out her catalog and looked up the horse's trainer. "That groom is working for Collazo. Now that guy is a *good* trainer."

Before long, Hunter and his new groom showed up. "There's my colt, Allie," said Christian. Hunter and the female groom walked in a circle under the covered paddock with other horses in the race.

"He's nice," Allie said, "not real tall, but good conformation, deep chest, straight legs."

"He's fifteen-three," Christian said, watching Hunter enter the number three stall. Price was already there with the valet, who held the jockey's saddle.

"Go on," Allie said. "You're the owner. You have the right to be in the stall while your horse is saddled."

Christian swung his leg over the chain, leaving Allie with the bettors who had come to view the horses before the race. He sidestepped a few horses still being walked and entered the open stall. Price was straightening the number blanket on Hunter's back.

"I see you didn't take my advice," Price said, glancing at Allie behind the chain. "But I guess I can't blame you. Half the track would like to sleep with her."

Christian took a deep breath. After the race, he'd tell this pompous trainer that his colt was going to Allie. He watched the groom who kept yanking on his colt's bridle and bit while Price placed the tiny saddle on Hunter's back and tightened the girth. Irritated, Christian finally spoke up, "He's standing still. You don't need to be so rough, jerking his mouth."

The groom glared at Christian. "It keeps him focused," she said, and led Hunter out of the stall to the grassy riders-up area.

Christian gave Price a nasty look, letting him know he didn't approve of his new groom and followed him out of the paddock.

Christian and Price stood under the trees in the center of the wide circle, watching Hunter and the groom walk the border. A jockey approached them, Price introducing him as Carlos, Hunter's jockey.

Christian shook hands with Carlos whose height was that of a ten-year-old boy, amazed that such small men had the strength to control their daunting mounts. Carlos was wearing a silver-and-black shirt and matching cap. With a start of recognition, Christian realized he was familiar with those colors from his father's many winner's-circle photos, hanging on the living room wall. The dates, races, horses, and jockeys differed in the framed pictures, but there was one constant—his father's silver-and-black silks. He massaged his jaw, feeling a mix of pride and sadness. His father's dream colt was running here today without him, and this would probably be the last colt, the last race for his father.

Price spoke. "Just keep him out of trouble, Carlos."

Christian jumped in with his father's words. "My colt tends to back off if he's crowded or gets dirt in his face, so run him on the outside. Take him wide, if you have to." The jockey nodded.

Price produced a toothy grin beneath his mustache. "Guess you do know a little bit about your horse."

The groom stopped Hunter long enough for Price to give Carlos a quick leg up into the saddle. The horses and jockeys filed out onto the track, where the pony riders took their leads for the post parade.

"Come with me, Christian," said Price. "I have box seats in front of the finish line."

"No thanks," said Christian. "I'd rather be on the rail near the winner's circle. Despite what you think, Price, Hunter's going to take this race."

"I hope you're right." Price cackled and left the riders-up area.

Allie came alongside Christian. "That bastard," she said, watching Price walk toward the grandstand. "So, getting nervous?"

"I actually feel butterflies in my stomach," he said as Hunter moved down the track.

She giggled. "His odds have dropped to twenty-to-one. Let's put some money on him."

They hurried to an outside betting window. "Thirty to win on the third horse in the fourth race," Allie said and handed the clerk the money. After getting her ticket, Christian handed the clerk a hundred dollar bill. "Same horse and race, but make it a hundred to win."

They reached the rail as the horses approached the starting gate. Allie glanced at the big tote board next to the finish line. "That's strange. Look at the odds on your colt now," she said. "He's going off at eight to one. Somebody likes him. They dropped several grand on him to win."

Christian barely heard her as Hunter was loaded into the chute.

Minutes later, the last horse was in the gate. The bell sounded, the doors flew open, and the horses lunged out. "And they're off," called the announcer.

Christian's heart sank when Hunter stumbled leaving the gate. By the time he recovered, he was dead last going into the first turn, a good eight lengths behind the pack.

"Damn, got a bad start," Allie said, "but it's a mile. He's got time to catch up."

"Come on, boy," Christian whispered. "Please don't let Dad down." The colt was coasting along the back stretch and still trailing the field. At the half-mile pole, he shifted gears and began passing horses on the outside.

"Come on, Hunter!" Allie screamed. "He's making his move!"

Christian froze. The lump in his throat prevented him from yelling. His eyes became moist as his colt gave the race all he had. Rounding the final turn, Hunter had moved into third place.

"And here comes Glade Hunter," said the announcer on the PA. Hunter was neck and neck with the front-runner on the rail when they charged down the homestretch toward the finish line.

Christian held his breath. Hunter blew past the other colt and took the lead. He continued to gain ground, leaving the field of horses in his dust.

"Jesus, he's flying," Allie cried.

Hunter crossed the finish line and won by five lengths.

Christian clung to the rail for balance, his heart pounding, and closed his eyes. "He did it," he whispered. "He did it for Dad."

After the race, Christian was in a daze. All the tension, excitement, and fear had been compacted into the two short minutes. Allie hugged his neck and said, "Congratulations, Christian!"

"Did you see him?" he mumbled. "He was unbelievable."

"I saw him." She laughed. "If he hadn't had that bad start, he would have never seen another horse. You got yourself a good colt. Come on. It's the winner's circle for you." She led him through the crowd toward a circular, red-brick wall with a flowered hedge. Allie stood back.

He turned and grabbed her hand. "I want you in this picture, too."

"I don't think Price will approve."

"Like I really care." Christian pulled Allie next to him. Soon Hunter and the jockey came in from the track. Price and his barn staff joined them.

"Congratulations," said Price. "You were right about your colt. He does have talent." The winning crew lined up and the groom held Hunter's head while the photo was taken.

The jockey hopped off Hunter and shook Christian's hand. "Nice colt, nice colt," he said.

Christian hugged the colt's neck and patted him while the tack was removed. He was more elated than he could remember. His horse had won and validated his and his father's blind faith.

Allie, however, was grim. "Christian, that man over there, talking to Price," she whispered. "He's the clerk of scales." Price gave Christian a quick glance and walked toward the administrative office.

"Oh, shit," she said.

"What? What's wrong?" Christian asked. "Who is the clerk of scales?"

Before she could answer, the loudspeaker announced, "Glade Hunter, the winner in the fourth race, has been claimed."

CHAPTER TEN

Christian stood by the rail in silence, too shocked to speak. He watched the red colt walk down the track and out of his life. So devastated, he hardly heard Allie say she was sorry. He had gone from euphoria to sorrow in minutes. "How could this happen?"

Allie rubbed his arm. "Horse racing is a tough business. It's all about winning and losing, and I'm not talking about money."

He turned to her. "But Price said no one would want him, with his history of workouts."

"It's surprising, but I should've guessed something was up when I saw his odds jump from twenty to eight. Someone had the inside track and knew you had a damn nice colt, despite his workouts. Unfortunately, there's no recourse. If you tried to buy Hunter back, you'd pay at least double, and while he's winning, he won't see another claimer."

"What am I going to tell my dad? He trusted me and I lost his horse."

"Show your father the catalogue and Hunter's times. He'll understand why your colt was in the claimer," she said. "I'm going back to the stables and find Jorge. That groom might know something about my gelding. Do you want to come along?"

"Why not?" Christian shrugged. "I'm dreading the trip to Ocala."

They climbed into Christian's SUV and drove past the barns to the stable where Jorge worked. He was walking a horse around the shed row, cooling him down after the race.

"Hey, Jorge," Christian said.

Jorge stopped walking the horse. "Mr. Roberts, I am so happy your colt won."

"Yes, but he was claimed," said Christian.

"I am very sorry."

"When you're done, we'd like to talk to you."

"Sure, Mr. Roberts, sure, I am almost done." After Jorge put the horse back in his stall, he walked to the shade tree by the parking lot where Christian and Allie waited.

"Jorge, if you don't mind my asking, why did Price fire you?" Christian said. "I thought you were doing a good job."

Jorge lowered his head. "I saw something and complained, but it is not wise for a groom to speak badly about a trainer, especially when the groom is trying to become a citizen here." He looked up with tormented eyes at Christian. "But I trust you, Mr. Roberts."

Jorge went on to explain that he had only worked for Price a few months and became distressed by the high percentage of horse injuries. Horses that had been broken and trained on soft slow farm track were never given time to adjust to the hard, fast racetrack. Far too many never saw a race and were lucky to walk away maimed but still alive.

"Sounds like Price," Allie fumed.

Christian frowned. "Why would Price do this?"

"Because he's got a big name and loads of rich clients," she said. "He has horses waiting to fill his stalls, so why waste time bringing one along? He works them hard to find out which ones will hold up. What else, Jorge?"

Jorge looked at Christian. "Do you remember the gray filly I was icing down before a race?"

"I remember, your sweetheart," said Christian. "You said she was a winning little filly."

"Yes, my poor sweetheart. She bowed a tendon in a morning gallop and the following day I saw Mr. Price give her a shot in the tendon and take off her front shoe. He told me to get her ready for the track. I argued and said she should not go out. That is when he fired me. Later I learned she broke her leg during the workout and had to be destroyed."

"Ah, shit," Christian moaned. "Why would that son of bitch work an injured filly?"

Allie walked in a circle, kicking at the dirt and cursing under her breath. She stopped and said, "Because of the insurance, Christian. The filly was probably a stake horse and insured for at least a hundred thousand. A bowed tendon usually ends a horse's race career, but it's not a life-threatening injury. The insurance will pay the vet bills but not the value of the horse. Price probably shot up her tendon with Carbocaine. Like Novocain, it numbs the pain, and taking off the filly's front shoe throws a horse off balance. That sucker killed her for the money."

Christian swept back his hair. "How can he get away with this shit?"

"Easy," said Allie. "A vet confirms the broken leg, puts the horse down right on the track, and fills out a report. By the time the insurance company is notified, the horse's body has been hauled to an African wildlife park and fed to the animals. Any proof ends up in the stomach of a lion." She turned to Jorge. "Do you remember the chestnut gelding that I bought from Price? You helped me load him."

"Yes, he was a friendly horse."

"Did anything happen to him before I got him? Maybe he got cast in the stall, wrenched a back muscle, something that might not show up on an X-ray but would slow him down?"

"I know of nothing about your gelding," Jorge said and turned to Christian, "but your colt, Mr. Roberts, I am not surprised he was claimed. The last time you were here, Mr. Price told me to take your colt out after you had left and show him to the sheik. Mr. Price told the sheik that your colt was very fast."

"So I was set up," Christian said. "Price knew Hunter didn't belong in that claimer. I should've listened to my father. Damn it, I should've called him."

"I must go back to work," said Jorge. "I am sorry about your colt,

Mr. Roberts, but glad you have found this nice lady. Your horses, they, too, were friends." He started toward the barn.

"Wait a minute, Jorge," Allie called. "What do you mean our horses were friends?"

"Your gelding and Mr. Roberts's colt went to the track together."

Allie walked to Jorge, determination in her stride. "Are you telling me that our horses worked in company with each other? They breezed together?"

Jorge nodded.

"That's it!" she said, "That's how Price cheated the track clock on the times."

Christian scowled. "I don't get it."

"Think about it," she said. "Two chestnuts breezing together in the darkness before dawn. The clocker can't tell which red horse is which. He relies on the trainer for that information. Price switched the horses' times. My gelding got your colt's fast time. Your colt got my gelding's slow time. That's how Price screwed us."

Christian began to pace under the tree, boiling. After a minute, he growled, "Give me your catalogue, Allie."

She handed it to him. "What are you thinking?"

He flipped to the back pages listing the trainers and numbers that represented the races they had entered horses that day. "Let's go."

"Where?"

"Back to the track," Christian said. "Price has a horse in the ninth race. He'll be at the paddock before the race."

"You can't prove that Price switched our horses' times, and if you accuse him of cheating us, you might get Jorge in trouble."

"I won't mention Jorge, but I do want to talk to Price," Christian said as they walked to his vehicle and got in.

"You don't look like you're just going to talk."

They drove back to the grandstands and, while waiting for the ninth race and Price, they cashed their winning tickets and went to the bookkeeper's office. Christian signed off on the purse and claiming checks so they would be mailed to him. They then went to an outside table near a snack bar with a view of the riders-up area.

"You're wasting your time, confronting that lying prick," Allie said, "He'll just deny everything."

"It didn't stop you." Christian's cell phone chimed. Not recognizing the number and fearing it might concern his father, he took the call. "Hello."

"Hey, baby, I've missed you," said Kate. "I figured about now, you're missing me. If you come back to me, I'll buy you a new boat, any kind you want. I promise I'll be good to you. Don't you see we belong—"

"Goddamn it, Kate. It's over," he growled. "I don't want your fucking boat. I don't want to be with you. Now leave me alone!" He closed his cell and shuddered, trying to throw off the additional irritation. He glanced at Allie. Over lunch she had said he was a nice guy. That nice guy was fast disappearing.

"Ex-girlfriend?" asked Allie.

"Don't want to talk about it." Christian rose from the bench, seeing the horses for the ninth race file into the paddock. He scanned the area for Price.

After a few minutes, Price strolled past the jockey door on the open corridor leading to the paddock. Next to him was the sheik. Four Arab men followed them. Christian walked to the riders-up area and leaned against a wall, waiting until the horses were saddled and had gone to the track.

Allie stood nearby. "This isn't a good idea. I can see it in your eyes. You're ready to lose it. Let's just go."

He didn't answer and stayed focused on Price. Allie was probably right. Confronting Price wasn't a good idea in Christian's present state, when his anger outweighed reason. Losing his boat and now Hunter seemed minor, compared to disappointing and losing his father.

The last horse and jockey filed out of the riders-up area, and Christian made his move. "I want to talk to you, Price," he shouted and marched across the grass with Allie trailing. The surrounding spectators stopped to watch as he met the trainer, sheik, and his entourage head-on.

Christian straightened, puffed up, his fists like loaded guns resting on his hips. "I know what you did, Price!" he yelled. "You fucked us. You switched our horses' workout times and lied to the clockers so you could sell Allie a slow horse for good money and talk me into a claimer, where the sheik got my colt cheap."

"That's a lie," Price retorted.

"You're a goddamn liar and a crook," Christian barked. "I can live without the horse and money, but cheating my dying father—I can't live with that."

Price moved closer to the sheik's men, obviously sensing that Christian's ranting and manner suggested violence. "You're full of crap," Price said. "I didn't switch any times. And you got no proof I did. You, that bitch," he nodded toward Allie "and your sorry-ass old man can go to hell."

With the blinding rage, Christian could barely breathe. "You son of a bitch!" He sprang past the group of men to Price and grabbed the front of the trainer's sport shirt, slamming his back and head hard against an oak tree. With his victim stunned, he raised his fist, planning to give Price the beating of his life. But before he could strike, the sheik's four men rushed in and wrestled his arms down. They punched him as Price scrambled away. Under a hail of blows to his stomach, ribs, and back, Christian collapsed on the ground and curled up into a defensive ball. The assault continued with the men kicking him.

"Get away from him," Allie screamed and jumped on the back of the biggest man. She pounded his back and shoulders with her clenched fist.

The hefty, bearded man reached back and swatted her off like an annoying fly. She landed on her bottom in the grass. "American women," he seethed, "they know not their place."

"Chauvinist pig," she lashed out and clambered to rise.

Two security guards dashed onto the scene, and the sheik raised his hand, signaling his men to stop the attack on Christian.

Allie scuttled across the grass on her hands and knees to Christian. "Christian, Christian, are you all right?" she asked and cradled his head.

He coughed and uncurled his body. "I think so." He puffed.

"He attacked me," Price screeched at the guards, his high-pitched voice cracking. "Get the police."

After several minutes, Christian held his bruised ribs and managed to stand, but the guards clasped his arms. The police, always stationed around the track, arrived shortly.

"I want to press charges," Price said to the officers. "He threw me against the tree and cracked my head. He nearly knocked me out. And he threatened me."

The officers cuffed Christian's wrists behind his back. When they started to escort him away, he pulled against their hold toward the trainer and Arabs. "If it's the last thing I do," he shouted, "I'm going to get you—you and your fucking sheik buddy."

"Did you hear that, officer?" Price said. "He threatened me again."

"It's no threat," Christian said. "It's a promise."

Christian was loaded into the back of a squad car and taken to the police station. He was charged with battery, fingerprinted, and placed in a jail cell that held several other men. He paced the bars, waiting to bond out on the misdemeanor charge. He had a few hundred on him plus his winning ticket money from Hunter's race, but it still wasn't enough. The bond turned out to be fifteen hundred dollars.

He called Allie's cell phone and told her he was a few hundred short of bonding himself out. He asked if she could help out. An hour later, an officer came to the jail and told Christian, "A little lady out front says she's here to post your bail."

He walked toward the front of the police station where Allie waited. They plunked down their cash, and he bailed out without the use of a bondsman. He signed the papers for a hearing date and glanced up at Allie. "I promise I'll pay you back."

"You better." Her smile dissolved into a frown, and she pushed his locks away from his face. "Jesus, you're a mess. Those dickheads really worked you over." She took a tissue from her purse and dabbed at the dried blood on his forehead and chin.

"Lately, I've been finding myself in more scraps."

Allie drove Christian back to his SUV in the grandstand parking lot and, by the time they hooked up his old horse trailer for the trip home, night had fallen on Miami. Towing the trailer, he followed Allie back to Myakka, making sure her worn-out pickup would make it. Rather than take the hectic I-75, she drove up the middle of the state on the rarely used Highway 27. Before Lake Placid, they turned off on State Road 70 and stopped in Arcadia for a quick bite. At midnight they arrived at her farm.

In the driveway, she got out of her truck, unfastened the gate, and walked back to him while he sat in his idling vehicle on the quiet country road. "I'd ask you to come in," she said, "but I know you need to get to your father's."

"Yeah," he said and exhaled. "He expected me hours ago."

"Don't be worried, your dad will understand about the horse when he hears what the trainer pulled. Losing the colt wasn't your fault."

"Yes it was. Dad wanted Hunter in a maiden special weight. I should've followed his advice. I'm afraid that losing Hunter—" He rubbed his forehead. "I'm afraid this will finish my father."

"I'm so sorry." She reached in the cab and brushed the locks out of his eyes.

"I don't have a horse anymore, but I'd like to see you again."

"Well, you certainly know how to show a girl an interesting time. You've got my card and number and know where I live." She climbed into her pickup, drove onto the property, and hopped out. Shutting the gate behind her, she waved to him.

He raised his hand slightly from the steering wheel and then watched her pickup travel down the long drive leading to the house. He put his SUV in gear and continued his journey to Ocala.

• • •

At three in the morning, he pulled up to his father's house and saw his mother's parked Lexus. Rather than go in and wake them, he leaned his head against the cab window and shut his eyes.

Several hours later, Juan tapped the window, and Christian stirred. "Good morning, Mr. Christian," Juan said quietly.

Christian eased out of the vehicle and noticed for the first time that Juan wasn't smiling. "Dad learned I lost Hunter in the claimer?"

Juan nodded. "I had to tell him when I came back from OBS."

"Shit," Christian said and rubbed his sleepy eyes and stubbly face with the heel of his hand. "Guess I'd better go in and try to explain."

"Mr. Christian, you should know that your father is not well. He took to his bed five days ago, and I do not think he will ever leave it. Your mother has called in the hospice nurses. His time soon comes."

Juan's words hit Christian like he had been doused with ice water, snapping him to full alertness. He hurried inside the house and found Rosa in the kitchen. "Is he awake?" he whispered.

"No, but go in," she said. "All night he asked for you."

Christian pushed open the bedroom door and slipped inside. His father lay on the bed, so colorless he blended into the white sheets. With each rise of his chest, his breathing was rattled like a rock tossing around in a can. "Dad?"

His father opened his eyes. "Christian, is that you?" he murmured into the oxygen mask.

"Yes, Dad, I'm back." He swiveled a straight chair near the bed and sat astride with his crossed arms resting on the chair back. "I'm sorry about Hunter. Price switched his workout times with a slower horse and lied to the clockers. Then he talked me into the claimer. But I should've called you."

Hank slowly shook his head, too weak to show much emotion, but managed to pull down the mask. "You did call, said you had a bad feeling about Price. I should've trusted your instincts and switched trainers. I'm just as much to blame. And when Juan showed me the racing catalogue with the colt's times, I knew why you had him in a claimer. I don't want you fretting and carrying this around, boy. What's done is done." He pointed toward his dresser. "Top drawer. There's a box. Get it."

Christian retrieved an old cigar box and sat down again. He took out The Jockey Club registration papers on a horse called Clever Chris. Also in the box were the horse's Florida-Bred and Breeders' Cup certificates. "Who is he?"

"I got the Jockey papers back a few weeks ago. He's a five-month-old colt in Texas," Hank said. "I still owe two hundred and fifty thousand on him. I'd hoped Hunter's purse earnings would pay him off so you could bring him home."

"Two hundred and fifty thousand." Christian whistled. "My God, Dad, how much did the colt cost?"

"Three hundred and fifty, and worth every penny." He pointed toward the side table. "Get me a drink. My mouth is dry."

Christian brought the glass of water to his father's lips and held it while his father took a few sips.

"That's better," Hank said. "Two years ago, when I found out I had cancer, I mortgaged the farm and made a down payment on the colt. I used the farm as collateral for the rest."

"Two years? You bought the colt before he was born?" Christian asked, studying the papers. "And Dad, these papers say he's by Chris and the old mare out back. He's a full brother to Glade Hunter. Why would you have to buy him?"

"He's not by Chris. I plucked Glade Hunter's mane and sent off his hairs for the DNA test and had the guy in Texas take pictures of the colt so I could fake the breeding and get him registered."

"You paid three hundred and fifty thousand for an unregistered horse?" Stunned, Christian stood and walked around the bed. "I don't understand."

"Sit down, Christian. This colt is really by Bold Ruler and out of a mare called Somethingroyal."

Christian had no sooner sat than he was on his feet again. "Bold Ruler? He died decades ago."

"That's right," said Hank. "This colt, *your* colt—he's a clone."

Christian became breathless. "Who is he? Who's the donor?"

Hank's lips turned upward, forming a slight grin. "The greatest racehorse I've ever seen. Secretariat."

CHAPTER ELEVEN

"Secretariat. How's that possible?" Christian asked.

There was a knock on the bedroom door, and Hank whispered, "We'll get to that later."

Christian's mother opened the door and peeked in. "Rosa said you were here. Maybe you can convince your father into going to a hospital."

"Not a chance," Hank said. "I'll be damned if I'll go out in a strange bed, drugged up, and stuck with tubes. I'm dying right here."

Her eyes filled with disapproval, but she said nothing. She turned to leave and added, "Hank, the nurse will be here in an hour."

After she had gone, Hank said, "Been alone fifteen years and now that I'm kicking the bucket, I got women hovering all around me." He glanced at Christian. "Don't get me wrong, I'm happy Angie's here. I look at her and the pain ain't so bad. Back to this colt. With Hunter gone, somehow you'll have to raise the money and pay off the cloning bill. The colt has to be picked up next month."

Christian's eyes went wide. "Next month?"

"This is the dream, Christian, my son owning the fastest horse in the world. I can go to my grave content, knowing this horse will make up for the past—make things right between us. Promise me you'll get this colt, son. Promise you'll do it."

Christian took his father's hand, and not even thinking it through, he said, "I promise. Whatever it takes, I'll raise the money and bring the colt home."

"Good, good."

Christian stood and paced the room, his head spun with figures while he did the math. Minus the trainer's and jockey's ten percent, he should get roughly twelve thousand from Hunter's purse, adding in a few thousand for Florida-Bred awards, and another twenty-five thousand from the claiming sale. He would also get thirty thousand from the insurance company when they settled the claim on *The Princess*. If he sold everything else he owned, it wouldn't amount to another ten, and the total would still be a long way from two hundred fifty grand.

Christian stopped, a thought occurring to him. "This colt can't be raced. He's illegally registered."

"He can be raced. The Jockey Club won't check his DNA again until he goes to stud. By then you'll have a cool ten million in winnings in your pocket. That colt will make you a rich man."

Christian straddled the chair again. "Okay, so I race the colt, but if the truth comes out he's a clone, I could face fraud charges."

"Help me sit up," said Hank.

Christian gently pulled him forward and stuffed pillows between him and the headboard. His father eased back, and said, "That's better. You wouldn't face charges. You're an innocent kid who got a horse and his papers from his father. I'm the guilty party. I falsified the DNA and his registration papers, and I'm listed as the breeder." Hank grinned. "That's the beauty of it. They can't come after me, because I'll be dead."

Christian scratched his head. "So you have this all figured out."

"I do, but, Christian, don't ever tell anybody about the colt's origin. Nobody can know he's a clone. If it leaked out that you knew, you, the trainer, and everyone associated with the colt could be implicated. Besides fraud charges, you'd lose the right to own Thoroughbreds and have to return all the winnings on the colt."

"What about the cloning scientists? They must know."

"They don't know squat. I used the name Jones when I signed the cloning contract and gave them the down payment in cash. I told them I got the DNA from a great barrel horse. Barrel horses don't have to be a registered breed. Those vets and scientists in Texas have no clue about what they have."

"So how did you managed to get Secretariat's DNA? He's been dead for years."

"When I was roughly your age, I read a little article on cloning. Apparently, a fly had been successfully cloned back in the fifties, and they had started working with mice. At the same time, Secretariat won the '73 Triple Crown and did it with class. He broke the track record at the Kentucky Derby and Belmont Stakes."

Hank cast his eyes on the wall and it seemed he had drifted to a different place and time. "My God, what a race," he mumbled. "Never saw anything like it. It made me cry. Plenty of Triple Crown contenders have won the Derby and Preakness, but they lack the stamina to finish that grueling mile and a half Belmont, but Secretariat did. He shut the critics up and won by an unheard-of thirty-one lengths ahead of the field. The whole country stopped for two minutes and watched that Belmont. It was unforgettable. Darn race still gives me shivers. If the clock hadn't screwed up in the Preakness, he'd hold that track record too. Since then, no horse has matched his times."

Christian heard the enthusiasm in his father's voice and, for a brief moment, the cancer and pain seemed to leave him.

"Anyway, I put two and two together," Hank continued. "I knew they'd perfect horse cloning someday. Secretariat was the ultimate animal and, alive today, he'd be the most expensive. In the eighties, I put my plan in motion when he stood at stud at Claiborne Farms in Kentucky. I scraped together a couple of hundred bucks and paid a young groom named Wendell to sneak into Secretariat's stall and take a vial of his blood. I froze it and waited, waited for science to catch up. Ten years after Secretariat died, they cloned the first sheep, Dolly, in '97. I knew it was getting close." He fumbled for his cigarette pack on the nightstand.

"Dad, you can't smoke around an oxygen tank," said Christian. "You'll blow the house up."

"Hell, I smoke in here all the time. Just turn the damn tank off."

"If you want a cigarette, I'll put you in the wheelchair and take you out on the porch."

"Forget it." He sighed and went on with his story. "Anyway, I heard that Texas A&M was cloning horses, so I mortgaged the farm, sent Secretariat's blood off, and prayed—prayed the DNA wasn't too old and my horses earned enough purse money to finish paying for the colt. My prayers were answered. A quarter horse mare got pregnant and Hunter showed real promise, but, then, go figure. I had cancer."

"Dad, how do you know the clone will be like Secretariat?"

"Because I had an independent vet X-ray him and send me the pictures," said Hank.

"What does that prove?"

"Most people don't know that Secretariat was a freak of nature. When he died, the vets did an autopsy and discovered his heart weighed twenty-seven pounds, twice the size of a normal Thoroughbred. His big heart allowed him to pump more blood and oxygen, giving him the speed." Hank smiled wide. "And guess what, according to the X-rays, your little colt has an oversized heart. If he develops Secretariat's tremendous stride and determination, no horse can beat him."

Christian stood, walked to the window, and stared out. "This is crazy. It's like science fiction."

"Yeah, but science fiction has a way of becoming reality," said Hank. "Remember, son, people who have imagination and take risks are the ones that come out ahead. I had the vision to see this dream. Now you need the guts to carry it out."

"All right." Christian sat back down. "Assuming, somehow, I find the money and get this colt back here. I raise him up and put him in a race. What then?"

"First of all," he said, "find yourself a good trainer you can trust."

Christian raised an eyebrow. "I do have a trainer in mind."

"Good. The colt will have to climb the ladder, a maiden special weight, an allowance, and then one or two stake races. Enter him in the Florida Derby and, when he wins, he'll be eligible for the Kentucky Derby and other Triple Crown races. I've already paid for the Breeders' Cup races. After the colt retires from racing, he'll have to be gelded."

"Geld him?"

"I told you," Hank said. "The Jockey Club does a second DNA test before a stallion goes to stud, and they'll discover the wrong DNA. Besides that, his foals will also show up with the incorrect DNA when tested for registering. You'll lose the purse money, and the horse will be worthless. You bring him home, claim he's sterile, and geld him. That will be the end of it."

"What a waste. How much is a Triple Crown winner worth?"

"In today's market, upward of half a billion." He took Christian's hand and squeezed it. "Most of my life I've had lousy luck. Never hit the big time with a great horse. Now I think God was storing up all my good luck for you, the son I neglected. That's why I believe this little red colt will be remarkable."

Christian grimaced. "Oh, Dad." He lowered his head on the bed. "I don't want you to go," he whispered. "I need you."

Hank stroked Christian's hair and sighed. "You'll do fine. If there's an afterlife, I promise I'll be looking out for you. You're a good boy, and you'll succeed where I have failed."

Under a massive oak, Christian stood in an off-the-rack black suit his mother had hastily purchased and stared in a daze at the ominous dark clouds moving in. The clear-blue morning skies had given way to the afternoon thunderstorms, typical of Florida in July. Nearby, the crowd listened to a reverend speak the final words over the coffin. A week after Hunter's race, Christian's father had passed away.

Christian knew it was coming, thought he was prepared, but the finality was overwhelming. The never-again part threw him, and he struggled with his emotions. He couldn't focus on the ceremony.

His mind kept churning with things he wished he had said, but now, too late.

Allie took his hand. He glanced down, grateful she had come, but he could only halfheartedly smile. He had called her the day before and asked if she would come up after the funeral and take old Chris and the two mares to her farm. Back in Sarasota, he hoped to find the horses a good home. She surprised him and had showed up an hour before the memorial service.

Next to him, he heard his mother's sniffles. Frank put his arm around her shoulders, comforting her. Yesterday, he had flown into the small Ocala airport. In the crowd, Christian saw Juan, Rosa, and Shirley, the bar owner, but the rest he didn't know and he was taken aback by their numbers. Most of them, horse people, he thought. They came to pay their last respects to a man who had shared the same obsession.

The memorial service ended with sprinkling rain and the loud rumble of thunder. The people scattered, rushing from the cemetery under the threat of an approaching storm. Christian and Allie were the last to go. They walked toward his SUV as a strong wind howled and knocked small branches out of the trees. With a crash of lightning, the black clouds opened. The couple managed to get inside Christian's vehicle and beat the torrential rain.

Christian didn't start the engine but sat silently. He watched the raindrops pelt the windshield and listened to the wailing gusts. He finally glanced at Allie.

"Until recently, I hadn't seen my father in years," he said, "but I really miss him. At the same time, I'm pissed I was deprived of him all that time, angry he dragged me into his damn horse business, then up and left me." His eyes welled up, but the tears never fell.

Allie clutched his hand. "I wish I could help you make sense of all this. I've only learned that when life sucks and hands me lemons, I try to make lemonade. It's a stupid old cliché, but it works for me."

"Lemonade, huh?" He turned to her. "If not for Hunter, I never would have met you. That's lemonade, I reckon. Allie, Dad gave me another colt."

By the time Christian and Allie pulled up to the farm, the sheets of rain had diminished to a drizzle. His mother, Frank, Rosa, and Juan were inside the house. The six of them sat down to a quiet dinner and discussed the next few days.

They decided that in the morning Allie, with Juan's help, would load the three horses in her trailer, and she would take them back to her Myakka farm. Christian, his mother, and Rosa would box up Hank's belongings. Christian would decide what he wanted and the rest—furniture, linens, food would go to Rosa and Juan. They could either keep or distribute the things to needy Mexican families.

After dinner, Frank took Christian aside, and they sat on the dark porch, drinking cocktails and talking about the farm and finances. Frank had reviewed the farm mortgage. With the sizable second loan and falling real estate prices, the farm had no equity left. Hank had also failed to make the last few payments, and the bank was threatening foreclosure.

Although Christian was supposed to inherit the farm, Frank advised him to let the bank foreclose. Otherwise, Christian would be saddled with huge mortgage payments. The meager profit if and when the farm sold was not worth risking bankruptcy and destroying Christian's credit. He agreed and thanked Frank.

"There's one other thing," Christian said, "but please don't tell Mom. I was arrested in Miami for battery. I bailed out, and the hearing is set for next week."

"Who did you punch?"

"I didn't punch anyone, Frank. I shoved a horse trainer against a tree after I learned he cheated me. It's bull. The guy wasn't even hurt."

"Were there witnesses?"

"Tons, I did it at the track."

Frank took a sip of his drink. "When I get back to Sarasota tomorrow, I'll give the Miami prosecutor a call. If that's all that happened, I might be able to talk him into dropping the charges."

"Thanks," Christian said, appreciating that Frank rarely lectured or criticized. His mother, however, was a different matter, sometimes forgetting he was grown. If she found out, she would likely give Christian a lengthy sermon for losing his temper and getting arrested.

Frank stood up from the porch chair. "I'm beat and ready for the motel. I better get your mother."

Frank and Angie settled into her car and drove to the motel. Rosa and Juan left soon after, leaving Christian and Allie alone.

"I better hit the road too," said Allie as they sat on the couch. "I want an early start. I told my neighbor who's caring for my horses that I'd be back tomorrow for the afternoon feeding." She stood and walked to the front door.

Christian had been stunned when Allie arrived in the afternoon and supported him during the funeral. After all, they had not known each other for very long. But he was further astonished with her appearance. Rather than faded blue jeans and a ponytail, she wore a short black dress, makeup, and her blonde hair tapered around her face and drifted to her shoulders. She was pretty before, but she had transformed into gorgeous. Being so distracted throughout the day, he could not recall if he had complimented her.

He rose abruptly and stepped to the doorway and her. "Allie, did I tell you that you look great?"

She grinned. "Several times."

"Oh, sorry." He hit his forehead with the palm of his hand. "Guess I'm a little out of it." He nervously shifted his weight from foot to foot. "Do you really have to leave? I mean instead of going to a motel, you could stay here—with me."

She reached up, and her hand traveled across his shoulder and up his neck where she finger-combed the hair hanging over his collar. “It’s tempting.” Before he could respond, she removed her hand and stepped back. “But no,” she said. “Neither of us is ready for another relationship. Let’s take it slow and just be friends.”

He lowered his head and nodded. She left the house and strolled to her truck as he followed. She started to open the cab door.

“Allie?” he said. She turned and faced him. “I appreciate your coming.” He leaned down and kissed her, intending a short goodnight kiss, a thank-you kiss, a *friend* kiss, but it evolved, neither of them wanting it to end.

She clung to his neck, holding him tight, and he wrapped his arms around her slender waist. They kissed until they were breathless.

“Screw friendship,” she gasped. “The minute I saw you, I wanted you.” Against the pickup, under the stars, with the cool night wind whipping around them, he made love to her.

Allie never made it to a motel. Christian swept her up in his arms and carried her into his old bedroom, where their passion continued late into the night. Curling his frame around her petite body, he clutched her and drifted to sleep.

The next morning, Christian opened his eyes, feeling whipped, but content. He stretched and put his hand out to touch Allie, but the double bed was empty. Startled, he sat up. Bright sunlight flooded the room, and he heard his mother and Rosa chatting behind the closed door. He glanced at his watch—nine o’clock. He slipped on a pair of cutoffs and walked into the living room.

“Late night, son?” Angie teased.

“Yeah,” he said, and pushed his hair back. “Is Allie here?”

“No, Mr. Christian,” said Rosa. “She and the horses were gone before Juan and I arrived. She must have hooked up her trailer and loaded them by herself.”

“While you and Frank were on the porch last night, Allie and I had a nice chat,” Angie said and folded towels that she placed in a box. "That girl's had it rough, but I think it made her self-reliant and smart. I like this one, Christian. She's a keeper."

"I like her too, Mom."

A few days later Christian helped Juan and a few men load the last of the furniture into a truck. They drove away and Christian found himself alone. He walked through the empty house that held only faded curtains and exited the back screen door. Under a large oak tree, he ran his hand over the trunk and the initials of his name, carved there when a child. Glancing upward, he envisioned his tree fort that his father had built. The few nails still remained in the bark.

The old homestead held fond as well as traumatic memories, and they all flooded back when he wandered the grounds. For the first ten years of his life, he and his parents had lived on the farm.

He walked to the exercise track and gazed at the small lake in the center. He had not cried over his father's death, but after taking in his farm, he felt the welling up in his chest, and warm tears spilled down his face, dripping from his nose and chin. This truly was good-bye, good-bye to the place his father loved, and good-bye forever to him.

"I promise, Dad," he sniffled. "I promise, if it's the last thing I do, I'll fulfill your dream. I'll get the colt and race him."

CHAPTER TWELVE

Christian drove back to Sarasota, hauling the old horse trailer that was loaded with tack, shovels, and barn equipment. He figured he could park the trailer at Allie's farm, and she might have use of the bridles, bits, halters, and exercise saddles. The back of his SUV held several boxes of photos and other personal belongings of his father. His father's exercise saddle also lay in the back, and Christian chose to keep it for himself.

His mind spun with the promise to pay off the colt in Texas and bring him to Florida, but coming up with that kind of money in a month seemed impossible. He had managed to sell the farm equipment—the tractor, grader, his father's old truck—all of which netted him another ten thousand. He had also called the Sailing Squadron, and they found a buyer for his Morgan's mooring site off City Island for a few thousand. Add Hunter's purse earnings, claiming money, and the boat insurance check, he had roughly sixty-five thousand. When he sold the McGregor for five, he would have a total of seventy thousand, the most he'd ever had in his life.

He briefly thought about all it could do: purchase a darned nice sailboat to replace *The Princess*, pay off the SUV loan, or upgrade and expand his business with more small boats.

In the end, he shrugged. "Christ, I am like Dad. It's all going to a frigging toss of the dice on a five-month-old colt."

He thought of ways to raise the remaining one hundred and eighty thousand. Selling his boat rental business—forget it. It wasn't worth that kind of money. Besides, he needed the income to live on.

A bank loan was also out of the question. He had gone through enough hell financing his expensive SUV.

His thoughts turned to his mother and Frank. They probably had the money in stocks and investments and, in an emergency, they would help him. But buying a horse? No way. His mother would throw a fit and disown him, saying he was insane like his old man. Christian didn't even want to go there.

He contemplated taking the money he had and betting the horses, but it was far too risky. He could lose everything. He rubbed his forehead and wearily huffed. *Wonder if the cloning scientist would accept payments?* he pondered. The man might consider it, knowing who the horse was, but asking for a payment option could also create a flood of problems. The foal was illegally registered, and the guy might turn honest and expose the hoax or he might keep the colt or even demand more money. *Who the hell knew the outcome?*

Christian's father had said to tell no one that the colt was Secretariat's clone. He decided to follow that advice. He was even forced to lie to Allie, saying the colt was a full brother to Hunter.

He reached Sarasota and turned off I-75 at the Fruitville exit, going east. Allie lived seven miles south of Myakka City near Myakka State Park. He came to her house and the ten-horse barn, opened the gate, and drove down the long drive. As he pulled up in front of the house, Allie came out.

"Hey, you," he said. "I brought you some horse stuff."

She smiled. "Great, I'll show you where you can park your trailer." She opened the passenger door and got in.

"You left without saying good-bye," he said as they drove toward the barn. The horses in the surrounding pasture spotted the trailer and raced to the fence out of curiosity.

"I figured you were pretty beat, so I didn't wake you. Go past the barn. You can park this next to my three-horse."

He pulled off the drive and backed the trailer into a grassy area alongside Allie's trailer. "How are Chris and the mares doing?" he asked and climbed out of the SUV.

"They handled the trip well and are doing fine. Your old stallion has been racing up and down his paddock like a colt. I love him. He was wormed and had his feet trimmed yesterday. He behaved like a perfect gentleman. For a stud, that's unusual."

"My father raised and trained him. I'm sure that's why Chris has good manners." He finished detaching the trailer. They got back into the SUV, and Christian drove to the barn. "I want to see him."

They entered the old hay barn that Allie had converted into a horse stable, with stalls on each side of a long aisle. "He's in the last stall," said Allie. "It's the only one with an outside door, leading to a big turnout."

The stall was empty, and the stallion was grazing in the large pasture of lush grass. Christian walked into the stall and from the doorway, he called, "Chris, come on, boy."

The stallion lifted his head, answered with a whinny, and trotted to him.

Christian smiled and scratched behind the horse's ears. "Good boy. I think you like this place and the pretty lady." He raised an eyebrow, looking at Allie.

Allie blushed slightly. "So tell me about this other colt. Where is he, and when are you getting him?"

"He's out West, and I'm supposed to pick him up next month, but my father still owed two hundred fifty thousand on him. I've got seventy and need to come up with another hundred eighty." He chuckled and shook his head. "You wouldn't happen to have that kind of change around I could borrow?"

Allie knitted her brow. "Two hundred fifty thousand?" she repeated. "Christian, Hunter was a nice horse, but he wasn't worth that kind of money, especially as a foal."

Christian saw it in her eyes; thinking that he and his dead father had to be stupid or nuts. "I know it sounds crazy, but this foal is very valuable." He already knew her next question, given the colt was too young to prove his speed and his pedigree was marginal.

"But why?" she asked. "None of it makes sense. The foal's mare is here. Why isn't the colt with her? Your father owned the stallion and mare. Why do you have to buy him? And the amount is outrageous."

He patted Chris once more and left the stallion's stall with Allie. Christian scratched his head and looked down, trying to think of away to explain. "I can't give you the details about the colt, and I'd appreciate it, Allie, if you just didn't ask."

She tilted her head, looking at him funny. "A mystery," she said. "All right, it's your business, but I don't have a hundred eighty thousand lying around to lend."

Christian's eyes gleamed. "I was just kidding about the money—don't want you thinking I'm a gigolo."

"Actually, you're an open book. I can tell you're a good guy, but a little naïve when it comes to women and horses."

"You're right about that. Got involved with a pain-in-the-ass woman—my ex-girlfriend—and with horses." He tossed his head back and stared at the barn rafters, trying to get a grip on the unbelievable path he was following. "I promised my father I'd raise a small fortune and get this colt, a colt that might not amount to anything. Calling me naïve is being nice."

They climbed into his SUV and drove to the house. "I have a pin hooker friend who might help you," said Allie. "He has a lot of wealthy clients who invest in Thoroughbreds."

"What's a pin hooker?"

"Usually they're trainers. They go to horse auctions and farms, and buy promising foals, yearlings, and two-year-olds. They train the horses and hope to sell them at a profit. Sometimes they have several people invest in a horse and take out shares. It helps make ends meet. I'd planned to do it with the gelding I bought from Price, sell shares in him after his first race." She breathed a sigh. "Sometimes horse deals blow up in your face."

They walked into her small, two-bedroom block house, and Christian looked around at the rustic cowboy items sprinkled among antique furniture. The walls were loaded with horse paintings,

Florida landscapes, and a few deer heads. "This place is cool, real homey."

"Okay, I'm going to call this guy," said Allie. "His name is Sam."

Christian relaxed on the overstuffed couch and listened to part of Allie's call in the kitchen.

"No, Sam, I don't know much about the colt except it's a five-month-old grandson of Hold Your Peace," she said. "The mare won a few grade-three stakes. Yes, it is a lot of money. No, the guy doesn't own a home, but he has a boat rental business in Sarasota. His name's Christian Roberts." Her voice became edgy. "Look, Sam, he's lived here all his life and is not a fly-by-night. I wouldn't refer him if I didn't trust him. Okay, just check around and get back with me."

Christian rose from the couch and walked into the kitchen. "That didn't sound promising, but I appreciate your trying."

"I kind of expected it with the information I had, but we'll keep our fingers crossed. You never know."

Over the next few days, Christian stayed with his mother and Frank until he could regroup and find a place to live. His business had suffered with his absences. One of the WaveRunners would not run since some idiot had rented and flipped it, getting saltwater into the cylinders, and one of the Hobie Cat's rudders broke in half when another fool ran the boat into a sandbar, going full speed. Jake didn't have the time or skill to fix them.

Christian would like to have spent his evenings with Allie, but instead he had to settle for phone calls. Late into the evening under an outside light, he sat in the Squadron's fenced yard, sweaty and dirty, while he overhauled the WaveRunner motor and fretted over money.

To add to his problems, he was getting anonymous phone calls. He would pick up and say hello, but no one would respond. He suspected Kate. Who else would call only to hear his voice?

On the third night, Christian sat on a bench and tightened a bolt on the motor that rested on the ground between his legs. The wrench slipped, and he smashed his thumb. "Damn it." As he grabbed his hand and tried to shake out the pain, he heard a truck pull up, then the slam of its door.

A minute later, Allie walked into the light holding a bag of burgers and drinks. "So this is how you spend your evenings."

His mood immediately lightened. "Hey, how did you get in here?" He grinned, standing up from a bench. He sidestepped the motor and strolled to her.

"A car pulled out of the gate, and I was able to drive in. You sounded a little down when you called. I thought I'd drive out and feed you, maybe keep you company. Have you eaten?"

"Not really. I had a late lunch, a hot dog at the bait stand. Actually, your timing is perfect. I've had it and am ready to call it quits." He took several strides to a water faucet and washed his hands. "This was a long ride for you, coming from Myakka. I really appreciate it."

"No problem," she said and set the food and drinks on the bench. "Besides, I have good news and wanted to tell you in person. Sam called. He's found some investors willing to give you a loan on your colt."

"You're kidding me!"

"No kidding." She smiled. "They want to meet you in a few days, right here in Sarasota at the Ritz."

He grabbed her up off the ground and hugged her. "Thank you, Allie, thank you." He set her down and gave her a long, slow kiss.

Their kiss was interrupted when Christian heard a sport car engine turnover—an all-too-familiar engine. He jerked away from Allie and heard it drive off beyond the boatyard. He ran through the shadows and rows of dry-docked boats. Reaching the chain-link fence, he stared out at the dark road leading off the island and caught a glimpse of the car, blue with distinctive Porsche taillights, and then it disappeared into the night.

Allie ran up beside him. "What's wrong?"

"Nothing, nothing," he grumbled, unable to hide the bitterness in his voice.

She stared down the road. "That's her, isn't it?"

"I'm pretty sure it was."

After work, Christian hurried home to his mother's, took a quick shower, and put on a tie and new tan linen suit, hoping to make a good impression with the investors. He drove to the Ritz-Carlton and left his SUV with a valet.

He glanced up at the tall, luxurious hotel and thought about his grandmother, how she hated the place. She was a Florida native, born in Sarasota, and was outraged, along with other locals, when the John Ringling Towers hotel, a 1920's historical landmark, was torn down to make room for the Ritz.

"Lousy carpetbagger developers, stinking Yankee commissioners, worthless historical society," she would rant, always getting worked up whenever they drove by the Ritz. "Darned northerners don't give a gal-darn about preserving Florida's past. They're only interested in progress, making a fast buck, and keeping the tourists and snowbirds happy." Snowbirds being part-time residents who lived in Florida during the winter months.

Christian smiled, reflecting on her and his grandfather, who lived in a little cottage surrounded by ancient oaks and citrus trees off Orange Avenue, south of downtown. His grandmother was a tiny woman with silver hair and steel-blue eyes. She had a fiery, outgoing personality and said exactly what was on her mind. She took pride in her roses and small vegetable garden where she grew okra, mustard greens, and tomatoes. His grandfather was a quiet, gentle man with white hair and glasses. He had once sold boats at a marina on the Whitaker bayou, but had retired. He enjoyed fishing and had passed his knowledge and love for the sport onto Christian.

At least once a month, Christian made a point of stopping by and feasting on his grandmother's southern cooking that always included pickled watermelon rind, grits, and fried green tomatoes. Every time he walked through their door, his grandmother would say, "Chrissie, what the devil you been eatin'? You're lookin' too thin, boy."

His thoughts returned to the present. He strolled through the Ritz lobby and entered the restaurant that overlooked a small inlet off the bay. He stopped in front of the hostess. "I'm Mr. Roberts. I'm supposed to meet—"

"Yes, Mr. Roberts, your party is waiting."

He nodded and followed her past tables of diners. In a far corner with a view of the water, she stopped at a table with two middle-aged, dark-haired men in black silk suits. One man with thick curly hair was huge, three times Christian's girth and easily twice his weight. The other guy was of average build with a pencil-thin mustache and receding hairline. Their dark hair and eyes and olive-colored skin suggested they might be Italians. With their looks and dress, they stood out in the room of lightly clothed diners like two crows among a flock of parakeets.

"I'm Christian Roberts," he said and shook their hands.

"Nice meetin' ya," the big guy said with a Brooklyn accent. "I'm Sal Lamotte, and this here's Vince Florio. Sit, take a load off."

Christian eased into the chair and thought, *Lamotte and Florio, definitely Italians.*

"You wanna drink?" asked Sal. Before Christian could respond, Sal snapped his thick fingers and called to a waitress several tables over. "We need a drink over here."

"So, do you want to hear about the colt?" Christian asked.

"Sure, sure," said Sal, "but we're really more interested in you." The waitress came to the table, and he asked, "What'll ya have, kid?"

"A Cuba Libre," said Christian, and Sal waved her away. "You're interested in me?"

"A hundred eighty G's is a lot of dough," said Vince, speaking for the first time. "And betting on a horse is risky, so we're betting on you. We've learned you're a local kid with ties to the community, makes you less likely to run off, and you've never been in trouble, another plus. You also gotta squeaky-clean little business, proves you're reliable."

"I see," said Christian.

Vince slicked back his thinning hair and ran his fingers over his mustache. "Let me spell out this loan for ya. We give you the money right now, and you got two years to pay us back with interest. Your horse comes through, you give us our money, and we go our separate ways."

"What kind of interest?" Christian asked as the waitress set his drink on the table.

"Hundred percent," said Vince.

Christian fumbled for his glass, nearly spilling his drink. He was not dealing with horse investors, but loan sharks.

"Relax, kid." Sal laughed. "We ain't havin' you for lunch."

Christian took a large gulp. "With interest, I'd owe you—"

"Three hundred sixty thousand," said Vince.

"What happens if my horse doesn't earn the purses, and I fail to pay you back within the two years?"

"Then you'll have to work it off," said Vince.

Christian swallowed and slipped a finger under his collar to loosen his choking tie. "My boat business doesn't make that kind of money, so what kind of work are we talking about?"

"You ask too damn many questions, kid," said Sal.

"No, it's okay," said Vince. "Christian should know what's in store."

Vince leaned back in his chair. "In a few years, I'm fixin' to move here from Miami and set up shop. Fact, I got an appointment with a realtor this afternoon. My business in Miami just ain't pannin' out."

"Too much goddamn competition," Sal grumbled.

Vince raised an eyebrow and turned to Christian. "Sarasota is a nice, quiet place, and you and your little boat rentals sounds perfect for an investment. And I bet you know these waters like the back of your hand, know where to find the fish."

Christian straightened in his seat. "Sure, I fish, fresh and saltwater, and I know how to find and catch them."

"The boss wants his own personal guide," said Sal. "He likes fishin' and gettin' on a boat, but—" He chuckled, his huge belly shaking like Jell-O, "Vince can't swim a stroke."

Vince glanced sideway at Sal and pulled out his checkbook. "You work for me, you'll be doin' pretty much what you do now—goin' on the water, handlin' a boat. So what d'ya say, Christian?"

"It's a damn easy job," said Sal.

Christian took the last swallow of his cocktail and played with the straw, contemplating. His instincts screamed walk away, don't take the risk—that Vince and Sal were shady. He also recalled his father once saying that the mob had ties in horseracing. If he took Vince's money and failed to pay it back, he might face more than an *easy job*. But a loan from these guys was the only way to get the cloned colt. "If my horse comes through, and I pay you back in full and on time, we part ways, right?"

"Absolutely," said Vince, who started filling out the check. "The worst that'll happen is you'll end up with a new fishin' buddy."

A week later at Allie's farm, Christian backed his SUV up to his father's old horse trailer as the sun rose on the horizon. He got out and hooked up the hitch while Allie watched. All the money had come in from Hunter's purse, awards, and claiming, along with the boat insurance payoff on his burned Morgan. Added to Vince's huge check, Christian had two hundred and forty-five thousand. The McGregor hadn't sold, and he was forced to borrow the last five thousand from Frank, using the lame excuse he needed to pay a bill, another white lie.

His life had become a mass of secrets and deception, and he hated it. He couldn't tell anybody about the colt's cloned conception, the fraudulent Jockey papers, or the money he had borrowed from loan sharks. Except for Detective Samuels, he also kept quiet about his suspicions concerning Kate—that she probably had burned his boat, maybe murdered her parents, and was stalking him.

All these problems were his, and he didn't see the need to involve and worry Allie, his mother, or Frank.

Hank had told him people with imagination and who took risks got ahead, but his father had failed to mention the enormous stress. And Christian wasn't gambling with just horses and money anymore, but his life. Borrowing from Vince wasn't smart and racing the illegal colt might land him behind bars, but he plugged ahead, fulfilling a promise and his father's dream.

Allie watched him attach the chains from the old two-horse trailer to his SUV. "Are you sure you don't want me to come with you?" she asked. "Meg, my assistant, needs the money and would be happy to feed my horses while I'm gone."

Christian straightened. "No, Allie. You don't need to know anything about this colt."

She lifted her shoulders with a shrug. "I don't even know exactly where you're going."

"That's right." He leaned down and kissed her. "I should be back in four or five days." He climbed into his SUV and shut the door.

"Okay," she said and leaned into the cab window. "I can't wait to see your mystery colt."

Christian traveled north on I-75 up the center of Florida. Before the Georgia border, he turned west on I-10 and headed toward Tallahassee and Alabama. Towing the cumbersome horse trailer that hampered his speed, he spent most of the day getting out of his lengthy home state. At night he reached the outskirts of New Orleans and decided to call it quits. He pulled off the highway and located a rundown Cajun restaurant, knowing off-the-beaten-path places were generally reasonable and offered better authentic food. He ordered a bowl of gumbo and feasted on boiled crawfish. Stuffed, he found a cheap motel and slept for the night.

Christian woke before dawn to start the second half of his trip. He drove through Louisiana and entered Texas. Before leaving home, he had contacted the scientist who ran the cloning department. He made the arrangements to pick up the colt for Hank Jones and would be paying with a money order. Purposely, he didn't divulge that Hank Roberts, alias Jones, had died, or that he was his son.

Christian reached Houston, got off I-10, and drove another hundred miles northwest to Bryan. By late afternoon, he arrived at the university and located the stables where the mares and cloned foals were kept. In the office, he gave the manager the money order, the shipping papers, and a copy of the cloning contract, saying that Hank Jones had hired him to bring back the colt. The man handed him a health certificate and said there was no guarantee on the colt, but once a clone survives the first six months, its life expectancy is the same as any normally bred animal.

The transaction was fairly cut and dried. Christian was grateful that he wasn't asked many questions concerning the colt. After the paperwork, he and the man left for the stables, and a young woman led the little red colt out of his stall.

Between his wide-set eyes he had a big star and narrow strip that traveled almost to his nostrils, and he had three white socks, two on the hind legs and one on the right front. The flashy little colt danced across the ground as he was led to Christian's trailer.

"He's really nice," Christian said.

"Yes, he looks more like a show horse than a barrel racer," the man said.

Christian chewed his nails and didn't comment.

The colt was given a mild tranquilizer and loaded into the straw-deep trailer. Christian gripped the steering wheel to stop his shaky hands and headed home with his precious cargo.

Christian drove straight through to Florida, stopping only briefly to water and feed the colt and himself. Possibly having a living legend in the old trailer, he was nervous and wanted the journey over. On the third morning, he reached Allie's farm in record time and breathed a sigh of relief.

Storm clouds blocked out the rising sun when he drove past the house and small lake. He pulled up to the barn, and Allie walked out holding a rake.

"How was your trip?" she asked.

He stepped from his ride. "Long and tiring. I haven't slept in a couple of days."

"I'll get him out. I have his stall ready." She opened the trailer door, put a lead on the colt, and led him onto the grass. The colt dropped his head and grazed while Allie walked around him, her roaming eyes studying every feature.

"He looks good, doesn't he?" Christian asked.

She didn't answer and continued to stare at the colt.

"Allie, what do you think?"

She glanced up. "This colt is not a full brother to Hunter. He's too damn perfect."

"He's a chestnut, like Hunter."

Her eyes flashed at Christian. "Don't try and sell me a load of crap, Christian. Now, what's the deal with this colt?"

"I can't tell you," he said quietly and dropped his head.

She gathered up the lead. "Come on, Mystery," she huffed. "Let's get you into your stall. I've got work to do." She led the colt into the first stall and released him. In passing, she glared at Christian and disappeared into the feed room.

Christian slipped into the stall and locked the door. "She's mad at me," he whispered to the colt. "Thinks I don't trust her with the truth." It was for Allie's own good. If the cloning hoax was discovered when the colt was raced, she could also get in trouble—lose her right to train and breed Thoroughbreds, or worse, she could be charged with fraud and face jail. Better she remain uninformed and blameless.

He sat down on the shavings, and the colt came over and chewed on his shirt. The little guy then lay down next to him as the cool wind swept through the barn and rain began to fall. Christian stretched out, using hay as a pillow and placed his arm over the colt's neck. His eyes were so heavy he could not keep them open, and he and the colt drifted to sleep.

The colt's excited, high-pitched whinny woke Christian in the afternoon and he staggered to his feet. The colt's chin rested on top of the stall door as he strained to look out of the barn at the other horses. He whinnied again, calling to them.

"You'll get your chance to play in those pastures," he said, patting the colt. He brushed the hay and shavings off and left the stall. His SUV was still parked in front of the barn, minus the horse trailer. Allie must have taken it to the back of the property and unhooked it. He climbed in his SUV and ran his hand over his mouth, wondering if she was still angry.

He drove to the house and knocked on the door.

"Come in," Allie called from in the house.

He trudged in and closed the door. "You still pissed at me?"

"Christian, I was married to a liar. I won't go there again. Never in a million years could your stallion and that old mare produce something that good. Did you buy a stolen colt and have to fake his papers?"

"No! He's not stolen." He rubbed his forehead. "Look, I can't tell you anything about that colt and, believe me, it's for your own good."

She stared up into his eyes. "What have you gotten yourself into with this foal?"

"I don't know." He stepped away from her and her accusing stare. "I really don't."

"All right, I won't ask about the colt again, but I understand why he cost so much. He's really beautiful." She walked up and pulled a flake of hay from his hair.

"So, I'm forgiven?"

"When I saw you sleeping in the stall with your arm around the foal—" She smiled. "How could I possibly stay angry at that kind of a guy?"

CHAPTER THIRTEEN

Christian began to spend more nights with Allie than at his mother's. In his spare time at the farm, he mended the fences, fixed broken water lines, mowed, graded the small exercise track with her tractor, and helped feed and care for the horses. Having grown up in Ocala, he did not see those chores as work, but part of country living.

After a few weeks, Allie asked him to move in. Although he had never roomed with anyone before, he willingly agreed. It made sense. He did not have the money to purchase another boat or the thousands required up front to get an apartment. Splitting the cost of utilities and mortgage payment helped both of them out financially.

The daily thirty-mile drive to his sailboat business was a drag, but living among the horses, wildlife, and this woman far exceeded the time spent on the road. He also fell in love with the Myakka area and its country folks who were a totally different breed compared to the Sarasota population that mainly consisted of northern transplants.

Most Myakka residents spoke with a slow southern drawl and a polite "yes, ma'am; no, sir." Their lives were focused on livestock, weather, and religion. Myakka City did not have a supermarket or any fast-food chains, but it had eight churches. The people were a rugged bunch, accustomed to hardships. They wore cowboy hats and drove pickups, but their true charm lay in looking out for one another.

Christian also discovered that he and Allie had a lot in common. Both were born and raised in Florida and shared the same interest in animals, nature, and the outdoors. Besides beautiful, she was smart and laughed easily. She did have a temper, but he rarely saw it. He realized he also was guilty of getting hot under the collar if shoved the wrong way.

As weeks turned to months, he started believing Allie might be his soul mate. The feeling seemed mutual. She let go of her hurtful past and suspicion of men and embraced him with fondness and respect.

Born and raised in Arcadia, Allie had not spent much time on the coast, so Christian introduced her to his interests. She took to the sea with zeal. He launched the McGregor, and they sailed up the bay with Allie eager to learn about the boat. In no time, she steered and tacked as well as hoisted the main, ran out the jib, and even launched the big spinnaker sail. They stayed several nights aboard, anchored off a deserted mangrove beach, and swam, crabbed, and fished. On the deck under the stars, they cracked open boiled blue crabs they had caught, and dunked the delicate white meat in melted butter, and dined on a few speckled trout that Christian had cleaned and cooked.

Allie leaned back on the open deck with the night breeze blowing across the bay and lifting her golden hair from her shoulders. "I love the country and my horses, but I could grow used to this lifestyle."

Back at the farm, Christian revived an old obsession, lost when he was ten years old. He started riding again. Weather permitting, he saddled up old Chris before sundown, and he and Allie hit the trails on horseback. When they saw deer, wild turkeys, gators, and wading birds, they shared the same enthusiasm. Christian had never been in such a compatible relationship. He and Allie were so similar.

The colt that had been registered as Clever Chris ended up with the nickname Mystery. The farm already held too many beings named Chris. Allie had placed him in a big pasture with a gentle older gelding, and he was growing faster than summer grass. Christian and Allie leaned on the fence one day, watching him charge in a wide circle around the pasture as the gelding grazed.

Christian laughed. "Mystery's created his own racetrack."

"He does this every afternoon, all by himself," said Allie. "It's like he's practicing."

A plane flew overhead, and the colt stopped and looked up. He watched the plane until it was out of sight.

"I've never seen that," Allie said, amazed.

"What?"

"A horse watching an airplane," she said. "God, he's intelligent. You can see it in his eyes. He doesn't think like a normal horse."

"Maybe he's not."

Everything seemed ideal in Christian's life. He was living in a great place, doing the things he enjoyed with the perfect girl. But his happiness was hampered with worries. Could he get away with racing the illegal colt? Could he pay off the loan sharks in time? Would Kate cause him more grief? He continued to get anonymous phone calls to his cell every few weeks.

One night at the farm, Christian sat on the couch next to Allie, watching TV. His cell rang, and he answered it. "Hello? Hello?" With no response, he closed the phone. "Damn it," he grumbled and tossed the cell on the coffee table. "I get these calls all the time at work. I think it's Kate."

"Kate?" Allie huffed. "Next time I'll answer your phone and give her a piece of my mind."

"No, you'd only make matters worse. You don't know her, Allie." He figured it was time Allie knew the whole truth about Kate. He explained that Kate had threatened him when they broke up and soon after his sloop was burned. Kate had also said her parents died in a car crash, but he later learned from a detective that she lied and her parents really died in a house fire.

"Jesus, Christian, she's deranged and dangerous. What are you going to do?"

"Ignore her," he said. "She'll eventually get tired of bugging me and go away."

"She's not going away."

He puckered his brow. "Why not?"

Allie cupped his jaw and kissed his cheek. "Because I've sampled the goods, and you'd be impossible to replace."

Summer quietly ended with no devastating hurricanes hitting the Sunshine State, much to Christian's and Allie's relief. Like most Floridians, they had followed the track of each storm that came off the African coast and traveled west across the Atlantic. It then became a guessing game if the storm would land on your doorstep in the form of a hurricane.

"I used to love hurricanes, the wind, rain, and the excitement," Allie said one night, "but, after the Summer of Storms when Charley, Ivan, Frances, and Jeanne, almost all category fours and all hitting Florida within six weeks, I had had my fill."

She explained that Frances and Jeanne had damaging winds and left Myakka flooded, but they were minor compared to Charley. "That hurricane was like a giant buzz saw when it traveled up the center of the state. It missed my farm, but I still lost the barn roof, back porch, fencing, and tons of trees, and then I was without power and water for ten days. I'll never get over the sound, like a freight train going past the house. The whole place shook and things fell off the walls."

"Allie, why didn't you evacuate?" Christian asked.

Allie frowned. "And leave my horses? Out of the question. After it was over, I drove to Arcadia to check on my parents. The road was covered with downed trees and electric poles. My parents were okay, but the poor little town suffered a direct hit. It was unbelievable; ninety-five percent of all the buildings were damaged or destroyed, huge semi trucks lying on their sides, and the trees sheered off or toppled over and stripped of every leaf. The worst were the cattle, dead and twisted in the barbed wire. It was god-awful."

"I remember that summer," Christian said. "It was great if you were a surfer."

She scowled and gave him a friendly shove.

With the cooler mornings in October, Allie began to train Mystery, who was eight months old. For twenty minutes a day, she put him in the round pen and taught him to walk, trot, and lope on command. She continued to comment on his mature look and stunning conformation, but never again questioned Christian about the colt's origin.

After work, Christian couldn't wait to get home and see Allie and the colt. He was ridiculously happy and prayed it would last.

On a Sunday evening, he and Allie had cleaned up and driven to his mother's for dinner. Being an old rodeo gal, his mother adored Allie. They had become so close that Christian thought it was a conspiracy.

When dinner was over, Christian asked Allie if she would like to stop in the village on Siesta Key and have a nightcap at the local beach bar before driving home. She agreed.

Christian was about to commit a blunder for men: never revisit old haunts with the new girlfriend when the old one might be waiting inside. As soon as he and Allie walked into the dark bar, he realized his mistake. Kate sat at the bar, surrounded by three men.

"Oh, shit," he mumbled and motioned with his head. "That's Kate on the end. I think we should go before she sees us."

Allie's eyes narrowed. "I don't think so. I'll not be run out of a bar by her." She slid onto an empty stool at the other end of the bar from Kate.

Christian took the seat next to Allie and kept his eyes down, pretending he had not seen Kate. He uncomfortably ordered their drinks and hoped for a lack of fireworks. Although Allie and Kate were vastly different in their looks, thinking, and nature, they did share a common trait—they were fearless.

Keeping his focus on his drink, he swirled the ice in his glass.

"Please, let's just drink up and go," he whispered. "I don't want trouble."

"Too late," Allie said, glancing past his shoulder.

Christian felt a hand on the back of his neck. "Chris, baby, it's so great to see you," Kate said. She leaned over and planted a wet kiss on his cheek.

He jerked back. "Kate," he said, acting surprised. "Hi . . . ah, how are you?"

Still holding his neck, Kate ran her fingers through his hair. "I think you know, baby," she said seductively. "I've missed you and all those nights in my bed." Her other hand moved to his leg and inner thigh.

Christian seized her hand. "Kate, this is Allie, my—"

"His girlfriend." Allie gritted her teeth. "Would you mind getting your hands off him?"

Kate took her hand off his leg while giving Allie the once-over. Still holding his shoulder, she threw back her head and laughed. "Chris, you're shitting me. You're dating this pathetic little tramp? You could do so much better, baby."

Allie lashed out, "At least he's no longer with a psycho bitch."

Christian hopped off his bar stool and stood between them. "That's it!" He threw a twenty on the bar and grabbed Allie's hand. "We're out of here."

As he dragged Allie toward the door, he heard Kate call, "Chris, when you get tired of the little slut, give me a call."

Outside, Allie ripped free of his hold. "That fucking bitch," she said and stomped toward his SUV.

He sighed and followed her. "I'm sorry, Allie. I didn't think she'd be there." They got into the SUV.

"Christian, how many times did you take Kate to that bar after dinner with your mother?"

"Pretty often, I guess."

She pursed her lips. "Well, I guarantee you every Sunday night that viper has been sitting in that bar, waiting for you to show up."

"You're probably right. Guess I wasn't thinking." He started the engine and pulled out on the road.

The following Monday morning, Christian's business was slow, and by the afternoon, dead. He let Jake go home early and packed up the sailboats and gear. On the grass, he squatted and rolled up a sunfish sail around the mast and boom. As he tied the sheets in a neat package, he heard over his shoulder a woman's voice. "Hi, baby."

Startled, he jumped up and blurted out, "What do you want, Kate?"

She sashayed closer, staring at his shirtless body. "God, you always look good. After seeing you last night, I realized how much I've missed you. I was hoping to get a sailing lesson." She was dressed in beach attire, a skimpy red bikini top with a matching wraparound skirt.

"That ploy is old. You hate sailing. Now, I think you should go." He walked to a nearby tree and grabbed his t-shirt from a branch.

She followed him. "Don't be so hostile, Chris. I just want to be friends and talk. We didn't get a chance last night."

"There's nothing to talk about." As he pulled the t-shirt on, he felt Kate's hand on his crotch.

"I think there is." She pressed her firm breasts against him, pinning him against the tree as her hand quickly slipped down his pants, seizing and fondling him.

"Stop it, Kate," he said. By the time he untangled his raised arm and ripped off the shirt, he was aroused. He feebly tried to remove her hand. His mind said no, but his sexual urges screamed yes.

"Just one last blowjob, please, baby." She knelt in front of him and exposed his penis. "Then I promise I'll leave you alone."

"I don't want . . . I don't want to do this." He panted, unable to think or muscle any willpower to stop her. For a minute he leaned against the tree and let her have her way as she stimulated every sexual facet of his body. He moaned softly, feeling his building climax.

The cell phone in his pocket chimed. For Christian, it sounded like a fire alarm, snapping him back to reality. His thoughts flashed to Allie and his commitment. He looked down at Kate. "What the fuck am I doing?" Miffed, he shoved her off.

She landed on her butt and glared up. "Yes, what the fuck are you doing, Chris!"

"I told you it's over." He fastened his pants and flipped open the cell, seeing a voice mail left by Jake.

Kate stood and composed herself. "I don't believe you, and your hard-on proves it." Her devilish green eyes narrowed in on him, and she slinked closer like a cat stalking a canary. "Face it, baby, you can't resist me."

"I can. Look, I'm very happy with Allie."

"That little slut? I can't believe you dumped me for her."

"Allie is no slut," he growled. "And for the record, I wasn't with anyone when we split up. Now we're done. I think you better go."

Her eyes began to water. "Chris, I never realized how much I loved you until you were gone. My life has become a living hell." She swept back her long brown hair as tears streamed down her cheeks. "Please, Chris, please take me back. I'm begging you," she wailed. "I'll do anything you ask, buy you a huge boat. We'll sail around the world. I can't live—I don't want to live without you."

"Jesus, Kate." He rubbed the back of his neck and watched her tremble and weep. For the first time in a long time he felt sorry for her. She was messed up, but she did truly love him. He walked over and embraced her. "Kate, I never wanted to hurt you. Get some help. In time you'll find someone else."

"I don't want anyone else." She buried her face in his bare chest, hugged his waist, and sobbed. "You're never coming back to me, are you?"

"No, Kate." Suddenly, he felt her nails digging into his lower back. "Shit!" He shoved her. "You fucking crazy bitch."

She glared at him through puffy eyes. "If I can't have you—" she paused, her eyes became distant, her voice turned icy and surreal. "No one will." She whirled around and started toward her car.

"Wait a minute, Kate," he called. "What do you mean? Kate, what do you mean? Kate!"

She kept walking and never looked back.

Instead of driving straight home, Christian stopped at The Gator Club on Main Street, needing a cocktail to steady his rattled nerves. He parked alongside the red brick building and walked into the quaint landmark bar.

Ann, the bartender greeted him with a smile. "Hey, Christian, haven't seen you in a while. Want the usual?"

"Yeah," he said glumly, removing his sunglasses. He took a seat at the end of the bar, away from the other patrons. He was in no mood for friendly conversation.

Ann served him his rum and Coke. "Still have the sailboats?"

He nodded and took a sip of his drink.

Her brow furrowed. "Are you okay?"

"I'm just a little beat."

She walked away, leaving Christian with his drink and thoughts. *Beat* wasn't the right word. He was worried about Kate's threats, but more so, he was angry with himself.

Why had he let this happen? As soon as Kate showed up, he should have hopped in his SUV and left, but instead he talked to her and let her touch him, seduce him, and scratch him. The worst was the minute when he had a lapse in judgment and self-control and submitted to the foreplay. It raced over and over in his head. What if his cell had not rung?

He took a large gulp of his drink. *She played me like a fiddle. Stupid. I'm such an idiot.*

Kate usually left him kicking himself. But this was different. There was Allie. He didn't consummate the sex with Kate, and therefore, in his mind, he had remained faithful, but it was a fine line, and how would he explain the scratches on his back?

He took another sip and thought about President Clinton. He

had gone before the TV cameras and nation saying, "I did not have sexual relations with that woman." Most people considered a blow job sex and labeled him a liar.

Christian was fairly certain that if he fessed up and told Allie the truth, she would be furious. He lifted his empty glass to the bartender, signaling for another drink. He needed more alcohol, more of a buzz to squelch the sick feeling that his moment of weakness might cost him his relationship.

He could keep his mouth shut and not tell. He could file it away under all the other secrets he kept from Allie—the cloned colt and the mobsters' loan. Allie believed he had borrowed the money from some nice horse people. He kept those secrets to protect her, but with this lie, he would be protecting himself and ensuring a future with this great, trusting woman.

He noticed the light fading outside and glanced at his watch. "Damn," he mumbled, standing. Time had flown in the bar. Allie would be preparing dinner and wondering where he was. He paid the bar tab and walked out.

Allie met him at the door. "I was starting to worry and getting ready to call you. Dinner's been ready for half an hour."

"Sorry," he said, brushing past her into the living room. "I stopped off for a few drinks, but I should've let you know."

She tapped her fingers against her lips and studied him. "It's no big deal. Your life is your own. You can stay out all night if you want. After all, we're just roommates."

He frowned. "Is that all we are? Is that all I am to you?"

"Of course, but I do appreciate the extra benefits. You're great eye candy and an incredible lay." She walked into the kitchen, and he heard clanging of pots and pans.

He followed her in. "I thought we had something—that you had feelings for me. What the hell's going on?"

She slammed a pot down on the stove and whirled around,

catching him in the crosshairs of her hard stare. "I could ask you the same damn question."

Christian was taken aback. He had seen Allie's temper, but he had never been on the receiving end. "You're mad because I had a few drinks and was late?"

"Think again," she snapped.

He leaned against the kitchen counter, baffled. *Is guilty stamped on my forehead?* His decision to confess or lie became a no-brainer.

"I had a bad day," he started. "Kate stopped by work. She threw herself at me and begged me to take her back. When I said no, she scratched my back and said that if she couldn't have me, then no one would."

Allie put ice into two glasses and filled them with rum and a splash of Coke, making the cocktails lethal. She stared up and gave him his drink. "You say she threw herself at you?"

His eyes shifted to the side, trying to decide how much to tell. *Fuck it.* He took a sip and set the glass down. "I was putting my shirt on over my head, and before I knew it, she had her hand down my pants, and then she started blowing me. I—"

"You let her?" she growled.

"It happened so damn fast, Allie," he yelled.

"And then you hopped on and screwed her. That's why your back is scratched."

"No! No, I didn't. I shoved her off me, and she fell on her ass. I swear." His eyes watered, the alcohol loosening the grip on his emotions. "I'm telling you the truth. I swear to God, Allie." He stared at the floor and said what he felt but had held back. "I love you, Allie. Please don't let this destroy us."

She walked over and lifted his chin. "Christian, God help me, I love you too. And I believe you."

He embraced and kissed her. The kiss turned to frantic fondling as they stripped off their clothes, never making it to the bedroom. He lifted her onto the kitchen counter and, driven by the day's anger, guilt, argument, and near loss, he made love to her. He was determined to prove his feelings and, with the rum high, he had more control. Allie climaxed several times before he did.

Allie dripped with sweat when she slipped past him to the sink and filled a glass with water. "Lord, Christian, you were amazing. I should let Kate work you up every day under that tree before sending you home." She took a sip of water. "You want to take a shower with me?"

Christian leaned over the counter, eyes closed, his head resting on his crossed arms. He breathed hard. "The tree?" He looked up. "How'd you know we were under a tree?"

"Because Kate called me," she said. "She told me you leaned against a tree, and she gave you a decent blow job. Then you made love to her. The sex was so hot that she left her calling card on your back." Allie set the glass down and turned to him. "She said, 'Search his big blue eyes and see if there's any truth in them.'"

Christian straightened. "Bitch! She planned it, even the scratch. She was trying to break us up." He turned and tossed back his damp hair. "And when were you going to tell me that she called?" he spouted. "Or did you even plan to tell me?"

"Of course I would have told you, silly." She smiled. "But first I wanted to look into your gorgeous eyes and see if you'd come clean."

He frowned. "You didn't trust me."

"You're one to talk," she sniped. "You do love your secrets and don't confide in me."

"They only concern the goddamn horse!"

"Okay, okay," she said, drifting to him. "My lord, you're sexy when you're fired up." She raised an eyebrow. "You want to go again?"

For the next month, Christian remained on guard, believing Kate was far from finished. If she had Allie's phone number, she also had the farm address. He installed motion-sensor lights on the house and barn and replaced the gate latch with a chain and a padlock.

Allie suggested he question his stepfather about the laws concerning a restraining order.

Christian made the call to Frank. "A petitioner," Frank had said, "must prove to the judge that the recipient has committed two violent acts against him."

Christian realized that Kate had committed only one when she scratched his back. He couldn't prove she had burned his boat or that she was stalking him. She had a clean record, since her parents' death had been deemed accidental.

Frank went on to say, "An order of protection is useless if a person is truly out to get the petitioner. A broken restraining order would just be tacked onto the other charges of assault or stalking. A petitioner also must appear at several hearings with the recipient before an injunction for protection is granted."

Christian thought, *Kate would love that, seeing the aggravation she had caused or it could piss her off, causing more problems.* Even with adequate proof and going through the hassle of obtaining a restraining order, he felt the whole idea went against his grain. After all, he was a tall, strong guy, asking for a protective order against a slight woman. *How wimpy was that?*

In the end, he blew off the notion, but did, however, mention to Allie that they might get a watchdog.

"I like dogs and have owned plenty," said Allie, "but they can be a hassle. Out here, neighbors shoot dogs that come on their property, since dogs kill more livestock than all the wild predators combined. The dog would have to be confined or trained to stay home. And a barking dog drives off the wildlife so you can kiss good-bye the foxes, raccoons, and deer that come in the yard, and Al would have to go. He'd love a doggy for dinner."

Al was a ten-foot bull gator that lived in the small lake behind the house. Like Allie, Christian had grown fond of the big reptile that sunned on the lawn.

"Forget the dog," he said. "Besides, Kate could be bluffing. Maybe she only wanted to worry me."

A few more months passed quietly, confirming that Christian might have been right about Kate. He and Allie celebrated his twenty-sixth birthday and the holidays in December.

On January 1, Mystery, like all Thoroughbreds, had a birthday, and was now considered a yearling, despite his true birth date in March. Allie began working the colt in the round pen under tack, introducing him to the snaffle, bridle, and small saddle. Instead of being kept in his pasture all day and night, the colt was brought into the barn every evening and placed in a stall down from Chris.

Allie was continually impressed by the gorgeous and fast-maturing colt. She gave Christian a questioning eye without saying a word.

"All I can tell you is he's going to be a great horse," he said.

As he and Allie's relationship grew stronger, closer, he more and more hated the lies and secrets. Unexpectedly, one of his secrets called in the evening.

Christian was watching TV when the phone rang, and Allie answered it in the kitchen. "Christian, there's a guy named Vince on the phone. He has a thick New York accent."

"Brooklyn." Christian sighed and stood. "He's the one who loaned me the money for Mystery." He picked up the phone. "Hi, Vince."

"So, how's my Florida boy doin'? Did you get your horse?"

"Yeah, I picked him up, and he's doing good. I should pay you back without a problem."

"That's great, just great, Christian," said Vince. "I like to keep tabs on people with outstanding debts. Make sure ya didn't skip town."

"I'd never do that."

"Relax." Vince chuckled. "I'm callin' 'cause I need a favor. I finally bought a place on Longboat, got a dock and boat. I'd like you and your little girlfriend, Allie, to come out and show me the bay—keep me off the sandbars; ya know, a little boat ride."

"How did you—" He glanced around the kitchen corner, making sure that Allie couldn't hear and asked in a low voice. "How do you know about Allie and get this number?"

"I told ya. I keep tabs on people. So, what do you say, Christian, Tuesday at five?"

"I'll come, but let's leave my girlfriend out of this."

"Don't fuck with me, kid," he snarled. "Bring her." There was silence for a moment. "Hey, I want to meet her, and it'll be fun." His tone was sociable again. "Grab a pen and jot down the address."

Christian wrote down Vince's address. "Okay, I have it."

"See ya Tuesday."

Christian felt the queasiness in his gut, the unsettling feeling that he had gotten Allie involved.

She walked into the kitchen. "So what did he want?"

He turned to her, replacing the distress on his face with a contrived grin. "He moved here and bought a boat. He wants me to show him the bay, Tuesday at five, so don't hold dinner."

At four fifteen on Tuesday, Christian drove alone to City Island and the Sailing Squadron. He preferred to defy Vince and risk his wrath than have Allie come and get mixed up in this deal.

He parked in front of the Squadron clubhouse and glanced at his watch. He had the extra time to slip out of his cutoffs and t-shirt into a warmer pair of jeans and long-sleeved shirt. In January a sunny, mild day could turn nippy with the setting sun, especially on the water. He walked into the funky little clubhouse bar carrying the change of clothes.

Several old guys sat at a table. One called out, "Chris, did they ever find out who burned your boat?"

"Nope." Christian felt a little guilty that he couldn't recall the old man's name.

"Darn shame," said the old guy. "You had that Morgan looking new."

Christian moseyed into the men's room and changed his clothes. He walked back out and glanced at his watch. "Gotta go, guys." He did not want to be late, but then again, did not care to arrive early and spend any more time with Vince than necessary.

He drove toward the New Pass Bridge that connected City Island to Longboat Key. New Pass allowed Sarasota Bay to flow into the gulf and had gotten its name many years earlier when the receding tide of a massive hurricane cut a path through the southern end of the barrier island.

At the top of the bridge, he glanced left at the gulf, amber and shimmering under a dying sun and blustery gray sky. *Yup, it's gonna be cold,* he thought and was glad he remembered a windbreaker.

He entered Longboat, and after few miles on Gulf of Mexico Drive, he turned right at a side street that led to the bay side of the key. At the end of the street, he pulled up to a monstrous white three-story house that faced the bay with a canal on one side.

The loan shark business must be booming. The house was easily worth five million. He left his SUV and walked to the ten-foot-tall front door.

Before he could ring the bell, the door opened. Vince met him with a wide grin. "Saw you pull in on the security cameras," he said. "Come in, come in." His smile melted away, and he knitted his brow, looking beyond Christian.

"She couldn't make it," Christian said before Vince could ask.

Vince's eyes flashed mean, his black saucers studying Christian.

Christian didn't flinch and stared defiantly back at him, communicating that if there were consequences, let's get it over with.

Vince's expression softened, and his mustache curled upward with a grin. "She couldn't make it, then she couldn't make it. Maybe another time."

"Maybe."

"Well, come on, the fellas are waitin' out back by the pool."

"The fellas?" Christian questioned.

"Yeah, Sal and some of the guys wanted to come along for the maiden run. None of us know shit about boats." They walked through the living room, and Christian glanced up at high vaulted ceilings surrounded by balconies that led to other rooms.

"Nice house," Christian said.

"Yeah, I picked it up for a song from a guy who owed me money. Besides owning and racing horses, I dabble in real estate and have some businesses in New York."

"I see," Christian said with a raised eyebrow. They reached the back door and walked out to the pool and patio.

"Hey, boys," Vince called. "Our captain is here."

Christian walked toward the poolside bar and four other men with dark hair who also appeared Italian. They held cocktails and were smoking long cigars. Sal, wearing a loose floral shirt, sat in a chair. His shadow was equivalent to several men. Two lean, thirtyish men stood behind Sal. Their black shirts matched their surly expressions. One man with a pockmarked face, high cheekbones, and a tight ponytail, seemed especially hardcore. His black soulless eyes followed Christian as if he were prey. The fourth man sat opposite Sal and was a short, curly-headed guy.

Although the men were well dressed and clean shaven, they had a sinister aura of grime. Christian had plenty of Italian friends, but these men gave him the willies.

"Hello," Christian said.

"Hey, kid," Sal said with a grin. "Where's the girl?"

"She apparently couldn't make it," Vince answered in an irritated tone. Sal became long-faced, and the other men's mood darkened into deadpan serious with all eyes focused on Christian.

Sal rocked his huge bulk out of the chair and stood. "Kid, maybe you don't understand. If you want to stay healthy, you'd better do what Vince says. Next time you're told to bring her, you'd better damn well do it."

For a moment, Christian stared at Sal and then shifted his gaze to Vince. "I'm not bringing her, not now, not ever. I don't want her involved. The deal and loan concerns only me, Vince."

The ponytail man clenched his fists and started toward Christian. Vince raised his hand, and the man halted.

Vince walked a half circle around Christian, stopped and kneaded his mustache. "Seems our boy is somewhat of a Johnny Reb. Let me straighten things out for you," he said. "When you took my money, your girl and the rest of your family became involved in our little deal."

Christian scowled. "My family?"

"Yeah, the mother and stepdad on Siesta," said Vince, "and your grandparents off Orange Avenue, or is it Lemon? I get these fuckin' fruit streets mixed up."

"Orange," said Sal.

"I like to call these people leverage," Vince continued, "in case you don't behave. You run, talk to cops or cause me problems then somethin' bad might happen to them. You got it now?"

"I got it," said Christian.

Sal patted Christian's back so hard he nearly fell over before he got his footing. Sal placed his weighty arm over Christian's shoulder, clutched him close, and leaned into his ear. "Look, kid. Just do as you're told, keep your mouth shut, and everyone will be fine. *Capisce?*"

"Sure, Sal," Christian said, and Sal freed him from the crushing hold. Christian stepped back and produced a Cheshire-cat smile. But beneath his affable appearance, he fumed. *How dare these sons of bitches threaten my girl and family.*

"Sal's right," said Vince. "We're always looking to adopt new talent, and you fill the bill."

It occurred to Christian that they were counting on his inability to pay back the loan. "It's getting late," he said. "Let's get this boat ride over."

"*Sì, andiamo,*" Vince said to the men.

The group walked down the lawn to the boat dock. When Christian saw the forty-foot Scarab tied to the dock, it all was adding up. The super-fast cigarette boats were high maintenance and gas-guzzlers. They were rarely used as pleasure crafts for fishing, but generally functioned as race boats, or possibly drug running.

The men piled aboard the open-deck boat with Vince taking the front passenger seat near the steering wheel. The other men got comfortable in the back seats. Christian stood alone on the dock, quickly realizing he was captain, deckhand, and tour guide. He untied the bow and stern lines from the dock cleats and tossed them aboard. He hopped on the Scarab and gave its bow a slight shove away from the dock.

"Key's in it," Vince said, lighting a cigar while Christian made his way past the men to the helm.

"So, kid, how's the horse?" Sal asked.

"He's doing fine. Should make enough to pay you back." He turned the key and the four three-hundred-horse Mercury engines fired up with a rumbling roar and deafened all other sound. "Where do you want to go?" he yelled over the noise.

"Wherever," Vince shouted with a wave of his cigar.

"It'll be a bit choppy tonight." Christian stood behind the steering wheel and eased the throttle forward. The sleek boat glided slowly past the wooden pole markers and entered the bay. As they reached the channel markers for the Intracoastal Waterway, he swung the bow north on the open bay.

Christian smiled at Vince, an illusory smile, as he thought about the man threatening Allie, his mother, and grandparents. Rather than intimidate Christian and make him behave with the leverage, they had enraged him. He shoved the throttle forward, and the boat dug in, nearly flying with the acceleration. With each ripple of a wave, the boat lifted, halfway out of the water, and crashed down hard, making for one rough ride.

Christian glanced back at the men, the crisp wind and sea spray blasted their terrified faces, the night beginning to close in as they clung to the handles and sides. The spilled cocktails and soaked cigars had already been discarded.

Sal screamed, "Slow it down."

Christian cupped his ear, pretending he could not hear or understand. He turned back, looking straight ahead and increased the speed. In minutes, they left Sarasota and were in Bradenton. He drove the boat with a vengeance and recalled Sal saying at the Ritz that Vince could not swim. In open water, Christian could easily spin the wheel, capsize the boat, and drown these rats. They had misjudged him. He would willingly die or kill for his loved ones. They also made the mistake of climbing aboard and entering his water world. Now they found themselves at his mercy.

Christian disregarded the no-wake zones, and the Scarab reached its maximum speed. The boat zipped under the Cortez Bridge, which was lined with glittering car lights.

"Slow down," Vince yelled, but Christian ignored him.

They shot past Palma Sola Bay and flew under the Holmes Beach Bridge. Christian looked to his left and saw the tip of Anna Maria Island and its piers. The light of a vanishing sun slipped beneath the watery black horizon of the gulf when they entered Tampa Bay and its rougher chop. With each wave, the Scarab lurched completely above the surface, flying temporarily.

Christian made a beeline toward Egmont Key and a huge freighter that had left the gulf and was cruising toward the towering Sunshine Skyway Bridge. *Even if we survive, these pricks will rethink using me.* He swung the Scarab toward the freighter and took deadly aim at its massive side.

"Stop, stop!" Vince yelled, but the men couldn't move or stop Christian. If they released their hold to get at him, they risked being tossed overboard. If they shot him, the boat would have no driver, and they would surely crash and burn. Christian had them by the short hairs.

Just before the Scarab collided into the freighter's side and exploded, Christian throttled down, spun the wheel, and brought the Scarab coasting alongside the ship, ten yards away. The Scarab idled and rolled in the giant ship wake as the freighter motored past.

Christian turned and smiled at the wide-eyed men who were soaked, pale, and still clutched the boat handles. "Are we having fun yet?"

Sal leaned over and vomited. The man with the ponytail leaped to a stand and shouted in broken English, "I kill you, you bastard." He stepped toward Christian.

"Try it," Christian shouted, taking hold of the throttle and preparing to gun it. "I'll flip this bitch in a heartbeat and kill all you motherfuckers!"

"Sit down, Vito," Vince said and released his hold on the handles. He glanced up at Christian. "You're one crazy little fucker, pullin' this stunt with me."

"I am crazy," Christian said, his heart pounding against his chest walls. "I get that way when my family and girl are threatened. We can keep this business between you and me, Vince, and things will be fine. But drag the people I care about into it, and someone's going to die. And I really don't give a shit if it's me or you."

For a long moment, Vince kneaded his thin mustache and studied Christian. Christian glared back, refusing to blink. Vince slowly grinned and turned in the seat to Sal. "Our boy's got moxie, Sally. What'd ya think we should do with this punk?"

"Well," Sal said and anxiously looked around at the choppy dark bay, "the kid knows these waters and can definitely drive the boat."

Vince laughed, sudden and hard. "All right, we'll keep him around and leave his girl and family alone."

On the return trip to Longboat, Christian drove the Scarab at a slower pace. The fright had worn off, and the men relaxed and talked about the nerve-shattering ride. At Vince's house, Christian guided the boat alongside the dock and cut the engines. He sprang onto the dock and nervously secured the lines. The playing field had changed. No longer having the upper hand, he wondered if he would pay the ultimate price for his defiance and putting them through the hellish boat ride.

Vito stepped off the boat and hovered near Christian. His intense glare conveyed he thought the same thing. Now safely on shore, he waited for Vince's orders to wreak havoc on Christian.

Vince put the matter to rest when he asked Christian, "How 'bout stoppin' by next week and takin' me fishin'?"

"All right," Christian said uneasily and glanced at Vince's men. With raised eyebrows, they also seemed astonished that their boss was giving him a reprieve.

As the group walked toward the house, Christian said to Vince, "We'll use my Whaler. It's set up for bay fishing."

"Bay fishin'?" Vince said. "I ain't interested in dinky little fish. I was thinking more about deep-sea fishin' and catchin' grouper."

Christian smirked. "Running thirty miles out and holding a pole over the side of a boat is for tourists, Vince. I'll put you on big fish, even grouper, right off your backyard. There're some decent artificial reefs in the bay off the John Ringling home and some great ledges near the bridges. The grass flats also hold good-sized reds and speckled trout. And you haven't fished until you've hooked into a big snook."

"Is that right?" Vince said. They reached the pool and walked in the house to the bar.

"They fight like a son of a bitch," Christian rambled on, concealing his fears and hoping to further defuse the earlier tense situation. "And right now snook are in the bayous, channels, and off the flats, seeking the warmer water during winter."

Vince fixed Christian a cocktail as he talked about fishing.

"I was standing on a high seawall," Christian said, "and hooked into a monster snook, a forty incher, but I forgot my damn net. When I hoisted the fish up the wall, the line was frayed and snapped, but the snook was so played out that it just floated below me."

Christian laughed. "I was so pissed I jumped off the seawall. Hell, the fish took off before I could grab its line, and then I couldn't climb back up the wall. I ended up wading barefoot through oyster beds to a boat ramp. Man, my feet were all cut up."

Sal laughed. "Dumb blond." The other men chuckled, except Vito. The ponytail man's somber fixed stare betrayed his loathing for Christian.

After a few drinks, Christian said good night. He climbed into the security of his SUV and felt relief wash over him like a warm shower. He had put on his poker face, played his best hand, and the gamble seemed to pay off.

Rather than treat Christian like a typical pigeon, Vince appeared to like him. But Christian wasn't a complete fool. Vince's friendly mood could change as fast as the Florida tropical weather, sunny one minute and storming the next. If cheated, Vince wouldn't hesitate to hurt him.

Christian drove toward Myakka and thought about the evening. It reminded him of scuba diving and messing with sharks. He always tried to get close to them, sometimes touching their dorsal fin or tail, close enough for the thrill without getting bitten. He was now diving in an underworld and getting close to a two-legged shark, a loan shark. In the end would he climb out in one piece?

I'd rather fool around with a big tiger shark. They're safer.

CHAPTER FOURTEEN

In February, Valentine's Day, Christian made dinner reservations at a fancy French restaurant for him and Allie, wanting to surprise her with a night out. As a teen, he had seen how his stepfather treated his mother.

"Indulge the woman you love, especially on her birthday and holidays," Frank had told him. "With the minor effort, she will return the favor tenfold." Frank was a good teacher, and Christian never forgot his lessons.

He rushed home early with a dozen roses and a small gift box containing ruby-chip earrings. The flowers, earrings, and dinner might set him back three hundred dollars, but the price was small, considering all Allie did for him.

After pulling up to the house, he ran to the barn to feed and care for the horses. He hoped to be finished with them and have himself ready before Allie came home. The Tampa meet had started, and she had a filly in a race at Tampa Bay Downs.

Christian had to jog when leading Mystery in from the pasture to the barn. To walk, he would be dragged by the rambunctious, strong colt. In his stall, Mystery tilted his head and begged for dinner, smacking, and chewing his lips.

"All right, Mystery." He chuckled and poured five quarts of oats and sweet feed into his feed bucket and tossed several plugs of hay into the stall. Although only a yearling, the colt was an eating machine, devouring twice as much as an adult horse.

Christian brought in two other horses that were also in training.

As he fed them, he heard Chris's nickering in the back of the barn. The stallion had the option of coming and going from a large outside paddock into the barn and his stall.

"I haven't forgotten you, Chris," he said, walking to him with a bucket of feed.

After an hour, he had the four barn horses watered, hayed, and fed and had taken care of the pasture horses. He raced to the house to shower, shave, and dress.

At six, he saw Allie's truck and trailer drive past the house, going directly to the barn. He stuck the earring box in his jacket pocket, grabbed the bundle of roses, and walked to the barn. Allie had unloaded the filly and taken her inside.

"How did she do?" he called when entering the barn.

Allie was in the filly's stall, putting a blanket on her. "Good, considering the competition," she said and fastened the blanket chest snap. "She got a third. At least the purse should pay for a few months of her board. How's everyone here? Did Mystery behave for you?"

"That colt is a handful. I don't know how you manage him."

"I told you to stop using a regular lead." She stepped out of the stall and locked the door. "He needs a stud chain when you—" She saw that Christian was wearing a black leather jacket and tie. "What's all this?"

He produced the roses that he had concealed behind his back. "Happy Valentine's Day."

"You're so sweet," she said and smelled the roses. "I'd kiss you, but I'm dirty."

"You need to hurry and get cleaned up. We've got an eight o'-clock reservation at a restaurant on St. Armands." He produced the box from his pocket and handed it to her. "A little something you might want to wear."

She opened the box and gazed at the earrings. She covered her mouth, and her eyes watered. "Oh, Christian, I've never received anything like this." Tears began to stream down her cheeks. "They're beautiful. You're so good to me."

"Hey, you treat me good, too." He leaned down and kissed her wet lips. "Now stop crying. You need to get ready."

An hour later, Allie had gone from scrappy little horse trainer to an alluring creature in her short dress with a plunging neckline. They drove to town anticipating a great evening.

At ten o'clock, Christian and Allie had finished dinner, and he suggested going to the club around the corner where they could dance and have a nightcap.

"I'm sorry, but I'm beat. Been up since four this morning. And I've been so busy I didn't get a chance to even buy you a card, but I had planned to make it up to you tonight."

Christian's eyes sparkled. "Forget the club. I prefer your plan." He nodded to the waiter for the check.

Forty minutes later, they pulled into the farm drive. Christian slammed on the brakes when he saw the open front gate. "What the hell?"

"Did we forget to shut it?" Allie asked.

"No, I got out and locked it." He leaped out of the SUV, and with the use of the headlights, he examined the gate padlock and chain. "The chain's been cut." He looked toward the house and barn. Through the trees he spotted light within the barn. "Someone's down there." He hopped into the SUV and raced down the bumpy dirt drive toward the barn.

When they passed the house, Allie screamed. "My God, the barn is on fire!" In seconds, the light had turned into a ten-foot blaze, fueled by the stacked hay bales stored in a corner. The SUV slid to a stop in front of the barn, and they leaped out. Christian caught a glimpse of a blue car, parked in the shadows beyond the barn.

"I'll get Mystery," he yelled and ran into the burning building.

"Wait, Christian. He won't leave his stall unless you cover his eyes," Allie shouted and disappeared into the tack room to fetch a blanket and lead rope.

Halfway inside the barn, Christian hesitated for a moment but ran on to Mystery's stall, believing he could hold the colt's halter and guide the trusting colt outside without a blindfold. Glancing down the aisle, he saw Allie open the first stall and lead the filly out.

Christian threw the stall door open and grabbed Mystery's halter. "Come on, boy," he said and tugged the halter. The colt took a few steps to follow, but with the snapping flames, he spooked and reared straight up. Christian was forced to let go and jump back or risk being struck by the horse's front hooves. Mystery reared again and then spun around within the stall, hysterically crashing into the stall boards.

Christian tried to approach the terrified colt's rear, but Mystery kicked out from fright. Christian ducked sideways as a back hoof nearly clipped his head.

A thought raced through Christian's mind. *Either the fire or this colt is going to kill me. No wonder horses die in barn fires.* Determined to save this one, Christian swallowed hard and pushed down his own panic.

His father had said, "A horse can sense human fear, and fear begets fear, just as calm can be transmitted to a frightened horse and quiet him." His father was always levelheaded, never losing his cool when handling an out-of-control horse.

Christian removed his jacket and stepped back into the stall. "Easy, Mystery, easy," he said softly. "Come to me. Come on, boy."

After a minute, the colt stopped hitting the boards and turned to Christian, who continued to beckon with a low, soothing voice. Mystery dropped his head and allowed Christian to approach his side.

"Good boy," he said and petted the colt. "Just be calm and trust me." Holding the halter, he slowly laced his jacket through the halter side bands and over Mystery's head, covering his eyes. "Okay, boy," he said quietly and stroked him. "Now let's get out of here." He led the blindfolded colt out of the stall, down the aisle, and past the roaring flames that lapped at the overhead beams. Christian and Mystery reached the driveway when Allie rushed to them.

"Don't free him," she said. "He might run back in. Put him in the pasture." She ran back to the barn for another horse.

Christian swung Mystery around and stared at the blazing barn. The fire had spread to both sides of the aisle and was billowing from the roof. "Shit," he said, seeing that Allie had disappeared into the smoke-filled barn. He hurried with the colt to the pasture, led him in, and shut the gate.

The sound of thundering hooves from the small frantic herd echoed beyond in the dark field. Once freed of the jacket and Christian's hold, Mystery whinnied and took off after them.

Christian gripped the top board of the fence, leaped over it, and raced back to the barn. Allie emerged from the heat, smoke, and flames with a horse.

"He's the last one." She puffed and walked the horse toward the pasture in her bare feet. She had removed and saved three horses to his one.

Christian opened the pasture gate for her. "What about Chris?"

"I don't know." She gasped, breathless. "His stall door was open to the outside. Hopefully he had enough sense to get out."

Christian ran to the side paddock and tried to see Chris, but it was too dark. He dashed back to the barn entrance. The building became an incinerator, the fire rapidly consuming the old dry wood. Looking in, he saw the blazing roof trusses.

"Chris! Chris!" he yelled and hoped the stallion would answer and reveal his location. Instead of a horse's whinny, he heard the blood-curdling shriek of a woman.

He ducked down low to dodge the raging flames and entered the barn. He heard Allie scream his name, telling him to come back. Almost crawling, he coughed and felt his way through the thick, blinding smoke. Halfway into the barn, he heard the scream again, coming from the last stall opposite Chris's. "Kate! Are you in here, Kate?" he called, making his way farther in.

"Chris," she screeched. "Help me, Chris."

He managed to open the stall door, and through the haze he saw the outline of a figure crouching in a corner. He heard a loud snapping overhead and leaped back as a few roof timbers fell into the stall, separating him from Kate.

Kate squealed and hopped around, her dress and hair on fire. He hastily unhooked the water bucket that hung near the stall door and doused her. She screeched and collapsed into unconsciousness. He leaped over the burning boards and scooped her up. He looked around and saw fallen and burning boards were everywhere. He was trapped. No way could he leave the barn by the way he came in.

He glanced at the strong two-by-six boards, making the inside of the stall, impossible for a horse or him to break. He hurdled over the fallen flaming beams and exited the stall. With Kate cradled in his arms, he kicked the plywood board panels at the end of the aisle. After a minute, several boards gave way. He ducked the flames and holding Kate, he crawled through the low opening. Choking and gasping for breath, he carried Kate to a small paddock, a safe distance from the barn and crumbled into the dewy cold grass. Behind him, he heard a loud crash and saw the whole barn had collapsed into a massive bonfire.

Over the roaring flames, he faintly detected Allie's wailing. She was calling his name near his parked vehicle on the drive.

"Allie, I'm here," he shouted.

"Christian! Christian, you're alive!" she yelled, her voice coming closer.

"I'm okay," he hollered and saw her image scaling a wooden fence to get to him. "Go back to the house and call an ambulance."

"Are you hurt?"

He glanced down at Kate, still unconscious. "It's not for me." The nearby blaze lit up the area and revealed Kate's injuries. Her hair was gone and half of her face and neck was charred black and bloody. "Oh, Kate," he groaned. "What have you done?"

Within ten minutes, the first Myakka fire truck and ambulance arrived. Christian had carried Kate to his SUV and placed her limp body in the open back. His eyes were moist, and he covered his mouth, watching the paramedics hook her up to fluids and give her oxygen. Allie took his hand, but said nothing.

He could not focus on all Kate had done to ruin his life. He thought only about the once-beautiful, vibrant woman who had laughed and made love to him. He kept reflecting on the last time they were together, how she had cried and begged him to come back and said she couldn't live without him. He had dismissed her like a nagging headache that wouldn't go away.

The bright paramedic light revealed that half of Kate's body was covered with deep, repulsive burns. If she survived, she would be forever scarred. No cosmetic surgery could erase those wounds. Never again would the stunning woman turn every man's head when she entered a room.

He walked away feeling sick with guilt. He knew Kate was unstable, psychotic. He should have convinced her to seek therapy or let her down easier—something. Down the fence line and in the shadows, he stopped, gripped the top rail, and hung his head. Allie walked to him and rubbed his back.

"Allie, how could I have let this happen?"

"It's not your fault, Christian. Kate was a sick firebug who was bound to get burned. That heartless bitch tried to kill my horses, and I have no doubt she murdered her parents. I'm sorry, but she got what she deserved."

He looked up as a medevac helicopter arrived and set down in the pasture, since it was a long way to the closest hospital. Christian and Allie watched as several firemen carried Kate's stretcher across the field and loaded her into the helicopter. A paramedic had said that she would be airlifted to Tampa General's burn unit.

Allie put her arm around Christian's waist, and they watched the helicopter lights move across the dark sky. "I know you feel bad," she said, "but it might have been you or me in that helicopter, or we could be dead."

He wiped the moisture from his eyes, using his sleeve. "You're right. But I knew this might happen and did nothing." He kicked the ground. "I should've taken the time and talked her into getting help."

"She wouldn't have listened. She only wanted to hear that you were coming back to her." Allie raised an eyebrow. "You're a strong, tough guy but have an awfully tender heart when it comes to animals and women. Right now you're wasting your compassion on a woman who didn't know the meaning of the word." She patted his back and walked to his SUV. She retrieved a flashlight and scanned the pastures, checking the horses.

For some time, Christian stood in the dark and watched the burning barn. Firemen contained the blaze and were hosing down the flaming timbers. Allie had returned from the pastures and stood near the squad cars, talking to the police who filled out their reports. A dozen or more trucks were parked down the drive and near the house. They belonged to the surrounding neighbors who had come to help.

Christian gripped his mouth. He had to get his act together. He walked to Allie. "I guess I need to build a new barn."

"Come with me," she said quietly and took his hand. She led him down the drive and away from onlookers. "There's a problem." She gathered up both his hands. "I checked Chris's paddock, and he isn't there."

Christian began to hyperventilate. If the stallion wasn't in the paddock, he had stayed in his stall and died when the roof collapsed. "No," he said, shaking his head. "He's not dead." He jerked free from Allie and walked toward the back of the property, shouting into the darkness, "Chris! Chris!"

Allie followed him. "He's not here. The paddock fence is intact, so he didn't break through it."

He stopped, looked up at the stars, and felt warm tears. *More fucking tears,* he thought and pictured the old bay stallion. For a stud, Chris was an exception, gentle and well behaved. He never kicked, bit, or even flattened his ears. Daily, Chris had never failed to trot to Christian, greeting him with his rumbling, deep-throated nickering.

Allie walked up. "I'm so sorry, Christian."

Christian embraced her and wept. "He didn't deserve to die like that," he stammered through his sobs. The ghastly images filled his mind of the stallion's death, his wide terrified eyes, his burning mane, and cooking flesh—the unimaginable suffering. Christian let go of Allie and sank to the dirt. Sitting, he clasped his legs and lowered his head against his knees and whimpered.

His thoughts drifted to his dead father and this stallion he had loved, gone now, both of them. A double whammy ripped at his insides.

Allie massaged his shoulders. Through the blur of tears, he glanced up at her, strong, silent, and composed. Women were supposed to be the weaker sex, but that was bullshit, probably a myth created by insecure men. Allie was living proof.

After several minutes, he sniffled, cleared his throat, and stood. "Damn, Allie," he mumbled, wiping his watery eyes. "This really sucks."

"Yes," she said and put her arm around his waist. Together they walked back to the burning barn.

Several hours later, the flames were extinguished, leaving only smoldering embers. Firemen packed up and left, along with the police. One by one, the neighbors also headed home with promises to lend a hand in the coming days. Vic, a lofty cowboy who raised rodeo bulls and lived nearby, offered the free use of some empty stalls. Mystery and the other three horses in training could be stabled there until a new barn was erected.

With dawn only a few hours away, Christian and Allie walked

hand-in-hand to the house. A chilly north wind howled and swept through the dark pastures. Christian felt weary and depressed plus filthy and cold. Sometime during the commotion, he had lost his leather jacket, along with everything else.

He squelched his sorrow and was determined to put the event to rest and move on. On the driveway behind him, he heard the rhythm of trotting hooves. "Allie, I hear a horse."

"It's one in the pasture. They'll be worked up for days."

"I don't think so." He stopped, took a few steps back toward the barn, and strained to see in the moonlight. Like a ghost, a horse emerged from the shadows and stopped several yards away.

"Hey, boy, what are you doin' loose?" Christian walked toward the animal and then recognized the distinctive long, black mane. "Chris," he exclaimed. "You made it, buddy!"

The stallion answered with a whinny and stepped to him. Christian threw his arms around the horse's thick neck and hugged him. "I'm so glad to see you, boy."

"I can't believe it," Allie said. "He must have jumped that five-foot fence. At his age, I didn't think it was possible."

The old bay stallion tossed his head up and down. Christian laughed. "He's saying 'Of course I could jump it.'" The horse nuzzled him and nibbled on his shirtsleeve. Christian stroked the stud's head. "You've made everything okay, Chris."

Six months after the barn fire, Christian stood near the farm track and watched Mystery gallop past with Allie on his back. The rising August sun lit up the horse's shimmering coat, a burnt orange, almost copper. The leggy colt was slightly short backed, according to Allie, with heavy bone, muscled shoulders, and a powerful rear end. He had a slight dish head, remnants of his Arab blood, with deep-set, intelligent eyes. Every time Christian saw him, he had to catch his breath. Mystery had developed into the most beautiful creature he had ever seen.

Allie circled the track twice with most horses, but with Mystery, she went four rounds, complaining the colt was still too chunky. Part of the weight was the result of his mass consumption of food: eight to ten quarts of oats and sweet feed daily and half a bale of hay. She wouldn't deny a growing colt the grain, but hoped to work it off with longer exercise time.

Allie pulled the colt up in front of Christian. He held the reins, and she slipped off.

"What do you think?" Christian asked, patting the colt's neck.

Allie swept the damp bangs off her forehead. "Well, he's very kind. Doesn't buck or give me trouble. He's also level-headed and doesn't spook easily. And he's so good-looking he has the makings of a terrific show horse, but—" she sighed. "Not a racehorse. So far, I'm not impressed. First of all, he's clumsy and overweight, and mentally, he acts like a clown. He has no interest in competing for the lead when Meg brings another horse alongside. Unfortunately, some Thoroughbreds never develop the right attitude."

Meg was a seventeen-year-old neighbor who lived a few miles away. She barrel raced her quarter horse, but for extra money, she came to the farm in the mornings and helped Allie exercise the horses, and afterward, walked and cooled them down. Allie said that Meg had a good seat, and learned quickly about the vast difference in riding a Thoroughbred versus a hobbyhorse.

"With Thoroughbreds, you tighten the reins, letting them take the bit, and they go faster," Allie had explained. "Loosen and drop the reins on their neck, and they slow to a stop." All other breeds of horses were taught the opposite, stop when a rider pulls back on the reins and go with a free rein.

Christian was quiet, unhappy that his gorgeous colt was not showing any signs of becoming a racehorse. He had assumed his father knew best and the cloned colt with Secretariat's DNA would also become a great Thoroughbred.

Christian wasn't merely disappointed, but also worried. If Mystery couldn't win his first few races, Christian would end up in Vince's debt.

Meg emerged from the barn, riding a black gelding.

"Hi, Christian," Meg said when she and the horse walked past Christian, heading toward the track.

"Hey, Meg," he barely responded, his thoughts still on Mystery, the money, the gangster.

In the barn, Christian held Mystery while Allie removed the colt's tack. "You do know that Meg has a terrible crush on you?" she said, giving him a tee-hee glance. "She melts every time you speak to her."

"Is that right?" he said unenthusiastically and stroked the colt's head.

Allie grew serious. "Don't get so down about your colt. Mystery is still young, and I just started riding him. Some colts don't get it together until they're three. He has plenty of time."

Her words struck him. *Plenty of time. Mystery might have it, but I don't.* He had to repay Vince by next summer. He watched Allie walk Mystery through the barn to a concrete slab out back to hose him down.

A white SUV pulled up to the front of the barn, and a thin, long-legged woman with light curly hair climbed out. She had the look, walk, and talk of a cowgirl, but she was Allie's vet, Betsy. Christian walked out to greet her. "Hi, Betsy."

"Hey, Christian," Betsy said. "Where's Allie?"

"Around back," he said. "She's giving Mystery a bath." He had come to know Betsy during one long, late night in the barn when he, Allie, and Betsy worked on a mare down with sand colic.

In spring Florida often suffered from drought that could turn the green pastures into brown stubble and a sandy wasteland. A horse that ingested too much sand, bad feed, or a poisonous weed could get a stomachache and die from rolling on the ground and tangling their intestines. With oil tubing, fluids, and walking the horse, Betsy had saved the mare that night without surgery.

Living with Allie on the farm, Christian was learning that the big, powerful animals were really fragile. They had delicate legs the width of a man's arm that had to support a thousand pounds while moving at forty miles an hour. One broken leg might cripple the other three with laminitis. They had touchy digestive systems that could host fatal conditions, and their flighty nature could send them crashing through a fence or cause them to remain in the security of their stalls even when the barn was burning.

Betsy's vet assistant left the passenger seat, opened the back of the SUV, and began taking out equipment.

Christian glanced at the equipment. "What's up?"

"I'm here to X-ray Mystery's knees," Betsy said. "See if they're open or closed. A young horse moving too fast can develop bone chips if the knees are still open."

Christian folded his arms. "According to Allie, going too fast isn't an issue for Mystery."

"He's still a baby." Betsy good-naturedly patted his arm. "Give him time." She strolled into the new barn.

His eyebrows rose. "Right," he mumbled.

Allie handed Mystery's lead to Christian. "You mind walking him a bit, so I can help Meg with the gelding and talk to Betsy?" Meg rode in and dismounted.

Betsy turned and stared at Christian and Mystery. "My word, Allie, he certainly is a handsome creature."

Meg chimed in, "Are you talking about the colt or Christian?" The four women giggled and gawked at Christian.

He felt the flush on his cheeks and took Mystery down the drive. On the return trip to the barn, Allie met him.

"That's good enough," Allie said. "He barely broke a sweat this morning, and I don't want to keep the vet waiting."

"Good, I've gotta get to work," he said and handed the lead to her. He slipped his Ray Bans on his face, kissed Allie's cheek, and patted the colt. He nodded to the smiling women. "Ladies, have a good day." He strolled up the drive to the house and his vehicle.

• • •

On the ride to town, Christian reflected that maybe he was worrying needlessly about Mystery and his lack of desire to run. Perhaps Secretariat had also started out fat, awkward, and slow. Like most people, Christian did not know the details about the legendary horse except that he won the Triple Crown, broke some track records, and was hailed as the best Thoroughbred of all time, although Christian remembered hearing his father argue that Man o' War deserved the title.

The question bothering Christian was whether a clone that resembled Secretariat in every physical way—red coat, three white socks, star and strip down the nose, great body, and large heart—would also inherit his talent and soul, his tremendous stride, and the competitive nature to dominate a field.

For several months, life had been good for Christian, and he hoped his luck would hold out. After the fire, the new barn had gone up within a week. Little Lenny, Allie's lanky blond cousin, had showed up with his bulldozer and pushed the rubble of burnt timbers aside and leveled an even pad. Christian questioned Allie about Lenny's name, since the young guy was far from little, but Allie said that his name had nothing to do with size, but that his father was also a Lenny. As a small kid, her cousin had gotten the nickname.

A lumber store delivered the materials for the barn on the following afternoon and told Allie that she could pay for them when her insurance check came in. Neighbors and friends chipped in, and they had a good old-fashioned barn raising. In days, the beams and sides went up. A roofing company set the trusses and the metal sheeting, while Christian and some of his friends built the ten inside stalls.

Unlike the old hay barn that had been converted into a horse stable, the new barn had exits at each end of the center aisle. The roomy stalls had two doors, one leading into the aisle, and the other a split door that opened to the paddocks outside.

Christian dug trenches and dropped in the PVC piping for

automatic waterers in the stalls. An electrician took another day to run the wires and hook up. The barn was finished in less time than it took Christian and Allie to apply the two coats of paint.

Kate had survived her burns, but faced months of reconstructive surgery and skin grafts. Christian had asked Allie about the wisdom of a hospital visit. Allie had said, "Go if you want, but I doubt Kate wants to see anyone in her state, especially you. And what purpose will it serve to confront her? She'll only lie like she did to the police."

Kate had fabricated a story to the detectives that she had come to Allie's farm to visit Christian, a dear friend, and saw he was not home. While waiting for him to return, she had gone to the barn to see the horses. She was smoking a cigarette and had tripped in her high heels and hit her head. When she came to, the barn was on fire, and she was trapped.

The evidence suggested a different story. Investigation showed the charred beams near the hay held traces of an accelerant. An empty gas container, not belonging to Allie or Christian, was found near the barn and had Kate's fingerprints on the handle. Two more full containers of gas were found near the house, suggesting that Kate also intended to ignite it. After reading Kate's statement, Christian informed the detective that Kate didn't smoke cigarettes.

Christian figured that somewhere between Kate's story and the evidence was the truth. She had started the fire in the barn, but before she got out, Christian had raced up in his SUV, probably startling her and blocking the only exit. She panicked and, fearing being exposed, she ran into a back stall to hide. She tripped and was temporarily knocked out. A lump on her forehead and mild concussion confirmed that this part of her story was accurate. The state's attorney charged Kate with arson, but the trial was pending until her recovery.

Christian took Vince on several fishing trips. The first time out, he rerigged Vince's spinning reel and pole, stripping it of the weights, wire leaders, and big hook. He told Vince, "You'd only catch channel cats with this rigging, and they're worthless."

On the end of the fishing line, Christian attached a three-foot, thirty-pound test leader line with a small hook and added a rattling, popping cork so the live bait floated, jumped at the surface, and looked natural. The rattle cork noise attracted fish.

On a grass flat in Sarasota Bay, Christian anchored his Whaler and pointed to a narrow channel that bordered a sandy shoal with mangroves. He told Vince they needed to get out of the boat and wade through the grass flats to the edge of the shoal, since a boat motor would scare the fish.

Vince grumbled about getting wet and wading fifty yards in knee-deep water, but his griping stopped after his first cast. When his shrimp hit the water, the fin of a large red broke the surface and gulped down the bait. Vince's pole bent close to snapping, and Vince struggled to reel in the fish.

"Holy Christ," Vince yelled like an excited kid. After a lengthy battle, he landed the thirty-three-inch red drum.

Christian began an uneasy friendship with Vince, although they shared little in common. Christian learned that Vince was a city guy, raised in the dingy alleys and rough neighborhoods of the North. He was old enough to be Christian's father and had crude manners and lacked culture. To Vince, a plate of spaghetti was fine dining, and he would not know a Picasso from a Rembrandt. His only interest was business and making a fast buck at someone else's expense. Morally, they stood worlds apart as well.

Christian, on the other hand, had grown up in Florida and lived for the outdoors and nature. He had seen snow only twice and would go insane up North if shut in without sunshine for half a year. He spent the better part of his life in Sarasota, an extremely culture-conscious town that had playhouses, museums, art galleries, and fine restaurants. Hidden among the Sarasota population were best-selling authors, renowned artists, actors, and musicians. Bumping into Stephen King in a bookstore, drinking with Dickey Betts in a lounge, or attending the film festival and talking to a movie star was not unusual for Sarasota residents.

Christian's mother and lawyer stepfather exposed him to the finer things in life and, with urging, he even had a few years of college under his belt.

Christian, though, could switch gears when hanging with blue-collar workers, boat people, and cowboys. Unconsciously his accent would even change to a southern drawl when he talked to the good old boys in Myakka. Allie had joked and said he lived a double life, being a redneck cracker and a classy gentleman in one package.

With Vince, however, Christian was at a loss. He could not relate to the guy on any level. Furthermore, he wasn't sure he wanted to. After their second fishing trip, Christian realized that Vince simply liked to fish, and unfortunately none of his associates shared his passion.

On one occasion, Vince brought up the earlier Scarab ride. "The ride back to the dock—I seriously thought about hurtin' you for pullin' that ballsy stunt," Vince said while reeling in his line. "But what saved you, what impressed me, was you weren't worried about your own skin. You were only concerned about your gal and family. Devotion to family is important to me, too. And from all reports, I've learned you're a straight shooter and a decent guy."

Vince shook his head. "Usually I deal with lying snakes, pathetic losers, or greedy, hardcore bastards like myself." He laughed. "You're a refreshing break, Christian. You look like a beach bum and act like a hokey boat kid, but I ain't buyin' it. You're smarter than you let on. I like bein' around ya."

Christian accepted the compliments with mixed feelings. Sure, he would be Vince's fishing buddy and show him a good time. They laughed and joked around, but beneath it lay Vince's unspoken words, "screw me over, and like you or not, you'll pay a dear price." Christian was playing with fire, getting sociable with the mobster, and in the end, he might get burned.

Christian often reflected on Vince and then on Mystery and his lack of performance. The two were closely connected.

CHAPTER FIFTEEN

Christian picked up the remote, turned on the TV, and watched a few minutes of the six o'clock evening news. The chatty newscaster did not fill the empty void in the quiet farmhouse. Christian switched off the set, stood, and looked out the window at the cypress trees that bordered the lake. Like a time gauge, the tree's bright-green needles of summer had turned orange and deep red with the onset of fall and now, in January, were dropping soon to leave the trees barren.

Where had the time gone, he wondered. Nearly a year had passed since Kate set fire to the barn, and last he had heard she faced a five-year prison sentence. His thoughts turned to Mystery. With New Year's, the colt was considered a two-year-old, his racing career soon starting.

Beneath the cypress, Christian saw four little brown shadows marching through the grass in single file, making their way to the back door. "Here they come," he said, watching the female raccoon and her three half-grown babies. He walked into the kitchen, opened the fridge, and grabbed a bowl of leftover stew he would not eat. He opened the back door, and the coons were waiting. Like little bears, they sat up on their hind legs and did a begging motion with their front paws.

"All right." He smiled and dumped the food onto the step, near his bare feet. "Some company is better than none."

The raccoons ignored him, accustomed to the handouts, and picked up each food piece with their front paws, held it, and ate with more manners than some children. With their cute little masks and fluffy ringed tails, the coons were charming. He never understood the repulsion some people felt toward the creatures.

A crisp winter wind blew his hair back as he gazed at the horizon of darkening trees beyond the pastures and the turquoise sky, laced with pearly lavender clouds. In the distant pine forest, he heard the yipping of a few coyotes, their populations on the rise in Florida, alarming the local cattlemen in Myakka, who occasionally lost a calf.

He closed the door and ambled back to the living room, facing another lonely night without Allie. Several days before, she had taken Mystery and two other horses to Miami. The Gulfstream meet had started. Rather than go to the Tampa track, she decided to take advantage of some vacant stalls at Calder, since the track was closed in the winter months. She entered the two horses in Gulfstream races only days apart. Although Mystery was not in a race, he needed his gate card and tattoo. Plus, raised on a quiet farm, he had to be acclimated to the racetrack commotion and to be exposed to the multitude of horses.

The colt had only marginally improved, but he at least was taking hold of the bit, a good sign, and was keeping more in stride with a companion horse. He still lacked the fire in his gut required to win races.

The phone rang and Christian raced into the kitchen, knowing Allie would call with her nightly report on what the horses had done that day.

"Hey," Christian said.

"Hey back at ya," she said, her voice cheerful.

"Well?"

"The filly got a second! And Gulfstream is a tough crowd. She even beat out one of Nick Zito's. I'm in the hotel bar, celebrating with Sam, you know, the pin hooker who set you up with the loan on Mystery."

Set me up all right, Christian thought. "So what happened with

Mystery today? You planned to work him three-eights with other colts." He heard her sigh.

"He did okay. He worked with some fast colts and got a thirty-eight."

He had learned that the time and conditions differed from track to track, so he asked, "How did he stack up against the others?"

"Dead last, but Christian, it just took him longer to find his stride. He was moving at the end."

"Christ," he mumbled quietly.

"Don't get discouraged. I think he'll come around." She laughed. "I'll tell you your colt sure stops traffic. Everyone loves him, he's so well-built and good-looking. Even that jerk Price had one of his assistant trainers ask me about your colt's pedigree. Another old trainer stopped me. Said he saw Secretariat train down here as a two-year-old, and Mystery was a spitting image—even has the same straight hind legs and sloping rump. That was awesome."

Christian fidgeted with the phone cord and nervously changed the subject. "So when are you coming home?"

"I'll be back tomorrow night, and I miss you, too. Look, I gotta go. Love you."

"Love you, too," he said and hung up, his mind on the old trainer. How many others might make the link that Mystery looks a heck of a lot like Secretariat? He walked to the living room couch and plopped down on the cushions. "Why be concerned?" he grumbled. "He's the prettiest colt in Miami, but he's can't run worth a hoot." He snatched up the remote, turned on the TV, and hoped for a distraction.

Five months later, Allie entered Mystery in his first race at Calder. Christian watched Allie squat down and take off Mystery's leg wraps. "We'll have to celebrate tonight after his win," he said.

Allie stood. "He should at least be in the money. He's the best colt in the field. The new snaffle has stopped him from dipping to the left, and the blinkers are keeping his mind on business, but there're no guarantees in a first race."

"He'll win. He has to," Christian said, confident that his clone was on the same path as the great undefeated Secretariat.

Mystery had improved over the spring. He was still chunky, but the colt had found his stride. He took hold of the bit and learned to switch leads after the turns so he wouldn't tire. More importantly, his competitive nature had emerged. His workouts were thirty-six in three-eighths of a mile. He was in today's third race, a twenty-five-thousand maiden special weight that was six furlongs.

Christian was so positive of the colt's victory he had told Vince to expect the purse money. It was June, and Mystery's slow development and adjustment into racing had hampered Christian's plan to pay off the gangster. Being a good trainer, Allie refused to push the colt until he was ready. She was unaware of the problems Christian faced if Vince's loan deadline wasn't met in July.

A man's voice came across the backside PA system, calling for the horses in the third race. A strong wind whipped through the barns, and Christian glanced up at the black thunderstorm clouds rolling in, signaling the end of spring drought. Tropical storms would become a daily afternoon event with the progression of summer.

"Hope the rain holds off," said Christian.

"Me too," said Allie. "I'm not sure how our boy will handle a muddy track." She tied Mystery's tongue down, so his breathing wasn't hampered in the race and slipped his bridle on. She led him out of the stall and guided the colt through the barns, being his trainer, exercise rider, and groom.

A week prior to the race, she had relinquished Mystery's morning exercise to an apprentice jockey named Jeffery, so he could get a feel for the colt. Although Jeffery had an English first name, he was Hispanic like most of the jockeys in Miami.

Christian carried a bucket of supplies and walked alongside Allie and Mystery. Normally, grooms brought the horse and supplies and met the trainer and owner in the racing paddock, but Christian didn't have that luxury. Ironically, he was probably the poorest owner at Calder, but had the most spectacular colt. Allie, Mystery, and Christian reached the track and walked along the outside rail, passing the lathered horses and their grooms headed for the barns after the second race.

Christian's hands grew sweaty, his heart pounded, and he felt like leaping out of his skin. The trio left the track and entered the riders-up arena. He glanced at Allie beside him. She was the picture of calm, leading the huge red colt, talking softly to reassure him.

They stopped before the saddling paddock, and Allie lifted Mystery's upper lip in front of an official who checked the colt's tattoo. "Clever Chris, fourth horse," the man said and marked his clipboard. "Good-looking colt."

They proceeded to the covered paddock and the number four stall, when a tremendous crash of lightning struck nearby. Mystery spooked and reared. Allie had to use all her strength to contain him.

"Easy, Mystery," she said and brought the colt's front legs back to earth. "You're not going to let a little lightning upset you." The colt quickly settled. They stared out the paddock as the storm let loose, the dark gray clouds releasing a deluge of rain. Strong winds whipped at the trees, and the outside spectators raced for shelter within the grandstands. Thunder shook the building and unnerved the horses.

Allie patted Mystery. "I'm going to walk him to keep him calm. With lightning, they'll delay the race." She led Mystery out of the stall and joined the other horses and grooms that walked in a circle under the sheltered paddock.

Christian kept looking at his watch while the storm wreaked havoc. The fast, dry track quickly turned into an obstacle course of mud and big puddles. Allie was right. Because of the chance that a horse and jockey might be hit by lightning, the third race was held up for fifteen minutes past the scheduled post time.

Finally there was a break. The storm passed, but the weather was still windy and raw, with sprinkling rain. Allie brought Mystery into the stall, and Christian held his lead. The jockey's valet handed Allie the saddle. After saddling Mystery, she adjusted the blinkers and led the colt out to the riders-up area where the jockeys waited.

She walked Mystery around the wide grass and treed circle, and Jeffrey approached. "I'm not sure how he'll handle this surface," Allie told him. "Let him level out and find his stride. Don't push or crowd him."

Jeffery nodded, and Christian gave the jockey a leg up into the saddle. Allie led the colt and rider to the track opening where a post pony rider took over, leading Mystery to the starting gate on the other side of the track.

"Well, this is it," she said. "If we hurry, we can still place a bet."

Christian tittered. "We won't make much money, even with a winning ticket." Unlike Hunter, Mystery's *correct* workouts were in the racing catalogue, and with the colt's fast times, he was going off with three-to-one odds, the second favorite.

"Doesn't matter. Come on." She grabbed Christian's hand, and they jogged to an outside betting booth, each plunking down twenty dollars to win.

Despite the drizzling rain, they rushed back to the rail and watched Mystery load into the starting gate. Everything happened too fast. Before Christian could absorb or enjoy it, the bell sounded, the doors opened, and the horses lunged out. Mystery gamely dashed out but was bumped and cut off by the zigzagging number two horse. Jeffrey had to check Mystery, pull him up, to avoid a collision.

"Shit!" Allie cursed. On the backstretch, Mystery was struggling in the mud and in last place. "Come on, boy," she said. "Level out, level out, get it together."

At the turn, Mystery began to gain ground, but faced a wall of horses. Jeffrey tried to squeeze him through on the rail, but another horse cut in front of them, slamming Mystery's side. Jeffrey checked him again to avoid the other horses' back hooves.

"Asshole, take him wide, goddamn it," Allie screamed to the

jockey who couldn't hear her. "The moron just checked him again." Angry, she looked down for a second, unable to watch.

"He's moving, Allie!" Christian yelled. Jeffery had found a narrow space between two horses, and Mystery blasted through, leaving three of them. Six horses still lay far ahead. Rounding the turn in the short race, Mystery flew over the puddles as the other horses seemed to just coast along. He plowed past two more and was neck and neck with the fourth horse on the home stretch.

"And here comes Clever Chris," said the track announcer. "He's moving fast."

"But he's running out of ground," Allie answered. "He'll never catch them." Mystery blazed down the track, passing the fourth horse and only a length and half behind three tightly packed front-runners. At the finish line and with one more stride, Mystery overtook all of them, but too late.

Allie was happily hopping up and down. "What a race! What a horse!"

With the loss, Christian was a little numb. "But he got fourth."

"It doesn't matter," she said, excitedly. "Did you see him move? He got bumped, cut off, was checked twice, and dealt with a sloppy track and an idiot jockey, and he didn't flinch. He moved through horses like a confident three-year-old and made up the distance in record time. Damn, Christian, you've got yourself one nice colt."

He swiped back his dripping wet hair and held his forehead. "I know, but he got fourth," he repeated. "I thought he'd be like Secretariat—that he couldn't lose."

"Secretariat?" She knitted a brow with puzzlement. "Don't you think you're aiming a little high? Besides, even Secretariat lost four races, including his first one."

Christian stood in a daze, as if a two-by-four had smacked him in the back of his head. Why didn't he know that information? Stupid, he thought. Up until today, he had never uttered Secretariat's name or discussed him with Allie. Fearing she might make the connection with the cloned colt, he even avoided bringing books or information on Secretariat into the house. With the race, he realized his mistake. He needed to learn about Mystery's famous donor.

Mystery, with the jockey, trotted up covered with mud, so thick that the dirt concealed his chestnut coat and forehead. Allie walked out on the track and held the colt's head, and Jeffrey demounted.

"This is a damn good colt," Allie ranted, eye level with the jockey, "and you rode him like a cheap nag through those horses. Instead of taking him on the outside, you rode him right up on their asses and risked clipping hooves. Then he got slammed on the rail and had to be checked for a second goddamn time. You cost him this race."

Jeffrey shrugged. "I did not take him through the field," he argued. "He took me." He held his saddle and walked to the scales, but stopped near Christian. "Your trainer— " He grumbled, glancing over his shoulder at Allie. "She is hot tempered, but the colt—never have I felt such power."

Allie removed Mystery's blinkers and doused his head with water, cooling him and getting the mud out of his eyes. Before going to the barn, Christian stroked Mystery's neck. "You did good, boy, real good." All the while, his mind was on Vince and the unpaid loan.

The following morning Christian was back at work in Sarasota and, as expected during the first part of summer, the boat rental business was slow. Standing on the white sandy shore dotted with seaweed and a few dead horseshoe crabs, he stared across the still, green bay. In the low tide, he watched a school of mullet darting over a shallow grass flat. Farther out, a flock of seagulls screeched and dove for baitfish. Several of their stately brethren, the pelicans, floated amid the hectic action. Although Christian had seen the view thousands of times, it never grew old.

Today, though, he couldn't enjoy it. Anxious and distracted, he turned away from the bay, birds, and fish and took the checkbook from his back pocket. Twenty-five hundred was the measly balance. In a few days, he could expect another twelve hundred from Mystery's fourth-place purse, but not enough, not even close. To offer it to Vince could be an insult.

He tossed back his head, closed his eyes, and felt the jittery tension within, a new feeling for him, but well known to addicted gamblers who bet, lost, and then felt the panic, since they lacked the cash to pay off the deadly loan shark.

All his life, Christian had played it safe and honest. What the hell had he been thinking when he jumped into the horseracing frying pan? It wasn't for money, power, or glory.

Buried deep down, he knew. He rubbed his left arm, the arm he broke when ten years old because he disobediently took out the gray colt and fell off—the broken arm that ended his parents' marriage.

If he fulfilled his father's dream and made Mystery the greatest horse since Secretariat, perhaps then he would squelch his nagging guilt. Reason told him he was likely blameless for their breakup, but his injury had coincided with the tragic loss of his home and father, scarring his childhood and leaving him with a lifetime of insecurity. With Mystery's success, he hoped to make atonement. He would prove, if only to himself, he was a good son. That he was okay.

In the rainy afternoon, Christian closed up shop, secured the boats, and put the equipment away. He slowly drove to Longboat Key and Vince's house. To avoid the man would only make matters worse. He knocked on the door, and Vince opened it.

"Fourth place, huh?" Vince said before Christian could open his mouth. "I watched the race on the cable channel. Come in. Never gamble on horses, sports, or people unless you hold all the cards and know the outcome."

"Right." Christian sighed and walked in with his head and shoulders drooping. "I guess it's no surprise that I'm not going to meet the deadline and pay you off." He pushed the hair back from his forehead and massaged his temples. "So what do you want to do, Vince, beat me up, break my legs? Just please don't involve Allie or my family."

"Lighten up, Christian." Vince said with an alligator smile.

"Don't plan on hurtin' my fishin' guide. Let's have a drink and celebrate our new workin' arrangement."

Christian sunk his teeth into his bottom lip and followed Vince to the bar. Over drinks, Vince confessed he had counted on Christian's failure to pay and laid out his new occupation. Using the Scarab, Christian would cruise twenty miles out in the gulf and pick up overseas goods, as Vince called it, from freighters entering Tampa Bay. "Do as you're told, and no one gets hurt."

"Overseas goods from south of the equator, I take it?"

Vince turned, giving him a sideward glance. "Just pick up the packages and don't fuckin' worry about what's inside."

"Okay, Vince," Christian said and took a gulp of his drink. Several moments passed. "I just don't understand. You've got plenty of men. Why do you need me?"

"You're a local kid with local ID and lanky with a mop of yellow hair. You're the typical type seen cruisin' in a speedboat, so you won't attract attention. The Coast Guard takes one glance at my bunch—dark-haired Italians in a fast boat—it's like waving a red flag. They don't exactly fit the profile of boaters or fishermen. Same thing happens to blacks and Hispanics in big cars running goods on the freeways. Cops get suspicious and pull them over."

Vince pulled out a cigar and lit it. "Besides, Christian, you've proved you got balls, can handle the boat, and know these waters. At night you can outrun or hide from the cops. Even if you're pulled over, your record is clean. Never been in jail except—" he laughed, "when you popped that horse trainer in Miami. Remember, I checked you out. You're known for bein' dependable and honest."

Christian set the glass down on the bar and inhaled deeply. "Then honestly, Vince, I'd prefer the broken legs rather than do what you ask."

Vince's expression darkened, his smile gone. "No, boy, no broken legs; this is a do-or-die thing. And because you're so devoted to your family and that girl, you'll do as you're told. They're the cards

I hold. Screw me over by runnin' or talkin' to the cops, and someone you love is bound to disappear."

Christian gripped the bar to conceal his tremors. The rush of emotions—anger, fear, worry—all hit him at once. He sucked up air and collected himself. "Fine, Vince," he said, barely above a whisper. "When do I start?"

"In a few weeks, I'll call ya."

Christian walked out to his SUV, climbed in, and started the engine. For a minute, he sat in the driveway and chewed a nail. "Jesus," he mumbled. "How did I get myself into this shit?"

Although shaken, he wasn't surprised by the conversation with Vince. Christian had seen the boat and knew Vince was crooked. Early on, the man made it clear he did not care about Christian's horse or boat business. He had loaned Christian the money because he needed a drug runner, one who could drive the Scarab like a madman through local waters. Christian, stupidly, had proved he qualified.

The reality hit him hard. He felt nervous perspiration popping out of the pores on his forehead. Wiping it away and pushing back his saffron hair, he straightened and looked into the rearview mirror at himself. *Dumb blond. Perhaps there's truth in those jokes.* His gullible personality occasionally got him into jams.

He left Vince's house, grateful for the long ride ahead. With plenty of time, he'd have his act together before he reached home and Allie. He left the barrier islands, made his way through the downtown area, and drove east.

He realized he wasn't above breaking the law. After all, he had just committed fraud by racing the illegal colt. And concerning drugs, he was far from sainthood. At parties, he rarely turned down a hit off a joint, and in the past he had trespassed and hopped many a cow pasture fence in late summer where he picked the purple and golden mushrooms so he and his buddies could hallucinate and trip all night. He had even given cocaine a try with Kate. Although the sex was incredible, he did not care for the uptight effect and never did it again.

He considered his hairpin temper and the past scuffles when a good-for-nothing pushed him too far, although up until Miami, he had never been arrested for assault and put in jail. Luckily, Frank had talked to the prosecutor and had Christian's misdemeanor battery charges dismissed.

Vince's gig, though, was a whole different animal. If caught hauling a mass quantity of drugs, he faced serious felony charges and a long prison term. If he refused, he put his family and Allie at risk, not to mention Vince's men would probably kill him.

"Fuck me," he cursed. "I'm such an idiot. Should've never taken Vince's money."

He looked at the overcast sky layered with black clouds. "Christ, Dad, when you made me promise to get the damn colt, did you have this shit in mind? I was happy, had a decent life. Now it's gone." He shook slightly and seethed. "You and your goddamn dreams."

CHAPTER SIXTEEN

A little more than two weeks had passed since Mystery's first race and Christian's visit with Vince. At the farm, Allie loaded Mystery into the horse trailer. "I can't believe you're not coming with us. You'll miss his second race," she said to Christian and shut the trailer door. "He's going to win."

"I'm sorry. I wish I could come," Christian said, "but Vince made plans for the fishing trip with friends. I can't get out of it."

"You don't need to explain," she grumbled. "I've heard it before. Without Vince's money, you wouldn't have Mystery. You owe him." She shook her head. "Vince is a Thoroughbred owner. You'd think he'd understand the importance of this race and postpone his fishing trip."

"You'd think," he said, "but apparently his friends are from out of town and don't have much time."

"Well, you can go to the dog track tomorrow and watch the race on their TV."

"I plan on it."

"Okay, wish us luck." She stretched up, embraced his neck, and they kissed.

"Luck." he said through his breath. Allie climbed into the driver seat of his SUV. His newer vehicle was more reliable for the long trip than her old pickup. The SUV and horse trailer traveled down the drive. Christian was left standing by the barn. In frustration, he punched the wall and watched Allie disappear down the empty road.

Everything he had told Allie, of course, was a lie. There was no fishing trip or out-of-town friends of Vince's. His whole life had become a jumble of lies—the cloned horse, the loan from a gangster, and now he could add drug smuggling to the list. The only truth was how he felt about Allie.

Allie had entered the colt in another maiden race, this time one going a little farther, seven furlongs, and Vince had called on the morning they planned to leave for Miami and told Christian he was needed that night to make his first run with the Scarab. Vince had probably given him little warning on purpose.

Allie had suggested scratching the colt and entering him in another race on another day, but finding the right race for Mystery might take a week or more. Christian wouldn't hear of it and gave the go ahead. The purse money was an issue, more important than his being there. He wanted to pay Vince off or at least start to.

Vince had been vague when Christian asked what would happen if and when his debt was paid off. "We'll see," Vince had said.

Christian held his tongue, despite the urge to question Vince and get a straight answer. The sick feeling that Christian had come to know, chewed at his insides. Had he unknowingly signed a lifetime contract with the mobster?

Christian drove to work in Allie's old truck. He checked the weather, tides, and sea chop. In the afternoon, the daily dark clouds gathered and the thunderstorms moved west from the center of the state to the Gulf and caused an hour-long downpour on the bay. With the lack of heat, the storms would disperse in the evening. Christian expected clear skies and calm seas for tonight's run.

Meg planned to feed the horses, so Christian had no need to return to the farm. At five, he packed up at work, changed from his cutoffs into jeans, and headed for Vince's house.

"Come in, Christian," Vince said after opening the front door. "We're in the livin' room."

"We?" Christian questioned and stepped inside.

"Yeah, Sal and Vito are here. You know Vito. He was with us

when we first took the Scarab out. He'll be goin' with you tonight."

"Great," Christian said sarcastically. He followed Vince down the marble-tiled foyer into the spacious living room with its contemporary furnishings.

Sal sat in a large stuffed chair and raised his cocktail glass when Christian walked in. "There's that speed demon," he cackled. "Every time I think about losing my lunch on that Scarab, I wanna beat your ass." He burst into a belly-shaking laugh.

Sal wore a constant grin; every sentence ended with a chuckle even when he threatened someone. Perhaps it was meant to throw a person off, since it was hard to tell if Sal was sincere or joking.

"Sorry I caused you to puke, Sal," Christian said quietly. He sensed someone behind him, a looming shadow that breathed down his neck. He swirled on his heels and saw Vito, standing only a foot away. "Hey, Vito."

Vito gave Christian an icy glare and sauntered past him into the living room.

Christian fidgeted, gnawed on his lower lip, and rubbed his clammy hands on his jeans. *Of all the bum luck*, he thought, *stuck on a boat with this guy.* He considered Vito the worst of the lot. With his harsh features, beady eyes, disgruntled personality, and his shoulder-length black hair slicked back into a tight ponytail, Vito resembled a water moccasin; dark, silent, deadly, with a nasty reputation to slither out of its way to bite you. The guy, it seemed, would rather cut a throat than smile.

"Take your shirt off, Christian," said Vince.

Christian frowned, but did as he was told. Vito came up and patted down Christian's pants, checking for wires, recorders, or weapons. "Clean," Vito said.

Vince nodded. "Just a precaution. Can never be too careful."

Christian put his shirt back on. "I'm not going to mess you over, Vince. I don't plan to spend the rest of my life looking over my shoulder."

They gathered around a table and looked at a map of the area. Vince pointed out where the Scarab would meet the large freighter, trail it, and retrieve the floating bags the crew tossed overboard.

Christian scratched his head. "Isn't using speed boats a little old-fashioned, Vince?"

"It is," said Vince. "In the seventies and eighties, we used fast boats and small planes to bring in goods, but we lost too much product to the feds and Coast Guard. We switched and began importing on large freighters, concealing the goods in shipping containers, but the cops went to drug-sniffing dogs in the ports. Nowadays, most goods are brought in over the Mexican border, but you can't trust those bastards. That's why we've gone back to the old ways and moved our operation to Sarasota. No one expects any trafficking to be done here."

"There's also no competition, like there is in Miami," said Sal, "Goddamn Haitian and Jamaican fucks."

At ten o'clock, Christian and Vito boarded the Scarab and slowly motored south through the dark bay. The water was pancake flat, with the lack of a breeze. A few miles away, the red-and-green lights of another boat streaked across the still water, probably a fisherman heading in for the evening. They entered New Pass and, to the left were the City Island jetties, a long row of boulders that sagged toward the water. Past the rocks was a seawall where a few late-night fishermen sat with their glowing lanterns. The lights hung just above the waterline to attract baitfish. On the Longboat side of the pass was a sandbar and beach lined with mangroves and Australian pines webbed throughout with hiking trails that wound their way through a bayside park.

The Scarab glided past floating clumps of still seaweed, telling Christian it was slack tide. "It's pretty quiet tonight and no incoming or outgoing current," Christian said, trying to make friendly conversation while keeping the Scarab barely above an idle in the no-wake zone.

Vito eyeballed him for a moment and then turned away.

Christian shrugged.

They motored past a marina, small restaurant, and bait stand on City Island and cruised under the New Pass Bridge. Christian eased the throttle forward, increasing their speed. South of the pass, large waterfront homes lined the shore, and across the water were the Longboat Key condos. In ten minutes, they entered the gulf and, a mile out, Christian opened up the Scarab. Vito sat in the passenger seat, clinging for dear life, as the boat leaped and crashed down hard in the open water.

Christian followed the GPS coordinates to the meeting place. After twenty or so miles, they arrived at the location where they would hook up with the freighter. He shut down the engines, turned off the boat lights, and waited in the dark silence. The Scarab gently rolled in the small swells.

"Everything okay, Vito?" Christian asked, still trying to be pleasant to the jerk.

"*Sì*," Vito answered, but his hands still gripped the boat handles.

Christian leaned back in the seat, propped his feet up on the dash, and tossed his head back, gazing at the night sky. Without city lights spoiling the view, the stars numbered in the millions. He felt no need to talk further to the man with limited English and a sour disposition.

Normally, he would have loved the tranquil setting on the gulf, but he hated this, being here, doing this, and wasn't fond of the company. After some time, Vito released his hold, cautiously stood, and scanned the dark waters. He pointed and said something in Italian.

Christian leaned forward and saw a green speck of light dancing on the black horizon. "Lights are too low for a freighter," he said, "probably a shrimper out of the panhandle or Louisiana." He wondered if Vito understood and rephrased, "No freighter."

An hour later, Vito excitedly rattled off more Italian, but ended the sentence in English. "There it is."

Christian stood and glanced at the boat lights high above the waterline as the large ship cruised toward them. "Yeah, that's our baby." He cranked up the engines, swung the Scarab around, and pointed to a hatch. "Get the light out."

Vito took out an enormous strobe light and scurried back into his passenger seat. They soon were trailing the freighter without lights. Vito flashed the deck, a signal to the crew to drop the goods overboard. The freighter never stopped or slowed, continuing its speed and course to the port in Tampa Bay.

Vito scanned the light across the surface and spotted the first of ten large duffel bags that had been tossed overboard. They were sealed in plastic and floated with buoys. Christian pulled the boat alongside the bag. It took both him and Vito to haul the hundred-pound package aboard. They carried the bag to the bow deck and dropped it down through top hull hatch. Christian scrambled back to driver's seat, and they searched for the rest. Forty-five minutes later, they had collected all ten packages and headed in.

Reentering Sarasota Bay was the tricky part, a time to get nervous, but all was quiet, not a boat light in sight. Christian slowly steered the Scarab wide around the moored sailboats off City Island and hit a switch that raised the motors' props halfway out of the water. The large Scarab glided over the shallows, never touching the grass flats, sandbars, or oyster beds below. He maneuvered the boat up a short, narrow channel shrouded with mangroves on each side.

Christian cut the engines, and the boat drifted perfectly up against a small dock. Alongside the dock was an obscure boat ramp with a parking lot. The ramp was sandwiched in between the park at the end of City Island and a wild-bird sanctuary, with a marine laboratory beyond.

At that laboratory, Al Gore had prepared his Democratic convention speech when he ran for president. An odd place, Christian thought, since the majority of Sarasota residents were Republican.

Sal stood on the dock with two other men and glanced at his

watch. "Right on time, kid," he said with a grin. A large, paneled bread truck and Sal's black Cadillac were parked near the ramp.

Vito tossed Sal a boat line. Christian hopped into the forward hatch and handed a heavy duffel bag up to Vito. He, in turn, passed the bag off to the two men on the dock. They hurriedly loaded the truck, concealing the goods behind bread racks, while Sal held the boat lines and supervised the process. Within fifteen minutes, the bags were offloaded and in the truck.

Christian wiped the sweat from his brow and lifted himself out of the deep hatch. "Vince didn't come?" he asked Sal.

"The boss doesn't get his hands dirty," Sal said, smiling. "You did good, kid, real good."

Christian nodded and watched the bread truck drive away.

Vito stepped off the Scarab and joined Sal on the dock.

"See ya next time, kid," Sal said and tossed the boat lines aboard. Sal and Vito conversed in Italian while they walked to Sal's car.

Christian pushed the boat nose away from the dock, leapfrogged over the windshield, landing behind the helm, and cranked up the noisy Mercury engines. He cruised toward Vince's house, feeling relieved that everything had gone so quickly and smoothly.

A thousand pounds of dope, he thought, trying to figure out its street value. Ten million, if the bags held pot, and an unimaginable amount if it had been cocaine. He huffed. *No wonder Vince wasn't concerned that I didn't pay off my measly horse loan.*

In the predawn hours, he pulled into the farm and caught a few hours of shut-eye. Soon he was up, helping Meg feed the horses and then hurrying off to work. At two in the afternoon, he left the business in Jake's hands and drove to the dog track near the Sarasota Airport. In the upstairs clubhouse, he entered the sparse bar. The majority of tables and stools were empty of bettors. At the bar, he took a stool in front of an overhead TV that was tuned to the Miami track.

After ordering a cocktail, he opened the catalogue he'd purchased downstairs and studied it.

"Who you betting on, son," asked an elderly man sitting on a nearby seat.

"I own a colt in the sixth race at Calder," said Christian. "He's the five horse."

The man looked at his catalogue. "Clever Chris. Says this is only his second time out, but last time he finished with a strong fourth. So you must be Christian Roberts."

"I am."

The man turned to the other men seated at the bar, a few older guys and some middle-aged workmen. "Hey, this young fellow owns a horse in the sixth at Calder, Clever Chris." He looked back at Christian. "Think he's gonna win?" All eyes focused on Christian and waited to hear the inside scoop.

"If the jockey doesn't fall off, he's a sure bet."

Christian had ordered and read several books on Secretariat. He had Amazon ship them to his mother's house so Allie wouldn't get suspicious and make the connection. He had only read about the horse's early racing career but learned that Secretariat was also a slow, clumsy clown as a two-year-old and was called a pretty boy with no talent. With his second race, Secretariat put a gag in the skeptics' mouths when the pretty horse easily won. Christian hoped now that his beautiful clone would follow in his famous donor's footsteps.

Everyone at the bar placed a bet on his colt, and the bartender turned up the volume on the TV.

The starting gate doors swung open, and Mystery was the last to leave, causing sighs at the bar. Christian wasn't worried. Secretariat was known for leaving the gate late and stalking the field from the rear. With the race half over, though, and his red colt still lumbered along in last place, Christian's faith began to wane. "Come on, Mystery," he whispered.

Going into the turn, Mystery began to move and pass the trailing horses on the outside. He had the same jockey, but this time Jeffrey followed Allie's instructions. The field rounded the turn, and the track announcer included Mystery's name. "Here comes Clever Chris. He's moving fast into third, overtaking Midnight Peace." The horses were on the homestretch, racing toward the finish line. "Clever Chris," said the announcer. "He's neck and neck with Leonard G."

Mystery surged ahead and left the other chestnut in the dust. "It's going to be Clever Chris," said the announcer. "Clever Chris coming to the wire, and they're not going catch him today."

The small group at the bar erupted with cheers as Mystery sailed across the finish line six lengths ahead of the second horse.

Christian stood at the bar, not remembering when he had left his seat. His mouth gaped open in awe, and he stared silently at the TV screen.

The old man patted Christian's shoulder, snapping him out of his trance. "Great race, son, great horse," he said. The other bar patrons came over and also congratulated him on the win.

Christian grinned. "He is a great horse."

At the farm, Christian stood in the stall and talked softly to Mystery while brushing him. "You like that rubbing, boy?" Ten days ago, Mystery ran his second race and came out of it not tired, but raring to go again. On the farm exercise track, Allie had to use all her strength to hold him back.

She leaned against the outside stall door and thumbed through the racing form. She glanced up from the paper when Christian began working on the colt's rump. "Be careful," she said. "He's so full of himself he's gone to kicking sometimes back there. He needs another race to burn off that energy."

Christian stroked the horse's neck. "You wouldn't kick me, would you, Mystery?" The colt nickered.

Allie laughed. "You do have a way with horses. You should have been a trainer."

"My father said that a few months before he died." He shrugged. "But I'm happy to be the lowly groom."

She leaned her chin on the stall door and looked at Mystery and Christian. "Never underestimate the groom. They clean the stall and wash, brush, feed, and handle the horse. They spend more time and get closer to the animal than the trainer or owner. A good groom knows when his horse is a little off. That knowledge can make or break a Thoroughbred. Ironically, grooms are the most overlooked, overworked, and least paid in this business. A horse can win the Triple Crown, and everyone gets rich except the groom. He can still walk away a pauper."

"Hardly seems fair."

"It isn't," she said and returned to her reading. "Next Tuesday, there's an allowance race at Calder for eighteen thousand for two-year-olds, winners of one race, seven furlongs. I think we should enter Mystery in it."

"Eighteen thousand? We're going down in purse money. At this rate, I'll never pay Vince off."

"It's July, and the purses are cheap down here. Besides, Mystery needs to get the experience and build his confidence. This time he'll face serious competition and won't be running against a bunch of sorry-ass maidens who've never won a race. If he wins it, I'll start looking for a bigger purse and race. We might have to take him north. But let's not count our chickens before they hatch. We'll see how he does."

"That works for me," he said. "I'm taking Vince and his friends fishing again Sunday night, so I can go with you on Monday."

Saturday morning at the marina, Christian sat at a shady picnic table with a book on Secretariat open in front of him. Occasionally, he glanced up and scanned the bay for his WaveRunner, skeptical of the renter. He also checked on some kids in his sailboats. His cell rang, and he saw it was his mother and answered.

"I got your message, Christian," she said. "You can't make Sunday's dinner?"

"No, Mom, I'm taking some people fishing Sunday." He rolled

his eyes with the fib. "Besides, Allie and I are leaving early Monday for the track. She'll be packing up the gear Sunday night."

"We'll plan for the following weekend. By the way, another package came for you."

"It's probably a racing tape I ordered on eBay. I'll come by after work and get it."

"I won't be here, but I'll leave it on the kitchen counter."

In the afternoon, Christian read the last page in the biography on Secretariat. "Jesus," he whispered, overwhelmed. "Damn horse was a phenomenon."

He read that Secretariat had not only won the Triple Crown, but also still held the track record for the Kentucky Derby and Belmont Stakes. In the Man o' War Stakes, a mile-and-a-half turf race, he had run with little effort against the wind in 2.24 4/5, matching the world record for that distance on *any* track.

Christian also learned that the horse made the cover of *Newsweek, Vogue, Time,* and other magazines. The articles were filled with praise, hailing him as the greatest racehorse of the twentieth century and, basically, the greatest animal of all time.

What moved Christian the most was the way Secretariat affected the nation. The horse was a shining star during the time of Watergate and the Vietnam War. This single creature uplifted an entire country. Everyone considered him a true American hero. He did not run for money, power, or praise. He ran for the pure joy of running.

Christian packed up at work and drove to his mother's house to get the old tape. ESPN had produced a show of the century's fifty greatest athletes. Secretariat, the only animal, came in at number thirty-five.

At his mother's house, Christian opened the package, grabbed a soda, and strolled into the family room with the tape. Luckily, their old VCR was still hooked up and working. In the empty quiet room, he leaned back on the couch, got comfortable, and pushed the remote key, expecting to watch a series of horse races.

Halfway through the tape, Christian found himself on the edge of his seat with goose bumps and a shiver going up his spine as he watched the super-horse.

In the Belmont, Secretariat was charging toward the finish line, an outstanding thirty-one lengths ahead of the field. Christian fell on the floor to get closer to the TV. "Oh, my God; oh, my God." He breathed hard, and his eyes watered while his heart pounded with euphoria. He knew the horse had won the race, a race that had captivated the entire country, but it was so long ago and he was ill prepared. He wiped the tears from his eyes, trying to recover from witnessing such perfection, such raw grit and speed, such magnificence. He recalled his father had said that he had cried, watching this race. No wonder. The tape scanned the crowd, moved, many spectators also were weeping.

Christian covered his mouth, sniffled, and stared at the blank screen. Is this what he had? Was Mystery, his clone, destined to shape history and touch every soul in the nation?

Barbaro, the injured Derby winner, was a sampling. The horse had captured everyone's interest and concern, but his fame was nothing like Secretariat's. The horse had raced in 1972 and had died in 1989, but his legend lived on, his name immortal. If polled, people might not know the name of the current vice president of the U.S., but the majority—rich, poor, young, or old, and horse lover or not—would know Secretariat, the name of the illustrious Thoroughbred. Christian's father had said that people who saw Secretariat win the Belmont could recall exactly where they were when they watched this race. The event was so huge, historical, and unforgettable.

Christian collapsed against the couch, grasping for the first time that his colt, if truly like Secretariat, was way bigger than his own little life with its goals and problems. His colt would steal every heart, influence millions of people, but when the racing was over, what then? They might discover it was all a lie, a hoax—an unregistered horse, illegally raced, a clone whose genes had been manipulated by science and men.

He stood and felt weak in the knees. Maybe Mystery is just a nice racehorse, and he'll win enough to get me out of hock, he thought, but he did not believe it. After reading everything about Secretariat, he knew Mystery looked, ran, and behaved identical to his remarkable donor. Being raised in a different environment had not altered Mystery or his course. It was only the beginning, and his colt was racing down the path of fame.

Several days later, Christian leaned against the rail at Calder, chewed his nails, and watched Mystery walk past in the post parade, led by the pony rider. Allie stood nearby with her gaze fixed on the colt.

Christian thought about two days earlier when he and Vito had taken the Scarab and made their second run in the gulf. The pickup and delivery of goods went as planned. While waiting for the freighter's arrival, Vito confessed that he hated boats and feared the water. Perhaps it might partly explain the man's disagreeable attitude. Every time Vito saw Christian, the man had to climb into a boat. Christian had hoped to see Vince and talk about the length of his employment, but Vince was in New York, leaving Sal, his second in command, in charge.

Christian's thoughts returned to the present as the horses had reached the starting gate and began to load.

Allie glanced at Christian. "You've been awfully distracted. Is something bothering you?"

"No, I'm fine." He winced, not having known his dejected mood had been obvious. Besides his other problems, he was dogged with a growing guilt concerning Mystery and whether the colt should be raced. He pointed at the gate, getting Allie's concerned eyes off him. "He's going in."

She turned and watched Mystery load.

The starting gate opened and, once again, Mystery was the last to leave. "Come on, Mystery," Allie shouted. "Get your act together."

"He will," Christian whispered, no longer doubting the ability of his colt.

Mystery hung back, trailing the other horses and, in the turn, he made up the distance with an explosion of speed. The other two-year-olds appeared to barely move as Mystery, big and mature for his age, stampeded past them. Allie yelled and bounced up and down as the chestnut colt dashed, unchallenged, toward the finish line.

Christian stood still, bit his lip, and watched. "Big Red," he said, unsure if he had mumbled or thought it. Mystery breezed by them, hardly breaking a sweat.

"Clever Chris, taking it by eight lengths," said the announcer.

Allie looked up at Christian. "Are you excited now?"

"Yes," he said with a smile. He felt like a kid in school who received an A on a test, but had cheated to get it, guilt hindering his joy.

Allie clasped his hand. "Let's go." She pulled him toward the winner circle. He stood next to Allie as she held Mystery's bridle with Jeffrey in the saddle while the photo was snapped. Christian took over, holding the colt while Allie removed the saddle and handed it to the jockey for the weigh in.

"Good, boy," Christian cooed and rubbed his colt's head while Allie talked to Jeffrey and ordered the picture from the photographer.

Christian heard a man's voice over his shoulder. "Nice colt. Would you be interested in selling him?"

Christian grinned and turned, but frowned upon seeing Price. "He's not for sale, especially to you."

"Well, think about it," said Price. "The sheik is offering a fair amount of money."

"Fair?" Christian glared. "What would you two know about fair? Speaking of it, what became of Hunter?"

Allie walked up. "Get the hell away from us, Price." She grabbed Mystery's lead from Christian and sharply swung the colt around, hoping to knock the trainer down with the horse's rump.

"Watch out!" Price yelled, jumping clear. Allie smirked and sauntered out onto the track with Mystery, heading toward the barns.

Price grumbled, "I see you're still with that little bitch."

"Yeah, I am." Christian glared. "What about Glade Hunter?"

Price ran his fingers over his mustache. "He was injured in a grade-three stake race last year."

"Did you kill him?"

"No," Price frowned, acting offended. "It was a hairline fracture. He was gelded and sold to a Miami woman who deals with polo ponies."

Christian picked up the bucket and remaining gear. He started to follow Allie and the colt who were fifty yards down the track.

"Christian," Price called. "Keep my offer in mind."

CHAPTER SEVENTEEN

Christian sat on the couch and stared at the TV. The weather forecaster pointed to the yellow, orange, and red swirls created by radar that represented a tropical depression named Blanche. She had swept through the Caribbean, crossed Cuba, and was headed for the Gulf of Mexico. With the warm gulf waters, Blanche was expected to pick up speed and turn into a hurricane overnight. Storm warnings had gone up from the Florida Keys to Tampa.

The colorful computer-generated spaghetti lines across the screen predicted the storm's path. Most lines had Blanche skirting the Florida coast and making landfall north in the state's panhandle, Alabama or Mississippi. As a native who had seen his share of storms, Christian knew not to completely trust the forecasts of computers, radar, and weathermen. A hurricane was an erratic and volatile creature with a mind of its own and could easily alter its course.

Although June was the start of the hurricane season, Christian did not start watching the weather until August when storms were the most active and destructive. It was August first. Christian wasn't overly concerned. Hurricanes, like mosquitoes, rain, and the sweltering heat, were part of a Florida summer.

He turned off the TV and walked into the kitchen. Allie stood at the counter and tossed a salad. He came up behind her and wrapped his arms around her waist. "Need help?" he asked, kissing and nuzzling her neck.

"No, dinner is ready, but you can do the dishes later."

"Hey, my mother didn't raise a male chauvinist. I got no problem with dish washing." He took a piece of carrot from the salad and popped it into his mouth. "Tomorrow we'll start feeling the effects of this storm. Should get a ton of wind and rain."

"Terrific," Allie murmured and placed the salad on the table. "That means I can't work horses on a flooded track. I'll have to put Mystery in the round pen so he can blow off steam. Otherwise he'll tear down his stall. What about you? Are you going to work tomorrow?"

"I'll drive in, but doubt I'll open for business. The bay will be too rough. If there's a super-high tide, I might have to drag everything out here and store it in the barn. If the pasture floods, I could tie Mystery to a WaveRunner and exercise him for you," he said, jokingly.

"I could picture that—him stomping you and the WaveRunner, and then he'd strangle himself. He doesn't like motors."

And neither did Secretariat, he thought and opened the fridge. "Want iced tea?" he asked and took out a pitcher.

"Yes, please." Along with the salad, Allie set a plate of fried chicken and bowls of collards, mashed potatoes, and corn muffins on the table.

He filled their glasses and took his seat. "Looks good, Allie." His cell phone rang. "Why do people call at dinner?" He flipped it open. Seeing the caller, he left the table and wandered into the living room for a private chat. "Hey."

"Hey, yourself," Vince said. "Tomorrow night you're on."

"What? You got to be kidding. Have you seen the weather?"

"This can't be canceled. Be here," Vince said and hung up.

Christian closed the phone and glanced at Allie in the kitchen. Fishing in a hurricane? She'd never buy it. "That was Vince," he said, sitting back down at the table. "Typical Yankee, he's freaking out about the hurricane and wants me to move his boat to a marina. I probably won't be home until late tomorrow."

"Can't you move it in the morning?" she asked. "I was thinking about coming to town and filling the gas cans for the generator, in case we lose power. Meg could feed the horses in the afternoon, and we can hang out on the beach and watch the storm come in. It'd be fun."

"I'll fill the cans," he blurted out, "You don't need to come in. I probably won't be home until after midnight, and I'll be too busy to hang out with you."

She looked at him strangely. "Doing what?"

Christian put his fork down, feeling his back was up against a wall. He couldn't come up with a believable answer and was sick of lying. "I have things to do that can't involve you. And please don't ask me what."

"Please don't ask?" she said, glaring at him. "Christian, it's bad enough I've had to deal with the lies and secrets about your colt and swallow the bullshit concerning those late-night fishing trips when you never bring fish home. Now it's running around all night in a hurricane with no explanation." She stood and dropped her plate of barely touched dinner into the sink. "In case no one told you, a good relationship is built on trust, but it's obvious you don't trust me!" She hurried into the bedroom.

He and Allie rarely disagreed, much less argued, but she was truly upset. For several minutes, he sat in the empty kitchen and rubbed his temples, while staring at the ruined dinner. "Damn it," he cursed and abruptly rose, rocking his chair so hard that it nearly fell over. His life had become a tangle of deceit.

He walked into the bedroom and found Allie with her face buried in a pillow. "I'm sorry, Allie." He sat down on the bed and ran his hand up her back. "If I told you what's going on, you might be hurt."

Allie lifted her head. Her eyes were moist and red. "I might be hurt? Are you seeing someone else? Was that really Vince on the phone?"

"Yes, it was Vince." He frowned. "Allie, I'm not messing around." He whipped out his cell phone. "Look, it's Vince's number on the caller ID."

"I don't need to see your phone." She wiped a tear off her cheek. "But, Christian, what am I supposed to think? I've seen how women flirt and throw themselves at you. You're a good-looking guy, but so was my ex-husband. I don't want to be a fool and be the last to know again."

He stood. "Damn it, Allie. I'm not your ex-husband!" He tossed back his hair and paced back and forth in front of the bed. "Fine, I lied about moving Vince's boat into a marina, and I know that looks bad, but I can't tell you what's going on. I can't tell anyone. I'm dealing with so much shit, and I'm sick of lying about it." He slammed his fist into his hand and shuddered. "It's killing me! It's just killing me."

She watched him for a moment. "All right, calm down."

He stopped pacing and looked at her, breathing hard. "You're the best thing going for me, and I'm scared." He bit his lip hard and rubbed his forehead from side to side. "Allie, I'm so damn scared that I might lose you over all this."

"Come here," she said and opened her arms. He crawled into her warm embrace, his soft place to fall. "You won't lose me."

He hugged her. "I'm sorry, I'm so sorry. I wish to God I could tell you everything, but I can't. Ever since I've gotten into this horse racing—" He shut his eyes. "It's like I've fallen into a pit that keeps getting deeper, and I can't climb out."

On the rainy bayfront, Christian stood on the Sailing Squadron dock and stared across the churning bay with its six-foot swells and whitecaps. Strong wind gusts tugged at his yellow foul-weather jacket.

Early in the morning, he and Jake had put his Whaler on a trailer and moved it, along with his small sailboats and WaveRunners, into the enclosed chain-link fence at the Squadron, deciding they would be safe enough. Last year, he had sold the McGregor and reimbursed Frank, so he was minus its worry. If the weather got worse, he still had time to haul his little fleet out to the farm. In the meantime, he ran around in the pelting rain and helped other people secure their boats in preparation of the storm.

During the night, the tropical depression had grown in strength. With the winds exceeding seventy-five miles an hour, Blanche became a Category 1 hurricane when she crossed the Florida straits and Key West. At dawn she had emerged in the gulf as a slow-moving category two. Hurricane warnings existed on Florida's entire west coast, along with small craft warnings. If Blanche maintained her course and speed, she would pass Sarasota at midnight, fifty miles out in the gulf. A voluntary evacuation order already existed for trailer parks and residents on the keys, but evacuation would soon turn mandatory with Blanche threatening to become a destructive category three.

Everyone was running for cover except Christian. Tonight he would take the Scarab twenty miles out in the gulf and straight into the thirty-foot-plus seas and more than ninety-mile-an-hour winds.

It's suicide. He glanced at the boats leaping up and down between the docks. Farther out in the bay, the fifty-knot winds were testing the moorings and taut lines of the anchored sailboats. A few, he was sure, would not survive. In the morning they would be found lying on their sides on some beach or smashed to pieces against the rocks. Times like this, he was grateful he did not live aboard a sailboat anymore.

With his jeans, sneakers, and hair soaking wet, he strolled down the slippery wooden dock and entered the clubhouse. He nodded to several members who sat around a table and drank beer. They excitedly talked about the hurricane, enjoying the cool wind, rain, and overcast skies, a nice break from the humid August heat that sapped the energy out of a person.

Christian swiveled a chair and joined the little party of year-round residents who were accustomed to hurricanes. He sat astride, with his elbows resting on its back. He added to the conversation, but his mind was on Allie, wishing she could be with him. It would have been fun.

After a while, he walked to the far side of the room, unzipped his waterproof jacket pocket and took out his cell phone. He pushed the keys, but once again, he got Vince's voice message.

Where the hell is he? Christian shoved the cell phone back into his pocket. Several times he had phoned and left messages, but Vince had not returned his calls. He hoped the guy would come to his senses and cancel the run tonight. But why should he? It wasn't his skin.

His thoughts drifted to Vito and his fear of boats and the water. Christian's lips curled mischievously into a grin. *It'd almost be worth facing a hurricane to see Vito crap his pants.*

At five o'clock, Christian ran through sheets of rain and fierce gusts and hopped into his SUV. He started the engine and turned on the windshield wipers, which swept away bits of leaves and twigs. The rain blew sideways and nearly caused white-out conditions. He sat in the idling vehicle and saw a huge uprooted tree that had fallen on a picnic table in the park. Smaller branches lay spewed across the roadway. The palm trees swayed, close to snapping.

He thought of his sorry choices, defy Vince and his mob buddies or take a boat out in a hurricane. *Either way, I'm fucked.* He took his cell out and placed a call to Allie. "How's everything?"

"It's windy and has been raining hard off and on," she said. "The power went out for an hour, but that's the norm for Myakka. I imagine it's worse on the keys."

"Yeah, blowing like a bitch out here," he said. "Ah, Allie, I just called . . . I called to say I love you." For a long moment there was no response. "Allie?"

"You really are in trouble, aren't you?"

"No, I'm okay." Saying he loved her out of the blue hadn't been smart, since those affectionate words were reserved for lovemaking or lengthy separations. She had sensed the latter. "Look, I gotta go. I'll see you later," he said, hoping to reassure her.

"I love you, too. Please be careful and come home to me."

"I will." He closed the phone, slid it into his pocket, and shook his head. *Damn her instincts. Why bother bullshitting her? She knows I'm not okay.* He put the SUV in gear and drove to Vince's house.

Christian removed his wet jacket and shook the droplets from his tousled hair before stepping into the foyer. "I've been trying to reach you, Vince."

"I know," Vince said. "I don't like discussin' things on a cell." He walked to the living room with Christian trailing. Once again, Sal filled a chair, and Vito stood and soberly stared out the sliding glass doors at the choppy bay. The mood in the room was grave. Not even Sal cracked a smile.

Vito turned from the window and rambled something off in Italian to Vince. His voice was elevated and nervous. No translation was needed. Vito wasn't happy about the evening boat ride.

Vince yelled something back in Italian. Vito shut up, turned back to the window, and sulked.

Christian walked to Vince. "I'm not scared of open water and storms, but this is crazy, Vince. You can't be serious about tonight's run. That Scarab isn't built to survive those rough seas. Even if we make it to the drop-off site, we'll never spot the bags in the dark with those huge waves. Plus, the boat will be rocking like a bitch. I have to stay at the helm and keep her pointed into the wind and waves, one big swell hitting her side will swamp or flip her. That means I can't help Vito. There's no way he can haul in a hundred-pound package by himself when we're bouncing around."

"*Sì, Sì.*" Vito chimed in. "Listen to *Signor* Christian," he pleaded to Vince.

"Look, goddamn it," Vince cursed. "The freighter can't pull into the port with the goods on board, and I'll be damned if I'll leave millions floating in the gulf. You two are going! *Capisce*?"

Sal shifted his weight and struggled to stand. "Boss, most the boys are out of town, and there's no extra help until morning, so I'll go with Vito and the kid tonight."

Vince frowned. "Forget it, Sal. You can barely get out of a chair.

You'd be useless on a boat." He rubbed his mustache and jaw. "I'll go."

"Boss, can't the drop-off be delayed until the storm passes?" Sal asked.

Christian swept his wet bangs back. "I imagine right now that freighter is moving at full speed, trying to outrun the storm. No way that ship captain will sit in the gulf and ride out a hurricane when the Tampa port offers shelter."

"That's right," Vince said and walked to the bar. "Plus, it has to maintain its schedule." He poured himself a straight shot of whiskey.

Christian raised his eyebrow. "Even with your help, Vince, it's still a hell of a risk. Trust me. You have no clue of how bad it's going to be. Can you contact the freighter and have them dump the bags in Tampa Bay? It'll still be rough, but we'll have a fighting chance."

"I said cell calls are risky," Vince said and gulped down the whole shot. "Someone might overhear the coordinates of the drop-off, and the cops will be waiting."

Amused at the ridiculous, Christian chuckled. "Vince, only a nutcase would be out in a boat or helicopter tonight. I guarantee, besides the freighter, we'll have Tampa Bay to ourselves. Even if the police show up, they'll never catch me in that Scarab and I know umpteen hiding places in the mangrove coves."

Vince wiped his mustache, contemplating for several moments. He looked at Christian and then turned to Sal. "You see, Sally. I told you this kid's got brains."

On a table, Christian leaned over a chart of Tampa Bay. He pointed to a location in the shipping channel between the Skyway Bridge and Egmont Key. "Here," he said to the men. "It's the shortest run to the intercoastal. Anna Maria Island should help block some of the wind." He relayed the coordinates to Vince, who contacted the freighter with the new drop-off point.

Because of the bad weather, they decided to come back to Vince's dock on the return trip and store the goods in his garage rather than go to the small boat ramp on City Island. With the police preoccupied with the hurricane, Sal would have no problem removing the bags from the garage and getting them to the bread truck in town.

While waiting to leave, Christian and the three men drank a few cocktails. Sal had made spaghetti and meatballs. Vince, Vito, and Sal filled their plates and sat down on stools at the kitchen counter. Christian stood and munched on a piece of garlic bread, but politely refused the dinner.

"No wonder the kid's a skinny twerp," Sal said. "What'sa matter, kid? Don't like spaghetti?"

"Love it," said Christian, "but facing those huge waves with a full stomach isn't smart, unless you don't mind seasickness and barfing all night." Vince and Vito glanced up at Christian and put their forks down, but Sal kept stuffing his mouth.

At midnight they bundled up and walked through the stinging rain and fierce wind to the dock and Scarab. Even in the little inlet, the waves caused the boat to bounce up and down, hitting the dock bumpers. Vito and Vince had difficulty climbing aboard.

"You better wear life jackets," Christian shouted over the howling wind and sprang onto the deck. He dug two vests out from the hatch and handed them to Vito and Vince.

Vince put the orange vest on and took a seat at the helm next to Christian. "Where's yours?" he asked.

"Don't wear life jackets," Christian said. "I consider it bad luck, plus I'm a good swimmer." He turned the motors over and called to Vito, "Push us off."

Sal had untied the lines and tossed them on the deck. "*Buona fortuna*, good luck."

Vito used the gaff to shove the Scarab's bow away from the dock. Christian quickly pushed the throttle and turned the wheel, guiding the boat clear of the crushing pilings. He nodded with approval to Vito, who scrambled back to his seat. After two trips together, the man had learned to be a deckhand.

Sal yelled from the dock, "*Dio ti guarda.*"

Christian glanced at Vince. "What did Sal say?"

Vince shuddered and gazed at the hellish ink water ahead. "He said, 'God watch over you.'"

They motored through the violent chop toward the middle of the bay. In the dark and sheets of rain, the boat lights were useless. Christian stood and steered the boat as Vito flashed the large strobe across the raven-black surface, hoping to spot the channel markers.

Although moving blindly with the lack of star and city lights, Christian instinctively guided the Scarab to the intercoastal waterway. "We should be coming up on the first marker," he called to Vito.

"*Sì*," Vito said. "There." He pointed and aimed the light on the marker only twenty yards off the port bow.

"How in the devil did you see it?" Vince asked.

Christian wiped the water out of his eyes. "I've lived on this bay." He glanced at his watch, figuring the time and distance it would take to reach Tampa Bay and the freighter. He didn't relish being there, but he was grateful they were avoiding the gulf. The brunt of the hurricane was hitting Sarasota and Manatee Keys as Blanche skirted the coastline going north. He eased the throttle forward and increased their speed. Scared stiff, Vito and Vince held on as the Scarab lunged, dipped, and rolled from side to side, fighting the large waves and intense gusts.

Christian stood, gripped the wheel, and steadied his footing. He glanced down at Vince, the boat dash lights reflected on his petrified face. "You all right, Vince?"

"I think I'm going to be sick. How much longer?" Vince yelled over the boat motor and wind.

"Half hour and we'll be in Tampa Bay," Christian said.

Vince put his hand up shielding his eyes from the smarting rain. "Christian, I'm glad I listened to you. In the gulf, we'd be dead."

"It ain't over. When we leave this protected channel and enter Tampa Bay, the chop and wind will be bad."

Sure enough, Tampa Bay was a nightmare. The giant waves resembled a watery roller coaster. The Scarab no longer blasted through the waves, but mounted each fifteen-foot swell and rode it up and down. At the peaks, the outboard motors whined and revved when their propellers came out of the water.

Christian chewed his lip, tasting the sea spray, and clinging to the wheel to keep the boat straight. It was nerve racking. One false move and the Scarab, like a surfboard, would go crashing and rolling under a wave rather than surging over it. Vince huddled below the windshield, head down, facing the floor. Christian glanced back at Vito, and their gaze locked, Vito's eyes wide, terrified, and beseeching.

"We'll make it, Vito," Christian called. For the first time he felt empathy for the gangster. Amid the sheets of rain and total blackness, he spotted the freighter's lights jumping up and down. Even the huge ship was having a bumpy ride.

"There she is, and right on time," Christian said and spun the wheel, forcing the Scarab to take on waves at an angle. More dangerous.

As they neared the freighter, Vito bounced off the boat sides, trying to stand and focus the light on the ship. He managed to motion to the deckhands who tossed out the goods. Christian steered the Scarab into the wake of the large freighter. Vince popped his head out to watch.

"When we reach a bag," Christian hollered to the men, "just grab it and throw it on the deck. I can't stop and idle. We'll stash them in the hold when we're back in Palma Sola and calmer water. If you miss one, it'll be a bitch if I have to go back for it."

Vito nodded, and Vince just stared, zombielike. Vito yelled in Italian and shined the light at the first bag.

"I see it," said Christian. "I'll come up on the starboard side. Use the gaff hooks." He steered the boat, and Vito handed him the light so he could focus on the bag. The two men, holding the six-foot gaffs, took up their position on the right side of the boat.

In the formidable seas, Christian guided the Scarab alongside the bag. Vito managed to hook its buoy line and pull the bag close.

With Vince's help, they struggled and dragged the first one on board, dropping it at their feet inside the open deck.

The second bag proved more difficult. As the boat cruised by, both men missed the bag with their gaffs. Not wanting to take the Scarab in a large circle to retrieve it, Christian sharply turned the wheel and, with the lift of a wave, the bag came within reach. He leaned way over the boat side and grabbed it while his other hand clung to the wheel, preventing him from falling overboard. He had it halfway out of the water, but was losing his hold and strength in the bouncing surf. Vito raced to the front and helped him lift it in.

Vito grinned, a first. "*Buono, buono*. You good guy, *Signor* Christian."

As the evening progressed, they found and retrieved nine of the ten bags. The last one eluded them. Christian was forced to swing the boat around, fighting the waves, and retrace their path. After a half hour, they located the final bag and tossed it aboard.

"*Andiamo*," Vito yelled.

"I agree." Vince puffed with all the exertion. "Let's get the fuck out of here."

"Don't need to tell me twice," Christian said and turned the Scarab south.

Vince crawled back to the helm and stood beside Christian. "You did a great job tonight, handling the boat in those waves." He clapped Christian's shoulder with affection. "I'm thinking about adopting you."

Christian grimaced. "Please don't." He suddenly caught a glimpse of something big and white, lit up by the boat's running lights, and dead ahead within a huge, rolling wave. "Shit!" He spun the wheel to avoid hitting it, but was too late.

The impact created a loud bang, scraping, crunching, as the Scarab came to an abrupt stop, jolting everyone and everything forward. Christian was slammed against the wheel and hit his forehead on the windshield. He collapsed unconscious beneath the instrument panel.

CHAPTER EIGHTEEN

Waves broke over the Scarab and flooded the cockpit. Christian was jarred awake, choking on saltwater. He managed to lift his head and lean against the boat bulkhead. For a few seconds he lay in a stupor. Another wave crashed over the Scarab, drenching him, and he snapped back to reality.

He noticed the two feet of water that sloshed back and forth within the boat while the silent, lifeless Scarab bumped around like a cork in the giant swells. His forehead hurt, and he touched it and felt the deep gash.

He sat up and remembered the monstrous wave and the object it held. With only a glance, he deduced it was the white hull of another boat, and then there was the crash and being thrown forward. He wondered how long he had been out—a minute, five, or maybe more. He listened, but heard only the roaring wind and gush of waves, hammering the hull. He pulled himself up and stood. The running lights still worked, giving off a dim glow. Beneath the steering wheel, he flung open a small hatch and rummaged around until he felt a flashlight.

"Vince, Vito," he yelled and scanned the light across the deck. They were nowhere in sight, but toward the stern, he noticed the nearly submerged motors. The Scarab was sinking. He kept calling and searching the dark waters.

Twenty yards away, his flashlight shined on the other boat they had hit. A large sailboat heeled over on its side, rising and sinking within each wave. It must have broken free of its dock or mooring and capsized in the storm. It floundered now a foot beneath the dark surface like a deadly reef, waiting to cripple an unsuspecting speedboat.

He felt the gushing water on his feet and looked down, shining the flashlight on the Scarab's cracked hull, a fatal wound for a boat. She would soon rest in a watery grave, becoming a host for crabs, fish, and barnacles.

On the starboard side, he aimed the light in the surrounding water and yelled, "Vince, Vince." He scrambled over the bags of floating drugs and hurried to the portside. Several feet off the bow, he made out an orange life jacket holding a limp body, facedown in the surf. A closer look exposed the distinctive black ponytail.

"Vito!" Christian rushed forward to the bow, lunged halfway over the boat side, and pulled the man's face out of the water. The running lights displayed Vito's open, dark eyes staring up at him.

Spooked, Christian jerked his hand away and clambered backward, unnerved by the dead man's gaze. He covered his mouth, and it took few seconds to collect his wits. "Vito," he said softer, not expecting a response. He reached down again and shook him. Despite knowing Vito was dead, drowned or killed by his injuries, Christian had to be sure. Reluctantly, he released his hold and let the bay and storm claim a man who, ironically, feared the water.

Despite the rocking boat and squall blasts, he stood up on the bow and maintained his balance, his surfing experience giving him the knack. He shined the light across the monster waves and shouted, "Vince! Vince!"

He caught a hint of orange in a steep wave thirty yards out. In the blinding rain, he pointed the flashlight at the next peaking wave and made out a figure in a life jacket. He dropped the light, stripped off his foul-weather jacket and shoes, and dove off the bow. He found the bay water warmer than the raw, cutting wind and icy rain. He surfaced and swam toward Vince.

"Vince, Vince," he said, reaching him.

"Christian," Vince responded weakly.

"Are you badly hurt?" Christian asked while treading water.

"My leg and chest, they hurt. What happened?"

"We hit a capsized sailboat."

"Vito, where's Vito?"

"He's dead."

"Oh, no," said Vince.

Christian glanced back at the Scarab. For a second he considered taking Vince back to it. More people survived a shipwreck by clinging to the overturned boat and waiting for a rescue than setting off and swimming for land.

The Scarab bow lights revealed the rising waterline. With waves breeching her sides and the hole in her bottom, she would be gone in half an hour and, with a hurricane, no one would be out on Tampa Bay to spot them until probably mid-morning. No sense in returning to the boat.

A large wave lifted them up and, at the peak, Christian caught a vague flicker of light on the Skyway Bridge. Oriented to his surroundings, Christian knew that Snead Island and Terra Ceia were south and the closest land. "We're going to have to swim for it, Vince."

"I can't." Vince gasped. "I can't make it."

"Yes, you can. Look, we're in luck. It's an incoming tide, and the wind is with us. I'll drag you. Lean back and kick." He grabbed the life jacket near the back of Vince's neck and started doing a sidestroke with one hand, pulling the man on his back through the water.

Vince kicked with his one good leg briefly, but quit and floated like a heavy log. After an hour, he mumbled, "Christian, Christian."

"What?" Christian puffed between gulps of air. He stopped swimming, taking a short break.

"Why are you doing this? You could leave me, let me drown. Then you'd be free of me and your debt."

"Don't tempt me, Vince." He panted and started swimming again. It was true. The gangster had him in a stranglehold—do the job or you and your family might suffer. With plenty of motive, Christian could easily let Vince drown, plus, dragging the weighty burden through the brutal seas, he was upping the ante of his own survival. Without Vince, he could swim to shore, no problem, and make it.

I couldn't live with myself, Christian thought and pressed on. God or luck had sent him a hurricane, a foundering sailboat, and crash, all to rid him of Vince, but he rejected the gifts. He knew his conscience would dog him the rest of his days if he deserted another human being, even Vince.

After several hours, Christian's leg and arm muscles burned with pain, and he neared exhaustion. Out of breath, he gasped and fought the waves that sometime engulfed them, but he kept going, encouraged by the lights he could finally see on Snead Island and Terra Ceia.

"Almost there, another mile, maybe two," Christian said between puffs. No answer. "Vince, you still with me?" he asked, and heard a groan. "Good, hang in there."

Hours later and a hundred feet from the dark beach, Christian stopped swimming and put his foot down. He felt the fringes of sea grass and closed his eyes with relief. Another forty feet, and he waded in the chest-deep water, towing Vince. The waves crashed over his head, but their wake helped push Vince toward shore.

Christian reached the shallows, grabbed Vince under his arms, and shuffled backward, dragging him onto the seaweed-covered beach. He collapsed on the sand next to Vince. "We made it." Vince didn't respond.

For few seconds, Christian thought he had died. "Vince!" He shook him and then leaned over, resting his ear on Vince's chest. He heard his beating heart and felt his rising and falling chest.

Vince moaned, barely conscious.

"Jesus, Vince, I thought you had croaked." Christian stood, wrapped his arms close, and shivered in his wet t-shirt and jeans. The cold rain and bitter wind penetrated his core. He glanced up and down the shadowy beach. "I'm going for help."

It was summer, the off-season, and with a looming hurricane in the gulf, most beach houses were vacant and dark. A block away, he saw an outside light and jogged toward it. Reaching the cottage, he climbed the wooden steps and banged on its back door. No one answered. He looked around the barren wooden deck for something to break the glass so he could get in and, he hoped, find a working phone.

He reached for a heavy conch shell and saw an inside light come on. He pounded the door again, and eventually an elderly man dressed in pajamas peered out the window at him.

"I need to call an ambulance," Christian shouted, rubbing his arms for warmth.

The man cautiously opened the door.

"My buddy and I were in a boat accident," Christian explained. "His chest hurts. He might have internal injuries."

"Oh, heavens," said the man. "What the heck were you doing out in a hurricane and in the middle of the night?"

"Look, just hurry. He's a couple of hundred yards down the beach." Christian pointed.

"Harold, who is it?" said an old woman behind the man.

"This young fella's boat went down in the storm, and he's got a hurt friend down the beach. Go call 911, Maud."

"Oh, my," she said and hurried off.

"Come in, come in," said the old man.

Christian stepped a few feet inside. "I gotta get back to him."

"Okay, but just wait here a minute. I'll give you a flashlight and blanket. As soon as I put on some clothes, I'll be down."

"Thanks," Christian said and stood by the door, shivering and dripping water. The man quickly returned with the light and quilt. Christian turned on the light and ran back down the beach.

He covered Vince with the blanket. "Just hold on, Vince. Help is coming." He felt a little lightheaded and sat down in the sand near Vince. He hugged his legs and rested his head on his knees. He still shook violently in the cold rain and harsh wind.

• • •

In the emergency room, Christian sat on a gurney in a hospital gown, a blanket covering his shoulders as a doctor stitched up his head gash. "Where's the closest phone? I need to get a ride home."

"There's one at the nurses' station," said the doctor, "but really, Mr. Roberts, I'd like you to stay twenty-four hours for observation. When you came in, that lightheadedness and shaking were the first stages of hypothermia."

"Hypothermia?" Christian questioned.

"Yes, swimming for hours in cold water lowered your body temperature. You can suffer from hypothermia, even in Florida during the summer."

"Well, I feel all right now and want to go."

"I can't keep you, but you'll have to sign an AMA—an Against Medical Advice release." The doctor finished and pushed the tray aside. "In ten days, your stitches can come out."

"Thanks, doc," Christian said and slid off the gurney. At the nurse's station he placed a call to Allie.

"Hey, it's me," he said.

"My God, Christian, it's five-thirty in morning. I've been up all night, worried sick about you. Where are you?"

"I'm at Manatee Memorial, the emergency room, but my SUV is still at Vince's, so I need a ride home."

"The emergency room!" said Allie with alarm. "Are you all right?"

"I'm fine. Got a few stitches on my forehead. Vince and I were in a boat accident."

"Jesus, you were on the water last night?"

"Can we please talk about it later? Right now I just want to get to the house, take a hot shower, and crawl into bed."

"With this rain, it'll take me at least forty-five minutes to get there."

"Okay, and Allie, could you bring me some clothes? Mine are soaking wet, and I'm wearing a hospital gown."

He hung up and turned to a middle-aged nurse, sitting in front of a computer. "I came in with a guy. Can you check and see how he's doing?" He told her Vince's whole name.

She tapped the computer keys and looked up. "Mr. Florio is in serious but stable condition—no visitors, unless you're a relative."

Christian leaned over the counter and flashed his pearly whites. "I'm his adopted son. I really would like to see him."

The nurse blushed with an ear-to-ear grin. "Oh, all right." She jotted down Vince's room number and handed him the paper.

Christian entered the hospital room and saw Vince lying on the bed with his eyes closed. With an oxygen mask over his face, he resembled Christian's father.

"Hey," Christian whispered, "are you sleeping?"

One of Vince's eyes squinted open, and his expression brightened in recognition.

"I'll let you rest," Christian said. "I just wanted to check on you before I left."

Vince frowned and moved his fingers, motioning him to stay. He pulled the mask down. "That boat trip—it cost me," he uttered. "It's your fault."

Christian raised his eyebrows. "My fault?" he said with an elevated voice. "Vince, there's no way I could've avoided that sailboat. I'm sorry you lost your shipment. I'm even sorry about Vito, but it couldn't—"

"Shut up." Vince scowled. "While you were draggin' me through the water, I was thinking—here I am a rich guy, risking going to jail, risking my life, and for what—more money? Christian, I thought I was a goner."

Vince took a deep breath. "They say a near-death experience can scare you straight. Fucker's true. So it's your fault I survived and am retiring. Quitting while ahead."

"That's good, Vince."

"All those Gs you still owe me—"

"I swear I'll pay you back."

"Will you please shut up and let me finish. You don't owe me a dime. That horse loan was obviously the best investment I've ever made. I'm just sorry I'll lose a good fishin' guide."

Christian smiled and lightly patted Vince's arm. "Get well, Vince. We'll go fishin' again."

Allie arrived at the hospital and gave Christian his change of clothes. They left the hospital under gloomy skies that hindered the morning sun. The couple walked through the shadowy parking lot with the wind whipping at their hair. The sprinkling rain and strong breeze were the remnants of Hurricane Blanche, which had moved north of Tampa.

Allie asked how many stitches he had received. He told her twelve. Other than that, she was unusually quiet.

He felt her silent questions boiling within her like a pressure cooker about to explode. They reached her pickup, and he asked, "How did the farm and horses make out in the storm?"

She spun on her heels and glared. "They're fine, Christian," she said in a huff. "They're in better shape than you. Now are you going to tell me about last night, or are we stashing it away with your other secrets?"

At her pickup he lowered his head and released a long, weary sigh. To say he wanted to discuss it later wouldn't fly, but should he tell her the whole complicated truth—the gangster loan on Mystery, his failure to pay the loan sharks that placed her and his family in danger, the drug smuggling, the reason he was out in a hurricane on Tampa Bay?

He was too exhausted to think clearly and come up with another halfway believable story. He glanced down at her determined little face. She wanted an explanation and wanted it right away.

He scratched his head and gave her a halfhearted grin. "Well," he started, "Vince and I weren't fishing."

"Really?" She rolled her eyes.

He glanced up, hearing tires squeal. A car raced through the hospital parking lot. He recognized Sal's black Cadillac. "Let's go, Allie.

I'll tell you on the way home." He opened the passenger door, and Allie walked to the driver's side and started to climb in.

The Cadillac slammed to a stop behind Allie's pickup and blocked it in the parking space. Sal, in the driver's seat, stuck his head out the window. "Christian, you little fucker," he shouted. "Don't you move, goddamn it."

Allie stood by the open door, her eyes the size of baseballs. "Who is he?"

"Get in the truck," Christian said. "I'll handle this." He walked to the back of the truck. Allie still stood by the open door, not budging. "Get in," he repeated.

Sal climbed out of the Cadillac along with three other men, their faces dark and mean. They marched up and surrounded Christian.

"What the fuck happened?" Sal yelled, inches from Christian's face.

"Have you talked to Vince?" Christian asked, forcing himself to stay calm.

"Fuck, no," said Sal. "I was waiting for you guys to come back so I could help unload the goods. Then some goddamn nurse called, said Vince was here and had been in a boating accident. Now what the fuck is going on?"

"Vince is okay. He'll tell you everything," said Christian, reluctant to discuss events in front of Allie. He turned to leave, but Sal grabbed the front of his shirt and slammed him hard up against the truck bed.

"Listen, you lil' shit," Sal growled, pinning and pressing his weight against Christian. "You might have Vince twisted around your finger, but not me. As far as I'm concerned, you're an arrogant prick that should've been taken out after that first goddamn boat ride."

"Hey, dickhead," Allie yelled and stepped to them. She pointed a gun at Sal's face. "Get away from him."

The men were startled, Christian most of all. She wasn't holding a little .22 girl's gun, or even a snub-nosed .38, but a .44 Magnum,

Dirty Harry's cannon. Two of the men reached for weapons concealed under their jackets.

"Pull 'em and I'll blow this fat fuck's head off," she said.

Sal glanced at his men, and with a slight shake of his head, they lowered their arms to their sides.

"Jesus, Allie," Christian said. "Put that gun away."

"Uh-uh." Her voice and stare were as steady as her gun hand. "Not till this ape gets his paws off you."

Christian looked back at Sal. "I swear I'll tell you everything, Sal. This is all a misunderstanding."

Sal released Christian's shirt and gave him slight shove. "Start explaining."

Christian's eyes darted back and forth between Sal and Allie's weapon. "It was all going as planned," he said. "We picked up the goods from the freighter, no problem, and were heading back from Tampa Bay when the Scarab hit a submerged sailboat. With those huge waves and the poor visibility, there was no way to avoid it. We crashed, and Vito and Vince were thrown clear of the boat. I found Vince, grabbed him, swam to shore, then called an ambulance. That's pretty much it, Sal."

"You brought Vince in?" Sal asked, more composed.

"Yeah," Christian said, "dragged him probably seven miles, halfway across Tampa Bay through the surf. He's not pissed at me." He looked at Allie. "Please put that gun down." She lowered the weapon and shook her head.

"And Vito?" Sal asked.

Christian looked down. "He didn't make it."

"Damn." Sal grimaced. "What about the goods?"

"There was no time to store them in the hatch, and they were on the open deck. They probably floated away when the Scarab sank. If they're found, the cops can't tie them to Vince's boat."

Sal rubbed the back of his thick neck. "Well, that's good, but a hell of an expensive loss." He looked at Allie. "This is the girlfriend you've been trying to protect?"

Christian nodded.

Sal exhaled a yuk-yuk chuckle. “Kid, that little doll don’t need your protection.”

“Apparently not,” Christian muttered.

Sal slapped Christian’s back. “All right, kid, you can go. If your story checks out with Vince, then you got nothin’ to worry about.” He motioned to one of his men. “Move my car so these kids can get out.”

“Sal, I’m sorry about Vito,” Christian said.

Sal looked down and nodded. “Yeah, he was a good soldier. He actually mentioned he was startin’ to like ya. For Vito, that’s a stretch.” The Cadillac pulled away, and Sal and his other two men walked toward the hospital.

Christian reached for the passenger door handle and saw Allie slide the .44 into its holster and place it back under the driver’s seat. She then climbed behind the wheel.

He got in, shut the door, and took a long, profound breath. “I can’t believe you pulled that gun.”

She started the engine. “And I can’t believe you got involved with those guys.”

“Those guys are loan sharks, mobsters. They wouldn’t have hesitated to kill you.”

“No kidding,” she sniped. She turned to him. “But Christian, if they had hurt you, I also wouldn’t hesitate to pull the trigger.” She drove out of the parking lot and turned toward home.

Christian caressed his jaw, feeling the five o’clock shadow, and watched her. Allie stood only five foot two and weighed roughly a hundred and ten pounds, but she was tough, the toughest woman he had ever dated. She trained and rode dangerous horses and held her own in the male-dominated world of racing and, rather than have a little pet pooch, she preferred to sit by the lake with her ten-foot alligator.

It shouldn’t have been an eye-opener that she hid a gun in her pickup and had no problem pointing it at four mobsters, threatening to blast them if they harmed her man. Damn, she was gutsy. Admittedly, she had said her only fear was of the heart, of loving and losing.

"Sooo," she said, breaking the silence. "This explains why you couldn't tell me about your evenings with Vince. The goods, I take it, were drugs."

"I think so. Allie, I hate lying to you, but you were safer not knowing, not being involved in my mess. Mystery didn't make enough purse money, and I couldn't pay back the loan on time. I had to work for Vince, picking up the bags with his boat. He used you and my family as leverage so I'd keep my mouth shut and do it."

He looked out the window and released a weighty sigh. "But it's over. I saved Vince's neck, and he's letting me off the hook."

"That's good news, but Christian, we've been together almost two years. Your problems are my problems. You should've told me."

CHAPTER NINETEEN

Mid-August and Christian found himself once again in Miami at the Calder Race Course with Allie. They stood by the rail and waited for the start of Mystery's fourth race. She had entered the colt in a mile-long allowance with a forty-thousand-dollar purse. If Mystery won today, he was on his way, the next time out a six-digit stake race. Allie had even started looking at upcoming races at Belmont and Churchill Downs.

Christian had tried to share her enthusiasm, but always the guilt of racing the illegal horse rolled in, squelching his excitement. The thought of deceiving millions of people caused him many sleepless nights.

Like the White Sox that cheated during the World Series, he would betray history if Mystery, like Secretariat, went on to win the Triple Crown. The money and fame that came with owning a spectacular racehorse was slowly taking a backseat to his guilt.

Only weeks earlier, he followed his conscience and saved Vince, not expecting any compensation. All his fears and worries had vanished by simply doing the decent thing. He could breathe again and, darn, it felt good.

He faced another dilemma with Mystery, do the honest thing—retire the colt, give up a ton of money, and betray his father's dream—or keep racing him and see how far he would go? Christian thought about his father's plan of racing the horse, making the money, and bringing him home. He could claim the horse was sterile, avoid the second DNA test required for a stud, and elude getting busted. The secret of the cloning would die with the horse and him. It was tempting.

Why, then, did Christian get a nagging ache in his gut whenever he thought about it? It had started after he read about Secretariat and found himself on his mother's living room floor, teary-eyed, after watching Secretariat win the Belmont. No one could possibly watch that mind-blowing race without getting a lump in his or her throat. It was simply miraculous, like watching a horse fly.

And who the hell was he, some Florida hick, to tamper with a phenomenon, to screw with a nation's trust and emotions, to screw with history? More and more, Christian felt sick about it.

"He's up against some of the best two-year-olds in Florida," Allie said, looking at the catalogue as Mystery walked toward the starting gate "And he's running a mile. He might run out of gas. We'll find out if he's only a sprinter."

"I don't think distance will matter," said Christian. He put his thumb to his mouth and chewed on the nail, nervous if his colt lost, more nervous if he won. After this race, he would have to make a decision. It leaned toward one that Allie wouldn't like.

The bell sounded and the gates opened. Mystery gamely lunged out, neck and neck with the pack of horses. Going into the first turn, he was running second, only a nose short of the front-runner.

"What the hell!" Allie screamed. "What the hell are you doing, asshole?" she screamed at Jeffery. "Slow him down or he'll have nothing left at the end."

Christian listened to her and grinned, accustomed to her getting worked up and cursing the jockey who was out of earshot.

"That's it!" she seethed. "That jackass will never ride him again."

At the half-mile pole, Mystery passed the front-runner and kept moving. With every stride he gained ground and increased the distance between him and the field of horses. Allie held her forehead and became quiet. Mystery approached the final turn all alone.

Christian covered his mouth and murmured, "Sweet Jesus." The other horses were so far behind Mystery that he could have trotted to the finish line and still won. Instead of slowing and tiring at the wide turn, he accelerated and appeared like a fiery red blaze. It became a one-horse race, Mystery competing against himself, each stride longer, faster.

The normally steady voice of the race announcer was screaming, "Unbelievable! Unbelievable, Clever Chris! He's all alone and moving at incredible speed."

Allie was hyperventilating. "He's—" She gasped, "he's moving too fast. He's going to break a leg. I've never seen a race like this."

Christian had, only a month earlier on a tape. His eyes watered as Mystery was halfway down the homestretch while the other horses were still rounding the turn.

"Clever Chris has at least a forty-length lead!" said the announcer. Mystery blew past the finish line, going faster in the end than at the start and looking like he could run all day.

"Clever Chris takes it," said the announcer. "Tremendous race. Ladies and gentlemen, Clever Chris's time was one thirty-three and one. That's—my word, that's a new track record. Wait a minute, he's also broken the Calder track record for three-year-olds going a mile. Ladies and gentlemen, you just witnessed greatness. Clever Chris has the makings of a true champion."

Allie slumped over, squatted on her heels, and held a post for balance. Christian's arms rested on the rail, and he buried his face in them and felt the welling up in his eyes, so overwhelmed he had to force himself to breathe. With this race, all his father's aspirations had come true.

After several seconds, Allie stood. "I'm not sure—" she said, also out of breath. "I'm not sure how many one-mile track records he broke today. I think he also broke Gulfstream's." She put her hand on Christian's shoulder, tugging at him to lift his head. "Christian, Christian."

Christian raised his head and tossed his hair back, trying to collect himself. Using his shirtsleeve, he wiped the moisture from his face and eyes. Mystery had followed in Secretariat's footsteps before, but today he had surpassed his famous clone donor, going faster at a younger age. The possibilities ahead were limitless. He turned to Allie. "I'm good. I'm okay. Heck of a race, huh?"

Mystery, with Jeffrey, trotted down the track alongside the pony rider. As they approached the grandstands, the crowd erupted with wild cheers. Christian and Allie walked into the winner's circle, but they weren't alone. Hundreds of spectators rushed to the circle, packing the outside brick wall. They wanted to see Mystery, a colt destined for fame.

Christian held Mystery's bridle and stroked the colt while the photo was taken. He glanced at the spellbound crowd, their eyes starry orbs. The men were clapping, shouting, and some held up their cell phones to take pictures. Many women were so awestruck that they openly wept. Numerous hands reached over the barrier, hoping to touch Mystery, hoping to touch an upcoming legend. Christian hung his head to avoid eye contact. It had started.

Christian led Mystery out onto the track, and Allie sponged the colt down with cool water before taking him back to the barn. She could barely contain herself. "I just can't believe that race. Do you realize you probably own the best two-year-old in the country?" She rattled on. "We're done with Miami. We're heading north and putting him in a grade-one stake race for a couple of hundred thousand. Then it's the Breeders' Cup for two-year-olds in the fall. Your father did register him in the Breeders' Cup, didn't he? I don't remember seeing the card."

"Yeah, he's registered," said Christian. "The card is stapled to his Jockey papers and Florida-Bred certificate."

Christian's cell phone chimed, and he took it from his pocket, but didn't recognize the number. "Hello?"

"Mr. Roberts," said a man's voice. "I would like you to come to the clubhouse so we can celebrate your win and perhaps discuss some business."

Christian noticed the foreign accent. "Who is this?"

"This is Sheik Abdul," he said. "We have never been formally introduced, but we met a few years ago when I claimed the full brother of your colt, Glade Hunter. You were rather unhappy at the time."

"Yeah, I remember you," Christian said, tempted to hang up. A thought then occurred to him.

"Shall you honor me with your presence? I flew in from Kentucky just to see your horse and this race. I must say, I was not disappointed."

"I bet you weren't. Sure, I'll meet with you." He closed the phone.

"Who was it?" Allie asked.

"Someone I need to talk to," he said and handed her Mystery's lead. "You go ahead. I'll see you at the barn in a little while."

She took the lead and gave Christian a what-the-heck's-going-on look. Before she could question him further, Mystery pulled and danced around on the lead, seeing the horses for next race coming down the track.

"Go on," Christian said. "I won't be long." She gave him a frustrated frown and walked off with Mystery, heading for the backside.

Christian, still carrying the bucket of horse supplies, took the elevator in the grandstands up to the clubhouse restaurant. He asked the hostess, a young woman, if he could stash his bucket behind her desk.

"Of course. Mr. Roberts, you have a super colt." She gave him an awkward glance. "Can I please get your autograph?"

Christian scratched his head. The entire restaurant must have seen him holding his colt in the winner's circle. "Sure, why not." He smiled, and she handed him a pen. He scribbled his name on her racing catalogue, realizing that as an owner of an illustrious horse, he also was fast becoming a celebrity.

He scanned the restaurant and saw the sheik, his four-man entourage, along with Price at a window table. Price stood and waved him over. As Christian strolled toward the sheik, he noticed the other diners were gawking, pointing, and nodding to him. A man rose from his seat and asked to shake his hand, congratulating him on the fantastic race. Christian thanked him and finally approached the sheik's table.

"Mr. Roberts, I am pleased you accepted my invitation," the sheik said and nodded to a large Arab man sitting near him. The man rose and yielded his chair to Christian.

Christian recognized the big man from the earlier scuffle with Price when Glade Hunter was claimed. The guy had knocked Allie down and commented that American women did not know their place. Christian felt the muscles in the back of his neck tense up with aversion, but he faked an easygoing grin.

The sheik motioned to the vacant seat. "Please, Mr. Roberts, sit. Would you like some tea?" he asked.

Christian eased into the chair and noticed the teacups in front of each man. Even Price had a glass of ice tea, obviously respecting the Arab custom forbidding alcohol. "No thanks, tea is for little old ladies." His eyes sparkled with insolence, and he turned to the waitress and ordered a cocktail.

The sheik's nostrils on his large hook nose flared with the affront, but he apparently choose to ignore Christian's rudeness and little-old-lady comment. "Your colt ran quite an impressive race."

"Yeah, I'm well aware," Christian said. "So, what do you want?" he asked, although he had a good idea.

"I am interested in purchasing him."

"How much?"

"One million," said the sheik. Christian stood and turned to leave. "Mr. Roberts, where are you going?"

"Sheik, there's a saying," said Christian. "Cheat me once, shame on you, but cheat me twice, shame on me. That's no offer."

"It's more money than you'll ever see," Price sneered.

"Is that right?" said Christian, leaning over and resting his crossed arms on the back of the chair. "I imagine that once the press hears about this race, I'll be flooded with offers, and they'll be for a hell of lot more than a million." He straightened.

"Wait, Mr. Roberts," said the sheik. "Please sit down. I was told you were a young man with no head for business." He glanced at Price. "But I obviously was misinformed. How much do you want for your colt?"

Christian returned to his seat, and the waitress placed his rum and Coke on the table. He took a long slow sip, set the glass down, and leaned back. "Sheik, every year you drop a small fortune at the horse sales, paying more than a million for some of those yearlings, not knowing if they can even run. I've been told my colt is probably the fastest two-year-old in the country. That's worth at least ten."

"So you want ten million dollars?" the sheik asked.

"No." Christian took another swallow of his cocktail. "I was lied to about Hunter's times and then cheated out of him in the claimer. Afterward, I was arrested and thrown in jail for shoving Price against a tree. I can deal with all that irritation, but what I can't forget or forgive—" His eyes narrowed, focusing on Price. "Going to my dying father and having to say I was sorry for losing his horse. That's gonna cost you extra."

"How much extra?" asked the sheik.

"Another ten million," said Christian.

"Twenty million!" said Price. "That's outrageous. The colt's run only one allowance race. He's not even a stake winner. The sheik won't pay it."

"I think he will," said Christian. "The sheik knows a great horse surfaces only once in a lifetime. Man o' War in the first part of the century, and Secretariat in the second half. I've heard Derby winners can go for fifty million. Twenty million is cheap."

"You are correct," said the sheik.

"I'll have a contract drawn up," said Christian, "that I'm selling you a two-year-old horse, and I'll guarantee he's sound and healthy, but that's all. Also in the contract, I want the chance to buy him back if you decide to sell."

"I will not be selling him," said the sheik. "My lawyers shall look over the contract before we exchange the money and horse."

Christian glared at Price. "Is this son of a bitch gonna be my colt's trainer? He's known for maiming and killing horses so he can collect on their insurance."

Price abruptly rose. "That's bullshit!"

The sheik raised his hand, motioning for Price to sit down. "I have never heard such things about Mr. Price, but I assure you that no harm shall come to your colt. He will have a round-the-clock security guard posted at his stall. As for Mr. Price, I have agreed to let him handle your colt, since he found the horse and kept me abreast of his workouts and races."

Price's mouth bent into a settling-the-score grin.

"All right," Christian said. "As long as there's a guard, I'll do the deal. I don't want anything bad happening to my colt."

"And neither do I," said the sheik. "My veterinarians shall be at your colt's barn first thing in the morning and perform the health examination."

Christian nodded. "My stepfather is a lawyer. He'll draw up the contract and fax it to me. If the deal goes through, I'll stop by the racing office and list Price as my new trainer. He can pick up the Jockey papers and give them to you. After the vet exam, your lawyers can look over the contract. We sign it. You give me a certified check, and I'll hand over the colt." He stood up from his seat.

The sheik also rose. "It has been a pleasure, Mr. Roberts. For one so young, you certainly are a shrewd businessman."

"I'm a fast learner," Christian said, and they shook hands.

Christian picked up the bucket and left the restaurant. On the long walk back to the barns, he pulled out his cell phone and called Frank at his law office.

He and his stepfather reviewed the details in the contract. The purchase agreement would state that for twenty million, Sheik Abdul was buying a two-year-old horse and nothing else—no mention that it was a registered Thoroughbred and could be raced or bred. Christian would warranty that the colt was free of liens and encumbrances and, on the date of exchange, the horse was sound and healthy. The sheik would give Christian first right of refusal if the horse was put up for sale.

"Twenty million," said Frank. "You actually have a horse worth that amount and a buyer for it?"

"Oh, yeah," Christian said. He had walked past the guard station and stood on the side of the road across from the first barn. "Frank, I need to ask you something, as my lawyer and not as a stepfather. If it's discovered that this horse has different DNA than from the horse listed on the registration papers, will this contract protect me from a lawsuit or from being charged with fraud?"

"Does this horse have the wrong DNA?"

"Yes."

Frank was quiet for a moment. "If the sheik signs this contract, it'd be hard for him to win a lawsuit, and a prosecutor would have an even tougher time proving fraud. First of all, you have only guaranteed a two-year-old horse. The horse's name and registration numbers are not on the contract, no mention that the horse is even a purebred. Did you make any oral promises to the sheik, like this horse will win races?"

"No, I was careful. I implied a little, said a Derby winner was worth fifty million, but I only stated that the colt was probably the fastest two-year-old in the country. And that's true. I even made sure that I didn't give the registration papers to the sheik. I said I'd list Price, the sheik's trainer, as my new trainer. That way, he goes to the racing office and gives the horse's papers to the sheik."

"It sounds like you've covered all the bases," said Frank. "I suppose you don't want to tell me the whole story about this colt?"

"I'd rather not, at least not yet."

"Well, this sheik is not going to be happy when he finds out you switched horses."

"Switched horses? I didn't—" A grin slowly emerged on Christian's lips as he thought about it. "Ya know, Frank that's an interesting concept. This sheik and trainer screwed me and Dad out of a horse. It's now payback time."

"Okay, I'll fax the contract to your hotel. Call if you need me."

Christian walked down the road and passed more barns. When he initially got Mystery, he had every intention of keeping his promise to his father and fulfilling his dream; race the colt, win the Triple Crown and Breeders' Cup, make a ton of money, and then retire Mystery and geld him. All the secrecy and lying would be over.

After learning how Secretariat had affected nearly every soul in the country, he knew it would never be over, though. The horse's fame would last a lifetime, a lifetime of deceit and guilt, the dream becoming an endless nightmare. The fame and money wasn't worth it, at least not to Christian. He had earlier decided that Mystery had run his last race, and he'd tell Allie everything, but then the sheik called, and he saw another way out, a way to get even.

He reached the small barn where the day's winning horses were kept until their blood and urine were checked for drugs. If a horse didn't pee, he could be there for some time. In the shade of a large oak, he leaned against the trunk and waved to Allie ten yards away where she walked Mystery around the small shed row.

She smiled at him, her eyes bright with elation. Like his father, she was a horse trainer with the same hopes and prayers—that some day a magical horse would come along and take her over the rainbow. That day and the big red horse had come.

"Shit," he said. He was about to shatter her dreams. How and when should he tell her that he had sold her magical horse out from under her? No doubt she would be extremely upset, probably furious.

All this time he had followed his father's advice and sworn to secrecy, not disclosing to Allie that Mystery was a clone, keeping her clear of the scandal. How could he explain the colt's sale without telling all? He wondered how she would handle it, being hot tempered when it came to her horses. Could she keep her cool when they signed the contract and the sheik and Price walked away with her baby?

"We're celebrating tonight," she cheerfully called to him.

He produced a phony grin and nodded.

To not tell her prior to the sale—my God, it would blow her mind. He pictured her bewildered face when they led Mystery away, followed by her questions, then the rage. Their relationship might not survive the betrayal.

At the end of the hotel corridor, Christian stood in front of the ice machine and filled a small plastic bucket. He slipped a few dollars in the nearby soda machine. With ice and a few Cokes, he trudged back to his room like a man walking to the gallows. Entering the room, he heard the shower water stop.

"Allie, you want a cocktail?" he called into the bathroom.

She stuck her wet head out the door. "I sure do," she said with a smile.

Her smile—so beautiful and sincere, never faked—it could light up the darkest room and ease his miseries. It told him how good things were. He wondered now if he would ever see that smile again. He picked up the rum bottle and fixed two cocktails. Holding a drink, he collapsed in a chair by the sliding glass doors.

Allie came out of the bathroom wrapped only in a white towel, the tresses of her blonde hair still dripping. "Where should we go for dinner?" she asked and picked up other drink.

"Allie, sit down. We need to talk," he said, his expression deadpan serious.

Her smile vanished, and she slowly sat down on the bed, facing him. "Christian, you're rid of Vince. You own a spectacular colt, and our life together, I thought, was pretty good, but you've been brooding for weeks. I hope you're finally ready to tell me what's eating you."

"I sold Mystery."

"What!" She leaped to her feet, spilling her drink.

"Sheik Abdul is paying me twenty million. They're picking him up tomorrow."

"No, no, no, Christian. Mystery's time was better than the best three-year-olds. He's got a great shot at winning the Triple Crown, Breeders' Cup, and even the Dubai Cup. The purses alone would be about twenty million. And after racing, his stud fee would be like Storm Cat's, five hundred thousand a pop, a minimum of fifty mares a year, that's twenty-five million the first year in your pocket. Even if you did sell him, a syndicate would probably give you half a billion for him. You're crazy to go through with this deal and, of all people, with that fucking sheik and Price."

Christian stood and stared out the glass doors at the empty racetrack below. "Mystery is not worth anything. And if I kept him, I decided today would have been his last race."

"What the hell, Christian?"

"Allie, he's a clone."

The vets and their assistants had come early in the morning. They took X-rays of Mystery, scoped his lungs, and performed blood work. In the end, the colt received a clean bill of health. Allie had held the lead and stroked him during the procedures, speaking softly to the majestic colt, her eyes slightly puffy and bloodshot from the previous night's tears. Mystery kept nudging her, waiting for his saddle, so he could go to the track for their daily exercise.

Christian had stood in the stall doorway and watched in silence. Since rising that morning, dressing, and driving to the barn, he and Allie barely spoke. After the night before, there was nothing more to say. He had utterly killed the fantasy.

She had learned everything about Mystery and the cloning. To his surprise, she never became angry once he told her, but was more in a state of shock. She tried to put on a strong front, saying horses, unlike cats and dogs, rarely had lifetime owners. She was used to losing horses. Mystery was just another horse passing through her life. That front didn't last long. She broke down and cried, her tears evolving to a numbing grief, as if a loved one had died. She was now going through the motions, like picking out the casket and burial plot, trying to get through the day and sale.

Christian was also despondent. He loved the horse, but he had found it was the best way to pull the plug and get resolution. He would get the money, and in doing so, take his revenge against the sheik and Price for cheating him and his father. When the sheik learned that Mystery could not be raced or bred, Christian figured he would easily buy back the colt.

A large limo pulled up to the barn. Price and the sheik and several of his men dressed in their Arab garb got out, along with two white men in dark suits, probably the lawyers.

"Mr. Roberts," said the sheik, strolling, along with his group, toward him and Allie, who stood by Mystery's stall. "You haven't changed your mind?"

"No." Christian shook his head. He handed the sheik an envelope containing the contract and health certificate. The sheik passed them to one of the suits.

Allie shuddered. "I can't do this. I'll be in your SUV." She hugged Mystery's neck and kissed his nose, and then walked off, wiping more tears away with her sleeve.

A lawyer read the short contract and looked at Christian with a baffled expression. He turned to the sheik. "Sheik Abdul, I urge you not to sign this contract. It does not have the horse's birth date, sire, or dam, or even the horse's name. The Jockey registration number is missing that would confirm you're buying a purebred Thoroughbred. Delay the sale for one hour, and we'll draw up a new and complete contract."

"Nope," said Christian. "We sign this one or nothing at all. I said I'd only guarantee a sound two-year-old, and that's all." He chuckled a little. "If you think I'm trying to pull a switch, you can check the colt's lip tattoo."

"Sheik Abdul," said Price, "this is the colt that broke a track record yesterday. I guarantee it. We'll have the horse and his papers. That's all we need. This contract is meaningless." The trainer was so eager to get his hands on Mystery that he was helping Christian make the deal.

The lawyer whispered into the sheik's ear. "My lawyer still suggests a stronger contract," said the sheik. "Surely, Mr. Roberts, you can wait another hour."

"Look, sheik," said Christian, "I was up all night with an upset girlfriend who's also the horse's trainer. She doesn't want me to sell and definitely thinks the colt is worth more. Maybe she's right. Maybe I need to hold off and consider other offers." He turned and took a few steps toward his SUV.

"Wait, Christian," Price called and turned to the sheik. "Sheik Abdul, you'll never find another colt like this."

The sheik ran his fingers through his beard. "You win, Mr. Roberts. Against my lawyer's advice, I will sign your contract."

Christian glanced back at them, crossed his arms, and hesitated long enough to make them sweat. He took a deep breath and exhaled. "Let's do it then."

After he and the sheik signed the contract, Christian was given the check. Price placed a lead on Mystery and brought the big, handsome colt out of the stall. With a toothy grin, Price displayed the colt before the sheik.

Mystery, unfamiliar with the strange handler, swiftly lifted a back leg and cow-kicked Price, hurting the trainer's leg and confidence.

Christian enjoyed watching a red-faced Price hobble from the minor injury. But when his colt was led away, Christian bit his lip and became solemn. Halfway down the courtyard, Mystery stopped and looked back at Christian. His large intelligent eyes seemed to question, "Why are you not leading me? Where is Allie?" Price tugged on his lead and got him moving again.

Christian felt sentimental moisture growing in his eyes. *Don't worry, boy. We'll be together again, I promise.*

Christian and Allie drove to the track office where he listed Price as his new trainer, giving him access to Mystery's Jockey Club papers. Price could then hand them over to the sheik.

Christian dropped Allie off at the hotel so she could pack and check out, and he headed to the closest bank and deposited the certified check for twenty million. Back at the hotel lobby, he picked up Allie. They stopped by the track and hitched up the empty horse trailer, exchanging only a few words.

During the first half hour of the trip to Myakka, the agonizing quiet continued with Christian looking straight ahead and driving while Allie stared out the passenger window.

She finally spoke up. "Now that you're rich, I guess you'll be moving out and taking off on that sailboat you've always wanted."

He puckered his brows in surprise. "I hadn't planned on moving out."

"Well, people and situations change with money. Your dream or scheme is over. You don't have Mystery anymore, so you certainly don't need me or my little farm. I just want to know where we stand."

Christian shook his locks and chuckled. "You sure don't beat around the bush. That's why I love you. If it's okay, I'd like to stick around."

"Really?"

"Yeah," he said with a smile. "I know the money might be a problem, but I was thinking we could spend some, fix up your place, and maybe build a small house on the back of the property for Juan and his mother. That way we'll have someone to take care of the horses when we sail the Caribbean in that new boat."

"Really?" she said.

"Yeah, really."

A few weeks passed after the colt's sale, and Christian sat in the kitchen drinking coffee before going to work. Despite his millions, he liked his work and never considered retiring. He figured that he would also grow antsy, sitting around the farm, and get on Allie's nerves.

He had called Juan and offered him a permanent job, helping Allie with the horses. Christian explained about a small house he would build for Juan and Rosa. Juan happily accepted.

Christian sat down with Frank and mapped out wise investments for his money after he finished fixing up the farm and buying the boat of his dreams.

There had been no word from the sheik, and Christian relied on the old saying, "No news was good news." The man was apparently pleased with Mystery. Christian just waited, waited for Price and the sheik to commit the crime and race the illegally registered horse.

Allie walked into the kitchen and slid a computer printout under his nose. "They've entered Mystery in a big stake race at Churchill."

Christian looked at the paper. "It's in two days. Guess it's getting close to pulling the rug out."

"You know this might come back and bite you."

"No way. I'm covered. The Jockey Club will be pointing the finger at Price, the sheik, or the breeder, my father, who's dead. I'm an innocent middleman who received a horse from his dying father. I had nothing to do with falsifying the breeding of the stallion and mare, sending in the wrong DNA, or registering the colt with illegal Jockey papers. And there's no proof whether or when Clever Chris was switched with the horse that the sheik now owns."

"What about the cloning trail?"

"I told you. All those contracts are in Hank Jones's name, even the pickup order. The scientists and vets were in the dark and had no idea that they had cloned Secretariat. They assured my father that they would destroy all DNA once the cloning was completed and paid for. They believed they cloned a good barrel horse. Even if everything came out, it's the same deal. With the DNA gone, there's no proof that the foal I picked up in Texas and the colt we raced are the same horse."

She sat down at the table. "So, you've got this all planned out."

"I do." He shook his head. "I'm sorry, Allie. I just couldn't keep racing Mystery. For the rest of my life, I'd have to lie to everyone I met. The guilt would eat me alive. I've learned that what a person needs and what one wants are two different things. I have everything

I need right here with you. I didn't want a famous horse bad enough."

He shrugged. "Maybe my father did. Maybe if he had lived, he would have taken Mystery all the way and been content to live the lie. That's not me. I took Hunter and Mystery and went down a crazy path, hoping to prove to a dead man—prove to myself—that I wasn't a lousy son. Turns out I'm okay. If you can't face yourself in the mirror, nothing else matters. God, nature, and luck created Secretariat. There should be only one. Cloning and racing Mystery was cheating."

She rose, slipped behind Christian's chair, and hugged his neck. "I think you're more than okay," she said and softly kissed his cheek. "You're just a little guilty of doing foolish things."

He breathed deeply and nodded. "I agree. Damn list of boners is endless."

"Nobody's perfect, except for me, of course." She giggled and stepped to the kitchen counter. Leaning against it, she faced him. "While on the computer, I pulled up some horse cloning articles. The dilemma you faced has become quite a controversy. The purebred horse registries are against cloning, saying man shouldn't be allowed to create a champion, whereas some breeders and owners want to register and compete with their clones. I can see both sides. Cigar won the Breeders' Cup but turned out to be sterile. Funny Side took the Derby, but was a gelding, and Barbaro won the Derby but had to be destroyed. Unless cloned, their bloodlines are lost."

She lifted an eyebrow and smiled. "And then there's the thrill factor, cloning dead champions so they can compete again. You have to admit watching Mystery, seeing Secretariat run again, was astounding. I'm glad I didn't have to make the decision, whether to race the fastest horse on the planet or pull him. I'd probably be like your father, deal with the lies, and let the world have another Secretariat, another Triple Crown winner. If nothing else, it'll be sweet when Price and the sheik take the heat."

• • •

A few days later, Allie and Christian drove to the Sarasota dog track, sat at the bar, and watched the TV screen. Mystery walked down the Churchill Downs track with other horses as they prepared to run a hundred-thousand-dollar grade-one stake race on turf. The catalogue listed Mystery as the favorite in the mile-long race, going off with two-to-one odds.

"I know it wouldn't be smart," said Allie, "but I still wish we had flown up for this race."

"Wish we had gone or wished we still had him?" Christian asked.

"Both," she said, pursing her lips.

The horses entered the gate and a few minutes later, the doors opened. Like in the allowance race, Mystery gamely leaped out with the other horses and quickly took the lead. His jockey never looked back.

Halfway through the race, Mystery pounded across the turf grass, continuing to widen the distance between him and the other horses. "Secretariat usually stalked the field and came up from behind," said Christian.

"Mystery might be the spitting image of Secretariat, but he's developed his own style of running. Come on, boy." She yelled out at the TV.

Again, Mystery cruised across the finish line all alone, the field of horses dozens of lengths behind. The TV announcers went crazy. "Clever Chris is the real deal. He has just broken Churchill's track record, going 1.34.63 for a mile on the turf. What a horse! What a horse!"

Christian said, "He is as good as Secretariat."

Allie sighed. "Christian, I think he's better."

Before going home, they stopped at a store. With cash, Christian purchased a disposable cell phone so his name would not show up on caller ID.

A few days later, he sat on the couch at home and picked up the throwaway, untraceable phone, knowing the sheik had received the purse money from the stake race. He hit the keys and made his anonymous call to The Jockey Club.

"Hi, I'm a groom for Ed Price who represents Sheik Abdul," he said to the woman. "Their horse, Clever Chris, just won a stake race at Churchill a few days ago. I don't want to get involved, but I think you should know that the real Clever Chris died, and Mr. Price and Sheik Abdul switched horses."

"How do you know?" she asked.

"I saw them cart off Clever Chris's body, plus that colt had a scar under his jaw. The horse they raced doesn't have a scar and scars don't just vanish. If you don't believe me, take another DNA test," he said and hung up.

Mystery never had a scar. He didn't even have a cowlick, a group of raised hairs commonly used to identify a Thoroughbred for registration.

The next day a man called Christian, saying he was from The Jockey Club. "Mr. Roberts, the Churchill Downs officials and I are investigating an inquiry made against Ed Price and Sheik Abdul concerning your formerly owned colt, Clever Chris. Did your colt have any scars?"

"Sure," Christian lied. "He got cut under his jaw as a yearling in a barn fire, although the scar is hardly noticeable unless you're brushing him. What this all about?"

"We were tipped off that Ed Price and Sheik Abdul might have switched horses and raced an illegal horse."

"That doesn't surprise me," said Christian. "A few years back I had a horse named Glade Hunter that had good times on the farm. Price got him and suddenly the colt's morning workouts were slow, and Price talked me into a cheap claiming race. The colt was fast again, wins the race, but he was claimed by Sheik Abdul. I know Price switched my horse's workout times with a slower horse and lied to the clockers so I'd lose my colt. Unfortunately, I can't prove it. I've also heard rumors that Price injures horses so he can collect on their insurance. Might want to question some of his grooms, especially the ones he's fired."

"That's terrible. I'll contact those grooms," said the man. "This inquiry on Clever Chris might come down to a question of DNA. I would also like to speak to Hank Roberts, the colt's breeder. Are you related to him?"

"He's my father, and I'd also love to talk to him, but he's dead. My parents were divorced, so I'm kinda ignorant about this horse business, but before Dad died he gave me Glade Hunter and Clever Chris. Since then, I've been learning."

"I believe I have enough information to start an investigation. Churchill's officials have already checked the colt claimed to be Clever Chris and found no jaw scar. We'll next pull the colt's DNA. Since you're not the breeder of Clever Chris, I doubt we'll need further information from you, but you might have to sign a statement confirming your colt had a scar."

"No problem. Happy to help," Christian said. He hung up and took a deep breath, glancing up at Allie. "I believe the shit is about to hit the fan."

The following week, Christian got the first call.

"Mr. Roberts, what horse did you sell me?" asked an exasperated Sheik Abdul. "This colt's DNA does not match his sire and dam. Where are his correct Jockey papers?"

"I don't know what you're talking about," said Christian. "You got the right horse from me. Ask Price. As you well know, he's notorious for switching horses. Regardless, I owe you no explanations or additional papers. If you reread our contract I only agreed to sell you a healthy two-year-old horse."

"Yes, yes, the bloody contract," the sheik grumbled. "Without the correct papers, I cannot race this colt. Not only that, The Jockey Club is accusing me of falsifying the papers and tattoos and racing an illegal horse. Churchill Downs has taken my racing license. I cannot race any horse in my stable until this matter is resolved. If it is not, I shall be forced to sell my horses or move them to Arabia so they can race."

"Gee, that's too bad. Well, good luck, sheik."

The next day a second call came from Price. "What the devil did you do, Christian," he raged. "You sold the sheik a colt with the wrong DNA. Since I'm its trainer, my license has been suspended while The Jockey Club investigates. It might become permanent. Plus, the cops have been called in. I could face criminal charges. The sheik is blaming me for this mess. All my clients have pulled their horses, since I can't race them. Your damn colt is putting me out of business."

"Some people shouldn't be in the horse business."

"Look, you son of a bitch, you better come up with the right horse papers and straighten this mess out or—"

"Or what?" Christian said. "Maybe finish that little business when I shoved you against a tree?"

Price was quiet for several moments. "You threatened me, said you'd get even. Goddamn it, you planned this, planned to ruin me! You fucker, you—"

"I am a fucker, Price, the kind you shouldn't have screwed." He closed the phone.

CHAPTER TWENTY

The still bay mirrored the rising sun, taking on a golden hue as Christian's Boston Whaler glided past the mangroves on Longboat Key. Only the boat's wake and an occasional splash from a jumping mullet disrupted the glassy surface. Christian maneuvered the boat up the small channel, and a great white heron squawked in protest at the intruder before taking flight. Up ahead, Vince stood on the empty dock with his fishing pole in hand.

Christian cut the engine, and the Whaler coasted up alongside the dock. "Hey, Vince."

Vince stepped aboard. "It's good to see you again, Christian."

"You too," Christian said, "although, I'm catching flak from my girlfriend. She's not happy we're still friends, but what the heck." He pulled a check out of his pants pocket. "Here's the money I owe you."

Vince looked at the check. "With interest too, but I said you didn't owe me."

"I know, but a deal's a deal. Are you ready to go?"

Vince grinned and stuffed the check in his shirt pocket. "Hey, I never argue when someone hands me money." He shoved the boat away from the dock as Christian restarted the engine.

Vince got comfortable in the passenger seat. "So your horse must've finally come in?"

"Yeah, he sure did. Made enough that I can retire. Let me tell you about this horse."

Besides Allie, Christian felt he could trust Vince with the whole truth about Mystery. Lord knows, the man had plenty of his own skeletons and would never rat out Christian. And who better to discuss and understand a scam than a gangster?

They had shared their life-and-death experience on the water, and their relationship had changed to one of mutual respect, but even prior to the boat crash, Vince, for some reason, liked Christian. Oddly, Christian also enjoyed Vince's company. Although crude and a little sinister, Vince was smart and full of useful advice, probably why he'd never seen a jail cell.

They motored to a grass flat, climbed out of the boat, and waded through the clear, knee-deep water. Casting out their lines, Christian told Vince the story, starting with Glade Hunter, his sick father, and how the crooked trainer switched the horses' workout times, causing Christian to place Hunter in a claiming race where the colt was lost to the sheik. He also mentioned Price's cruelty, numbing the gray filly's injured leg so she'd break down and Price could collect on the insurance.

"That bastard," Vince commented. "Ya know, I care more about my horses than people."

Christian continued and told Vince about Mystery, the cloning, the races, and then defrauding the sheik and Price.

Vince knew about track rules, Jockey Club registration, and DNA tests. When Christian finished, Vince turned to him. "That's brilliant, Christian, just brilliant. I've always said you have brains, but never realized you were so devious. That's the perfect sting."

"Not quite perfect." Christian raised an eyebrow and reeled in his cast line. "After the DNA test that proved Mystery was worthless, I thought there'd be no problem buying the colt back. With the sales contract, the sheik has to give me first right of refusal. I called the sheik, offered him millions for the colt, but the guy is really pissed off, said he'd never sell Mystery back to me."

"That's a damn shame. I hate those Arab pricks," Vince grumbled.

Christian saw a swirl of water and a three-inch fin gliding across the surface near Vince's cork and pinfish bait. "Vince, get ready."

Vince's reel clicked a few times and then the bobber vanished from the surface with the fish taking the bait. Vince gripped his bent pole as his reel zinged with more line going out. The large silver fish leaped several feet above the surface, exposing the black line running along its side near the back. "Holy shit," Vince yelled. "It's huge. Looks like a tarpon."

"Nope, it's a snook," said Christian. "Now, don't force her, let her run, and tire. She's got sharp gills that can slice your finger open and break line, so keep her on a straight run."

"It's a girl?" Vince muttered, struggling with his pole.

"Boys don't grow that big."

All talk of horses, Arabs, and scams had ended.

At Allie's farm, several white pickups that belonged to the bricklayers and building contractor were parked along the back fence. Nearby, a large semiflatbed holding concrete blocks sat near the house pad, and a Bobcat unloaded the cargo. Christian watched for several minutes and nodded to the contractor in charge of building Juan and Rosa's new, two-bedroom house. He turned and walked up the drive to the barn.

Juan was in a stall, brushing Glade Hunter. "Good morning, Mr. Christian," he called.

"How's my boy today?"

"Happy, very happy," said Juan. "I am so glad you found him and bought him from the polo people. Do you wish me to saddle him so you can ride?"

Now a confident rider, Christian had retired old Chris as his pleasure horse and replaced him with the spirited younger gelding. He walked into the stall and scratched Hunter's forehead. "Can't today. I promised Jake the day off, so I have to work the marina." He glanced out of the barn. "The contractor is moving right along on your house."

Juan ran a rubber currycomb over Hunter's back. "My mother and I cannot say enough to thank you."

"Hey, thanks for accepting my offer. It frees up Allie so we can go away without worrying about the horses." He left Hunter and Juan. Standing in the aisle, he glanced at an empty stall, two doors down, Mystery's old stall. His shoulders drooped, and he took a sad, deep breath.

Every time he reflected on Mystery, he felt the chest ache from his heart sinking, the sickening remorse that he had betrayed the horse, a horse that had given his all and made Christian wealthy.

He walked up to the house and his vehicle and drove to the marina.

Because it was a fall weekday, the place was quiet. Several young guys rented out his WaveRunners and a newly married couple took out a Hobie Cat. Other than that, business was slow, allowing Christian to kick back in a chair and thumb through a boat magazine, circling ads, looking for his dream boat. Although he had the money to buy whatever he wanted, old habits die hard, and he was searching for a steal.

The sun began to set, and Christian called it quits. He wrapped up the sails and locked up the loose gear. In the parking lot, he noticed his SUV was the only vehicle. Everyone else had gone home. He started to climb in when he saw the flat front tire.

"Shit." He flipped out his cell phone and called Allie. "Hey, I'm going to be a little late. I got a flat. Must've picked up a nail."

"That's a bummer," she said. "Are you going to call road service to fix it?"

"I could change ten flats by the time they got here. I should be home in an hour or so."

He closed the phone and got out the jack, tire iron, and spare. Squatting in front of the flat tire, he loosened the lugs before jacking the SUV up. He heard another vehicle pull in and park on the other side of his but ignored it, figuring it was another boater, going out for an evening cruise. He perceived the sound of footsteps behind him, but stayed focused on the last lug that would not yield.

"Trouble?" asked a man's voice.

"Yeah, flat tire, and this sucker won't budge," said Christian, putting all his strength into turning the iron. Suddenly, he was jerked up from the squatting position, and a sting hit the side of his neck. He caught a glimpse of three men before his body went limp and he collapsed into unconsciousness.

Christian woke in darkness and felt lightheaded and nauseated. As his mind cleared, he realized he was lying on his side with his wrists bound together behind his back. The vibrating floor told him he was in the back of a moving van. Since it was night, several hours had passed since he had been taken from the marina.

"Mr. Price, he wakes," said a man's voice with a Middle Eastern accent.

Christian looked up. Sitting nearby was a large, dark complexioned man, perhaps an Arab. Price sat in the front passenger seat, and a third person drove the van.

Price turned around in his seat and stared down at Christian. "Hello, Christian." He snickered. "I see the horse tranquilizer is finally wearing off."

Christian's head swayed with dizziness, and he tried to sit up, but couldn't. His ankles were also bound. "Price, what the fuck is going on?"

Price chortled. "Did you really think you could rip off the sheik, and there'd be no consequences?"

"Where are you taking me?"

"On a long, one-way trip," Price said.

Christian struggled against the tight, painful ropes while his mind raced, wondering how he could escape.

"You be still or I kill you now," said the man, nearby. He lifted his hand. The dim dash lights revealed a revolver pointed at Christian.

"Try to avoid that, Abbas," Price said to the big guy. "I don't want blood left in this van."

The van that had been traveling at top speed began to slow and then made a left turn. It bumped and rocked. They were obviously on an unpaved road.

"Almost there, Christian," said Price. "Time to say your final good-byes."

"Price, you and the sheik won't get away with this. Everyone knows you're pissed over our horse deal."

"Generally, a murder investigation requires a corpse. That's why we didn't knock you off at the marina. Where you're going, no one will find your body, so it's feasible you just skipped town with those millions. Secondly, a certain pin hooker named Sam mentioned you'd borrowed a sizable amount of money from loan sharks to get a horse. If you disappear, the authorities will be questioning your gangster friends."

"I paid off the loan. The cops won't be looking at them."

"Well, even if the cops suspected the sheik," said Price, "they can't even give him a parking ticket. He's an ambassador in this country and has diplomatic immunity. And the sheik is giving me an alibi for doing you in."

The van rolled to a stop, and Christian swallowed hard, forcing down the growing lump in his throat. Not only would he die, but his killers also might get away with the crime. Price and the driver opened their vehicle doors, and the inside cab lights came on. Christian saw two shovels and a flashlight resting nearby.

The back van doors opened, and Price and the driver stared in. Christian got a good look at all three of his captors and recognized Abbas, the large man beside him. Although he now wore pants and a shirt, he was the Arab who shoved Allie at the riders-up area and had later yielded his chair to Christian when he had a sit-down with the sheik in the clubhouse restaurant. The driver looked Arab as well.

"You two grab him," Price said to the men. "I'll get the shovels and light."

The men took hold of Christian's arms and pulled him out of

the van. He heard a deafening sound, the boisterous chorus of croaking and chirping created by millions of frogs and insects. He looked around, and the sky was a pitch-black of nothingness. Except for the countless stars overhead, the sky lacked the distant glow of a city. He was deep in the country and a long way from help. Following Price and his flashlight, the men held and dragged Christian through heavily wooded pines, cabbage palms, and scrub oaks.

"Where are we?" Christian asked with a low voice, trying to act calm, although terrified. His heart raced, his breathing was heavy, and a nervous sweat dampened his shirt.

"The Everglades," Price answered and trudged ahead. "The best spot to dump a body and it's on our way back to Miami."

Ironic, Christian thought, a place he had cherished was to be his gravesite. His mind drifted to Allie and the life they might have had. He breathed deeply through his nose to stop the moisture from forming in his eyes. Among his enemies, he was determined to go out strong rather than a crying, pathetic slob.

The men had walked nearly fifty yards from the van when Price stopped. "This is far enough. No one will find him here." The men released Christian, and he fell on his side into the dirt and leaves.

"We untie him," said Abbas. "He digs."

Christian looked up, praying Price would go along. Untied and holding a shovel, he might get the chance to bash in their skulls and get away.

Price looked down, shining the light on Christian's face. "No, you two will dig the hole," he said to the men. "This slinky bastard is a fighter. Turned loose, we're asking for trouble."

Christian closed his eyes, his glimmer of hope gone. He relayed silently, *Dad, if you're up there, if you're watching over me, please help. My promise to you has brought me to this.*

The two Arabs picked up the shovels and began digging a three-by-six foot pit while Price stood over Christian with a handgun aimed at his head.

"Got nothing to say?" Price asked.

"No." Christian lifted his head as high as he could and glared at Price. "Just go ahead and shoot. Let's get it over with."

"I don't plan to shoot you." Price smirked. "Makes too much noise, even out here, and leaves a bullet as evidence. These Arabs love their jambiyas. Abbas brought along a special one so he could gut you like a fish."

Christian laid his head back on the ground. "Price, I figured you didn't have the balls to kill me yourself."

The two men returned to digging, and the smaller man mumbled something in Arabic to Abbas.

"What'd he say?" Price asked.

Abbas leaned on the shovel handle. "My friend says this one is no dog. He does not cower and whine when facing his death."

"He will when you stick him," said Price.

After a half hour, the two men had excavated a pit several feet deep. "That's good enough," said Price, and the men climbed out of the hole. Abbas pulled out his Arab jambiya from a sheath that hung from his belt. Under Price's flashlight, he displayed the curved dagger with a jewel-crested handle. He grabbed Christian's hair and yanked his head back to expose his throat.

"Not here," said Price. "His blood will attract scavengers that might dig him up. Kill him in the hole."

Abbas, using his foot, shoved Christian into the pit. His body hit the moist ground with a thud and dirt fell on him. He managed to look up. "Fuck you, Price. I hope you burn in hell."

Abbas stepped down behind Christian and bent over. He clutched Christian's hair again and pulled his neck back. Christian breathed hard, closed his moist eyes, and waited for the blade to slash his jugular.

Gunshots rang out. Abbas collapsed like a rhino on top of Christian.

"Let's get out of here!" Price screamed and returned fire.

More gunfire echoed through the trees, along with the excited yells from several male voices. Christian detected the thumping of running feet and the crash of saw palmettos as people raced through the underbrush. Abbas did not budge or breathe, confirming he had been shot to death.

Unsure of what had happened, Christian frantically wiggled, trying to worm his way out from beneath the heavy corpse. If he could get out of the hole, he might be able to slither across the ground and hide in the brushes before Price returned.

The woods were suddenly silent. Except for the sound of the nocturnal swamp creatures, the running feet, gunshots, and yells had stopped. Christian lay still and listened for several long, agonizing minutes, his sweat dripping and stinging his eyes. He then heard the low drone of approaching voices.

"Get that prick off him," said a man, "and get him out."

Abbas's body was pushed off Christian who squinted with the glare of bright flashlights on his face. Two men lifted him out of the hole and laid him on the ground.

"Untie him," the man said. "Kid, are you okay, kid?"

Christian knew the voice. "Sal, is that you?"

Sal chuckled. "Yeah, bet this is the first time you're happy to see me."

Freed of his bonds, Christian sat up. "Shit, man, I've never been happier to see anyone."

Sal laughed again. He reached down and grabbed Christian's chin, turning and examining his face. "Did they hurt ya?"

"I'm good." Christian attempted to stand, but his legs were like rubber, and he crumbled to the dirt. His body trembled.

"Sit a while. You've had a pretty good scare," said Sal. "Your adrenaline is screwin' with ya. You're probably also sufferin' from a little shock." Sal turned to another man. "Go to my car and get a blanket out of the trunk."

Christian stayed on the ground and held his crossed arms. He stared down at the lifeless man in the hole and reflected on his own mortality. "I thought I was dead," he murmured.

"It was close," said Sal. "We were afraid to shoot while that fucker pointed a gun at your head." He took out his cell phone and placed a call. "We got him. Caught up with them on US 41 in the Glades. Yeah, he's a little shook up, but all right. Okay, we'll see ya in a few hours." He closed the phone.

Christian looked up at Sal. "That was Vince?"

Sal raised an eyebrow. "Ever since you told the boss about your scam with these assholes, he's been worried."

"I never dreamed they'd come after me."

"That's cause you're wet behind the ears. If you're gonna mess with bad guys, ya'd better learn to think like 'em. Vince figured you might get targeted, so he had one of our guys tail you. Our man saw the kidnapping and called in the troops."

Sal pulled out a foot-long cigar and lit it. "We had to drive like maniacs on that freeway to catch up with the van. Then they pulled off on this damn trail, and we had to walk through this fucking swamp. And, kid, I'm scared to death of snakes." The man returned with the blanket, and Sal wrapped it around Christian's shoulders.

"Thank you, Sal. I owe you my life." Now that it was over, Christian couldn't contain his emotions. He sniffled and wiped his runny nose and damp face on a corner of the blanket.

Sal patted Christian's back. "It's all right to be upset, but when we get back, it's Vince you oughta thank. Never realized how much the boss cared about you until these stinking Arabs nabbed you. Jesus, he went ballistic."

Sal took a puff from the cigar and watched the smoke trail disappear into the night. "Ya know Vince was married twenty-somethin' years ago. His wife was a pretty blonde with big blue eyes, but that little gal could dish out some shit. Vince just took it. He adored her. Anyway, they had a son, looked like his mother, but the baby died after a few months from crib death. Soon after, Vince's wife overdosed on pills. Losing his family that year, it nearly destroyed the boss."

Christian gazed at the ground. "He never told me any of this."

Sal flicked the ash off the cigar. "He don't like talkin' about it. Ya know, I couldn't figure why the boss put up with your bullshit and let you walk that first night after the boat ride. Got me to thinkin'. Standing up to him, cocky as hell, you acted just like Vince's wife and, if his boy had lived, he'd be your age and probably resemble you. Then, to top things off, you pulled Vince from the drink and saved his neck. He's proud of you, kid. I think Vince sees you as the son he might've had."

Christian nodded, more to himself than to Sal. He understood at last. "I like Vince, too."

"Well, we need to get going. Think you can make it to my car?"

Christian managed to stand but was still wobbly. He gazed up at the stars and thought about his real father. *Thank you, Dad. You said you'd look out for me.*

They walked through the woods toward the dirt road. Christian glanced over his shoulder, hearing men's voices in the distance. Through the brush and trees, he saw beams of flashlights. "What about Price and the other guy?"

"Don't worry about it," Sal said. "Let's just say they'll never bother you again."

On the ride back to Sarasota, Sal and Christian sat in the backseat with one of Sal's men driving. Sal took out his cell phone and handed it to Christian. "Better call your girl and make up some excuse that you're staying out tonight. You're not in any shape to go home. And it's wise she don't know about tonight."

Christian took the phone, glancing down at his filthy clothes that were also stained with the dead man's blood. He tapped the keys. "Hey, Allie."

"Christian, I was just leaving for the marina. I tried to call you a million times and have been worried sick."

"I—" He coughed and cleared his throat. "I'm sorry. Sal and Vince stopped by. We had a few drinks, and I lost track of the time. And I lost my cell on a dock. It fell into the water. That's why I'm using Sal's. Listen, I'm a little wasted, so I'm crashing at Vince's. I'll see you in the morning."

"Fine, but I wish you'd find better drinking buddies."

He glanced at Sal. "Isn't there something about not judging a horse by his color? Believe it or not, Sal and Vince are good friends."

"Whatever, Christian," she said. "Love you, see you in the morning."

"Ah—Allie, I love you, too. Really, really love you."

She giggled. "Maybe you shouldn't drive. You do sound a bit smashed."

Two week later, Christian and Allie were sitting in the kitchen having lunch when a large white horse van bearing the sheik's stable name pulled into the farm. Allie looked out the window. "What the hell? What's the sheik's van doing here?"

"I have no clue," Christian said. They walked outside and approached the van. The driver and another man left the cab.

"Are you Christian Roberts?" the driver asked.

"Yes," said Christian.

The driver nodded to the other man, who proceeded to the back of van and opened the door. "I need you to sign off on this horse," said the driver. "Sheik Abdul say he has no further use of it."

Allie followed the other man to the back. He led the horse out, and she screeched, "It's Mystery, Christian!"

"I don't understand," Christian said to the driver.

"Look, I'm just the delivery guy. Do you want the horse or not?"

"Absolutely," Christian said and signed the shipping paper.

After the van left, Christian walked down the drive toward the barn with Allie leading Mystery. "Why do you suppose the sheik gave Mystery back to you?" she asked.

"I'm not sure, but I'm betting Vince had something to do with it. Last time we fished, I told him everything about the cloning and scam and mentioned I was bummed because the sheik won't sell Mystery back to me."

"Vince? You really believe he has that much pull, especially over a sheik?" she asked when they reached the barn.

"People don't argue with Vince."

Allie swung Mystery around in the aisle and led him into his old stall. "Well, the man does owe you his life. Maybe Vince did get Mystery back for you."

A few hours later Christian left the farm and drove toward Vince's house on the key, wanting to learn if he had anything to do with the sheik returning Mystery. And, if so, thank him.

Vince opened his front door. "Christian, this is a nice surprise. Come in."

Christian walked inside. "I also got a nice surprise a few hours ago. The sheik returned my colt. I'm guessing you had a hand in it."

"Well, indirectly." Vince grinned. "After that unfortunate incident in the Everglades, Sal and a few of the boys flew to Kentucky and met with the sheik. One of his men had apparently lost a fancy curved knife. Sal returned it to the sheik and said that if anything else happened to you, more than a knife would go missing. With the disappearance of his trainer and the two Arabian men, the sheik got the message. Learned you had some scary friends. Sal also mentioned you'd like your horse back."

Christian thought of the power play of shady characters within the Thoroughbred business, an American gangster flexing his muscles against a wealthy Arab sheik who was probably acquainted with more than one terrorist—not your everyday playground.

"Thank you, Vince."

CHAPTER TWENTY-ONE

In the barn, Christian took the tack off Hunter after an hour-long ride in the woods and picked up a currycomb. On the crisp winter day, the chestnut gelding didn't even have saddle sweat marks. While Hunter ate hay, Christian groomed the red coat and reflected on his father.

Dad had said, "I'm going to make things square between us." His father had lived up to his promise, the dream fulfilled. Christian couldn't imagine a more perfect life. He had given his boat rental business to Jake but built a large garage on the farm where he could walk out the door and restore old sailboats at his leisure. The diversion gave him a sense of accomplishment, and he was too young to retire.

He had also found and purchased the sailboat he'd always wanted, a forty-seven-foot Catalina with all the luxuries necessary to sail around the world, if he so desired. The sloop was docked at Marina Jack a few blocks from the Sarasota downtown waterfront. Rather than have the inconvenience of paddling in a dinghy to an offshore boat, he could park his SUV, walk down the dock, and step aboard.

Allie continued to train and race a few horses, but with Juan's help, it was more of a pastime rather than hard daily work, and she didn't have the pressure of making ends meet.

Mystery, initially, had a rough time adjusting to retirement on the quiet farm. The first few months he would whinny in the morning, wanting someone to climb on his back and exercise him on the track. Instead, he was turned loose in a large pasture where he revisited his old foal habit and raced in a large circle, quitting only when lathered and breathing hard.

It distressed Christian, watching the magnificent colt tear up the pasture in frustration. With a Thoroughbred's competitive nature, Mystery truly loved and missed racing, and he had the potential to be the greatest Thoroughbred alive. Instead, he had sadly ended up on a little-known farm in a little-known place. Secretariat probably experienced the same bewilderment when retired in his prime.

With the arrival of the first quarter horse mare, Mystery's focus shifted from racing to breeding. Although he couldn't produce a registered Thoroughbred foal, his stud card began to fill with warm bloods, quarter horses, and Arabians, the mare owners hoping to produce a foal with his looks and speed for barrel racing, jumping, and other hobbyhorse sports.

Mystery didn't seem to mind that they weren't Thoroughbreds. After all, a girl is a girl. He settled down, content with his new role as a stud.

As Christian left Hunter's stall, Allie walked into the barn. "I finished packing your SUV and am ready to go," she said, "unless you've changed your mind. We could stay home this weekend."

"No, I want to go," he said and patted Hunter good-bye. "I just need a quick shower, and we're off."

They walked up the drive to the house, and Christian cleaned up. His mind wasn't on the lazy days ahead of sailing and fishing aboard the boat, but on the small box holding a diamond ring that he had hidden from Allie in his dresser. She truly was his soul mate. They shared the same goals and mind-set, enjoying and loving similar things. She was beautiful, confident, and smart, but also scrappy, refusing to take flak from anyone, including him. He had met his match and was totally in love with her. The time had come to take the next step, pop the big question, and make a lifetime commitment.

Although Allie had told him she would never remarry, he felt sure she had changed her mind, especially when their discussion turned to kids. They both wanted a few, someday.

After dressing, he slipped the ring into his jacket pocket and hoped to surprise her on the boat with the marriage proposal. While they drove toward town, Allie glanced at Christian. "You've been awfully quiet today, in your own little world."

"I have stuff on my mind."

"Stuff, huh?" she said. "You never said how lunch went with your mother yesterday."

He gave her a sideward glance. "Lunch was fine. Mom's fine. Everything was great."

"It was just a little unusual, you and your mom meeting alone for lunch."

"Is it okay that I spend time with my mother?" he sniped. *Damn her instincts. She knows something's up, knows when I'm being less than truthful.* There was no lunch. Instead his mother had helped him pick out the ring.

"Jeez, Christian, don't be so grumpy. I think it's great you had lunch with your mom."

Christian shoved his sunglasses against the bridge of his nose and swept back his hair. Time to get off this subject before he really blew it. "I'm stopping at Hart's for bait and ice. Do we also need to hit the grocery store before we go to the boat?"

"No, we're good. I packed a cooler."

At the marina, they made several trips from the parking lot and SUV to the dock and sailboat as they unloaded ice, the cooler, bait bucket, and clothing. After stowing everything on the sailboat that had been appropriately named *Hank's Dream*, they motored out of the marina, hoisted the main and jib, and sailed out Big Pass located between Siesta and Lido Keys. In the gulf, they headed south with a strong northwesterly wind riding their back. Christian launched the large yellow spinnaker and a few miles offshore, they rode the up and down two-foot swells. Moving at a pretty good clip, they reached Charlotte Harbor within five hours and entered its wide mouth and calmer bay waters.

In the late afternoon, Christian lowered the sails and dropped anchor off Pine Island. He went below deck and took a fishing rod down from the rafters. "Allie, you wanna fish?"

"I'd rather go ashore and look for shells," she said, walking down three steps into the cabin. "Would you mind inflating the dinghy?"

"No problem," he said. On the top deck he opened the stern hatch and pulled out the rolled-up rubber dinghy that was stored with the dive gear of tanks, fins, masks, spearguns, and regulators. He flipped on the compressor and inflated the dinghy. After several minutes, he tossed the small raft over the portside and tied its bowline to the ladder attached to the stern. "It's ready, Allie," he called into the cabin.

"That was quick," she said, bounding onto the deck. "I made a salad for dinner, and there's steak, just in case you come up empty handed."

He frowned. "Woman, you have such little faith. You'll never starve with me on the water."

She kissed his cheek. "Maybe I should make a video of you and send it into *Survivor.* You'd probably win another million."

"Those idiots," he said, shaking his head. "I guarantee I wouldn't go hungry on an island, but I doubt I'd win on that show. I'm not a very good liar."

"Oh, I think you're pretty good at it, just not with me." She climbed down the ladder and got into the dinghy.

"Wait, take your cell in case you have trouble. I'll get it." He grabbed her cell phone out of the cabin and handed it to her as she stood in the dinghy, holding the ladder.

"Thanks," she said and slipped it in her pocket. "I'll be back in a few hours," she called and rowed toward shore.

"Dinner should be caught, cleaned, and cooked by the time you get back." Taking his rod, he baited the hook with a shrimp and cast it out into clear water. He watched Allie. She reached the white beach a hundred yards away and pulled the dinghy up on shore. She strolled down the long, empty beach with the backdrop of sea oats and Australian pines. Every so often she'd reach down and place a sea treasure into her small, mesh bag.

His attention was diverted when he felt a nibble on his line. With a slight tug he set the hook, and the battle was on. His pole curved with the taut line, the fish refusing to yield.

"Man, what do we have here? Acts like a big ray." After a good fight, he managed to get the fish off the bottom and bring it alongside the boat. "Oh, woman of little faith," he repeated and beamed, staring down at the doormat-size flounder on the end of his line.

"Hello, baby," said a woman's voice behind him.

He dropped his pole and wheeled around. The fish took off, pulling his rig over the side. He swallowed hard, too astonished for words, as he stared at Kate and the revolver in her hand.

"You seem a little shocked." She snickered, stepped up out of the cabin, and sauntered onto the deck.

"Yes!" He cleared his throat. "Hell, yes, I'm shocked. What . . . how did you get here?"

"I've been keeping tabs on your new boat. When you and your little whore were in the parking lot unloading stuff, I slipped aboard and hid behind a berth. I waited for this goddamn boat to stop moving and for her to leave. I wanted some time alone with you."

"I thought you were in jail."

"No, baby. When you have money and good lawyers, you end up with probation."

"So what do you want, Kate?"

"Your life." She grinned. "I told you, Chris. I can't live without you, and I meant it." She removed her sunglass and tossed back her hair, revealing the scarred side of her face. "And I certainly don't want to live like this. I thought about suicide, but that just didn't seem fair, letting you live on with that slut."

He glanced down the beach at Allie.

"Oh, don't worry about her," said Kate. "After I kill you, she's next."

He had to stall for time. "I think I need a drink. You want one?" He took a step toward her and the cabin, causing her to raise the gun with alarm. "Come on, Kate, I've never known you to turn down a drink," he said with a seductive low voice. He removed his sunglasses and flicked back his blond hair so she could see his often-called bedroom blues. Ramping up his charm, he would require every bit of it to distract and overpower her without getting shot.

With the tilt of his head and easygoing smile, she relaxed. "Sure, why not? One last drink." She followed him down into the cabin.

He took a Bacardi bottle out of the galley cabinet. "Rum and Coke okay?"

She nodded, watching his every move while he fixed their cocktails. "I'm glad the bitch left so we can talk." She sat down at the table opposite the small kitchen.

Christian placed her drink in front of her and leaned back against the sink counter, facing her. He picked up his glass, took a sip, and casually slipped his other hand into his baggy pant pocket. "You don't need to kill Allie. She's got nothing to do with us. I met her long after we broke up." While he talked, he opened his cell inside his pocket and felt the keys, pressing the speed dial number to Allie's phone.

"Defending her isn't helping," Kate grumbled. "It only makes me want to kill her more." She took another gulp of her cocktail.

"Fine," he said. "Let's talk about us. I've missed you."

"Bullshit."

"No, it's true. No one gives a blow job like you. You know how to press my buttons." He deeply sighed. "I definitely miss those long nights, us tearing up the sheets."

"God, I've missed them, too." She finished her drink, set the glass down, and stared at him. "You were the perfect lover."

"Still am." He smiled. "We could have one last fling—give a condemned man his last wish." He took her glass off the table and refreshed her drink, making it strong. He hoped Allie was overhearing their conversation so she'd call the police and stay away from the boat.

"That's tempting." Kate stood and looked out the port window toward the shore and dinghy.

He set her cocktail down on the table. "Allie will be gone for hours," he said. "We have the time."

She sat back down at the table. "Take off your clothes." He pulled off his shirt. "Now the pants," she said with a wave of the gun.

He unfastened his pants, letting them fall to his ankles, and stepped out of them, standing before her totally nude.

She took a sip and leaned back. Her plump lips curled. "Baby, you do have one gorgeous body. Did I ever tell you that your dick is just like my daddy's?"

Christian grimaced. "Your dad's?"

"That's right. I must've been five or six when I started blowing him, and at nine, we made love. It was so romantic, Chris. Dad liked to do it by candlelight. Every time I see fire, I think about Daddy and those nights. But when I turned fifteen, he stopped. He didn't want me anymore, didn't love me." She scowled. "Just like you."

"Jesus, Kate, I'm so sorry." Molested by a pedophile father, no wonder she was so screwed up. "Let me help you. We'll find a good therapist and I'll—"

"Shut up," she growled. "I don't need a therapist!" She took her drink and guzzled it. Christian lowered his eyes and was quiet.

After a minute, she composed herself and smirked. "Anyway, I killed him, along with my pathetic mother, and now I'm going to kill you. Nobody hurts me and gets away with it."

"Okay, Kate," he said softly, "but you could at least blow me before I die." He moved closer, hoping with two cocktails in her, she'd be easier to entice and drop her guard. "Please, Kate?"

"Chris, you're such a little boy, thinking you can trick me."

He gnawed a fingernail and exhaled a dismal sigh.

She studied him for a minute and then shook her head. "Baby, you're so damn irresistible when you chew your nails and pout. All right, clasp your hands behind your head and don't try anything."

He put his hands up and walked to her. She pressed the gun into his side, below his ribs, and fondled him with her other hand.

He closed his eyes and concentrated hard on Allie and their lovemaking. He had to be believable. Failure to become aroused would prove he didn't want Kate. He softly panted with the stimulation.

"You're such a good boy," she said and stroked him. "Always so willing."

With Kate distracted, he took the opportunity to strike. He unclasped his hands and grabbed the revolver, but before he could point the barrel away from him, it fired. The bullet hit his side. The excruciating pain forced him to release the gun, and he doubled over, collapsing on the floor.

"Goddamn you, Chris!" she yelled, standing. "You've ruined everything." She moved closer, aimed the gun at his head, and growled, "Baby, it's time for you to go."

He cringed, held his side, and looked up. "Don't do it, Kate." He heard a slight click, but it wasn't from Kate's gun.

Kate's whole body jolted. She gulped and her eyes widened. Her gun hand shook as she tried unsuccessfully to steady the weapon and kill him.

Christian then noticed the blood oozing down her white blouse and the speargun tip protruding out of her chest, the spear traveling clean through her body. He ducked and rolled away. The gun fired a second time. The bullet hit the wooden cabinet just inches above his head. Kate fell to the floor and lay nearby.

Allie ascended the remaining steps into the cabin, soaking wet from her swim to the boat, and held the empty speargun shaft. She kicked the revolver away from Kate's hand and stared at her for a moment.

"Is she dead?" he gasped and managed to sit up and lean against the cabinet.

"Yes," said Allie. She set the shaft down and bent over him, examining his injury. "We need to get you to a hospital."

He glanced at Kate a few feet away, lifeless with a blank eerie stare and blood trickling from her unforgettable full lips. He shuttered and looked away. "You heard us on your cell?" He grimaced with the pain.

"I did," Allie said with a raised eyebrow. "I'm just sorry I didn't get here sooner." Like when she wrangled a dangerous horse, her voice was amazingly calm. She took a towel and applied pressure to his wound. With his phone, she called the police. Despite that she had just killed someone, she remained unflustered and in control.

She closed the phone, squatted near him, and held his hand. "They'll be here soon. Just lie back down and take it easy."

"You said—" He puffed. "You said you wouldn't hesitate to pull a trigger to save me."

"Now you know I meant it." She cupped his cheek. "But Christian, don't you realize you also saved me. Before we met, I resented men and was determined to live alone. Then you came along. You restored my trust and put love back in my life. You changed everything for me."

Several days later, Christian rested comfortably in a hospital room. His mother sat in a nearby chair. The Coast Guard had come to Pine Island and airlifted him to the closest hospital. The following day, the police arrived and questioned him, saying Kate's death was clearly a case of justifiable homicide. His boat was later towed back to Sarasota and docked at Marina Jack's.

Allie walked into the room and kissed his cheek. "How do you feel today?"

"Still hurts," said Christian, "but the doctor says I should be able to go home in a day or two."

His mother rose. "Allie, I'm going downstairs to get some coffee." She left the room, and Allie sat down in her chair.

"So you're going home soon," said Allie. "Will you be recuperating on the farm or at your mother's?"

"Let's put this to rest, so you know where I live." He reached under the sheet and produced a small box that Frank had retrieved off Christian's sailboat. "I wanted to give you this on the boat last weekend, but there were slight complications." He chewed his bottom lip and offered her the box.

She took the box and slowly lifted the lid. Her mouth gaped open. Her eyes grew big, staring at the ring and then him.

"Will you marry me, Allie?"

She nodded. A tear coursed down her cheek. She took the diamond ring out and slid it on her finger. Like their life together, it was a perfect fit.

Printed in the USA
CPSIA information can be obtained
at www.ICGtesting.com
CBHW020735051023
1160CB00009B/2